...ections by E...

...people may like to know

...like...to have some

...a...told with myself

...looked & how I

...ite well remember

...being taken a little

...daisies, as children

...my surprise and joy

...saw a whole-field of

THE CHOSEN

Also by Elizabeth Lowry

The Bellini Madonna
Dark Water

THE CHOSEN

Elizabeth Lowry

riverrun

First published in Great Britain in 2022 by

riverrun

An imprint of

Quercus Editions Limited
Carmelite House
50 Victoria Embankment
London EC4Y 0DZ

An Hachette UK company

A CIP catalogue record for this book is available
from the British Library

Hardback 978 1 52941 068 6
Trade Paperback 978 1 52941 069 3
Ebook 978 1 52941 071 6

This book is a work of fiction. Names, characters,
businesses, organizations, places and events are
either the product of the author's imagination
or used fictitiously. Any resemblance to
actual persons, living or dead, events or
locales is entirely coincidental.

10 9 8 7 6 5 4 3 2 1

Typeset by CC Book Production
Printed and bound in Great Britain by Clays Ltd, Elcograf S.p.A.

Papers used by riverrun are from well-managed forests and other responsible sources.

For my parents

Your novel seems sometimes like a child all your own &
none of me.

Emma Gifford to Thomas Hardy, 1874

Nothing but the illusion of truth can permanently please,
and when the old illusions begin to be penetrated, a more
natural magic has to be supplied.

Thomas Hardy, 'The Science of Fiction', 1891

'Who are you? Won't you say
Who you may be, you man so strange,
Following since yesterday?'

Thomas Hardy, 'The Chosen', 1922

The Going

B Y TEN TO EIGHT that morning he is already sitting at his writing desk with a shawl around his shoulders. It's a Wednesday near the end of November and just beginning to rain, a damp wind rising.

A quarter of an hour ago he woke from a dream in which he crawled across a deserted shore towards a cliff. At the top of the cliff stood a castle – shattered, perilous – which he had to reach. The cliff sides reared sheer and slippery, and every grain of the ashen sand glittered with menace, but he knew with the certainty peculiar to dreams that he was equal to the ascent. Though the dream was full of fear it was also tinged with desire, and with a defiance that came close to joy. He got out of bed with his heart beating hard, dressed hurriedly in the old trousers he likes to wear while working, and came straight to his study.

Voices drift from the kitchen below, where Jane Riggs, the cook, is getting breakfast under way. Later there will be bacon sprinkled with brown sugar; toast, marmalade, tea. Later he will walk to the back gate to take stock of the clouds balled over the distant heath. Later again he will change into a clean shirt and his Norfolk tweeds. He will go down to meet callers. There are always callers.

But for now, he will write.

Not a sound comes from above. Emma must still be asleep in her attic bedroom. She won't stir early when it rains; she hates the rain.

He's glad. After their quarrel yesterday (was it a quarrel? He sat gripping the arms of his chair, not saying much, simply trying to breathe while her rage and contempt broke over him) he doesn't want to be troubled by the sight of her. He wants, in fact, to forget all about his wife. He's irritably aware of her maid, Dolly, leaving the kitchen; the jig of the girl's light footfalls tapping up the servants' staircase, along the landing, then on the attic steps beyond his study door.

A sudden movement in the window catches his eye. Raindrops swell on the pane and plough down through his reflection. Despite the overcast day a glow is gathering in the sky, a nimbus of ghastly light trapped in its watery atmosphere, inflaming the sheets of plate-glass with red smears. He sees an elderly little man in a frayed shirt, half asleep, enclosed by peeling furniture. He seems to himself very small, very dry, very white. His features are worn and blurred and ruinous, the lips trembling, not so much from age as from an excess of introspection. Behind him stretches the room, streaked and stained, its faded coral walls distempered by the morning light. It's crammed with paper of all sorts. Newspapers. Books. Periodicals. Heaps of paper: cairns, slipping ziggurats.

Eight o'clock on a November morning, and he is an old man in ragged trousers, entombed by paper, with a rumbling stomach.

He gets up and draws the curtains. Then he sits, pulls the shawl over his head, and selects a pen from his pen tray. He touches the plaque on his table which he likes to stroke for inspiration. *Write,* it says, *and with mine eyes I'll drink the words.* The sensations of his dream still attend him: inchoate desire; an excitement, an apprehension of his own energies, that isn't yet happiness, and offsetting these, that feeling of dragging through sand or ash, of having to make an immense effort, of being about to be knocked back by something or someone –

He will go on, he will begin the climb.

He turns to the poem he drafted a week ago. It's a promising start, but it needs building out. Here, revealed in a burst of confidence, the sort of writer's luck that can visit him even after all these years, is a house – a cottage, really, like the one in which he was born. A young boy is going up to bed. His father traps and sells birds for a living and the house is filled with cages. The boy hates his father's trade, but this is how they have always managed. *My business 'tis to earn,* his father says, *yours to be taught.* Up the boy goes, groping for the dark stairs. As he goes, he runs his fingers over the cage wires. They make a sound like the strings of a harp. *Harp-like,* yes. The boy will escape this house, the darkness. He will find a different way. He will find freedom, but he won't survive it. What about the birds? The birds will remain.

He levers the lid off the inkwell, wets the nib of his pen. *Like those in Babylon,* he writes, *Captive they sung.*

There is a loud clatter down the steps, followed by a frantic hammering at the door. It slams open before he can speak.

He looks up, astonished. Dolly stands in the doorway, her collar askew. The servants know that they aren't allowed to enter this room when he is working.

'Whatever is the matter?' he asks.

Slack Dolly. A girl so slovenly and easily distracted that he has to restrain himself from raising his voice at her. There are many girls, spirited, intelligent girls, languishing in service for want of a better start in life. Dolly isn't one of them. She's a servant by nature, ready to place her neck under any boot. Anger would be as wasted on her as on a dog or a cat. Em never notices Dolly's shortcomings; or rather, she notices them, but is prepared to dismiss them. She probably expects Dolly to be even worse than she is.

'Sir, please come quickly. Miss'ess is terrible ill.'

He moves his blotter half an inch to the side. For a few minutes he carries on writing. Dolly takes a step into the room. The transgression is so flagrant that he is lost for words. He merely says, 'Your collar is crooked.'

'Yes, sir. Only, please come.'

He shifts his papers about, closes the inkwell. Finally he shrugs off his shawl, rises, and begins to climb the attic stairs with Dolly following. As he does so he notes that a fine skin of dust dulls the splintered skirting. A cobweb shivers from the banister, brilliant and fresh. Another dereliction, but a remarkable thing in its way. He halts, points to it mutely, glances around, and finds to his surprise that Dolly's lips are pinched as if she's getting ready to spit at him.

He takes the last three steps without haste, his irritation mounting. There's a slanted batten door at the top, made of the same splintery wood as the stairs. Though it's flung wide he knocks cautiously.

'She won't hear 'ee, sir.'

He goes in. He is stooped in the cramped vestibule to the loft that his wife refers to as her 'boudoir'. The floorboards are stained black and the ceiling slopes meanly. It's like stepping into a coal scuttle. He hasn't come up here for weeks – months, perhaps. Now he stops, ambushed.

He's forgotten how dingy it is. There is no natural light; the air seems clotted. Everything is the colour of burnt potato. The door to Dolly's room on his left is ajar, disclosing a wicker laundry hamper and a clothes horse where a pair of wet stockings is making a puddle. In the sooty darkness he picks out a sewing machine with some cheap stuff trapped under the needle. Over it all hangs the tang of distilled flowers, an artificial, exaggerated smell that he associates with womanhood itself. He has to will himself to continue down the corridor, past the two carpet sweepers posted at the end; to turn the corner and approach the brass lock of his wife's bedroom.

As soon as he crosses the threshold he recognizes that something is badly wrong. Emma is in her bed, wearing a nightgown he has never seen, embroidered with violets and fastened with a single button at the neck. Her hair is tossed about her face, except for a lone squiggle stuck to her forehead. She is moaning.

'Em, Em,' he tuts. He sits on the mattress and puts his arms around her. He hasn't touched her in many years, and through the fabric of her nightgown her flesh is unpleasantly hot. 'What's the matter?' he asks. 'Don't you know me?' But she doesn't reply. 'Call the doctor,' he tells Dolly. 'Get Dr Gowring.' Dolly attempts to back out past him. When she reaches the door he does what he's never yet done in the twelve months that she's worked for them, and shouts. 'Run!'

In the silence following Dolly's departure he studies Emma carefully. She's no longer moaning. Her eyelids are half parted, but her lips are firmly shut. He brings his mouth to her flushed ear. 'What's this, Emmie? What is it?'

5

But he knows what it is. She has never looked so aloof, so dismissive. Between his speaking to her and taking her in his arms, she has gone.

How much time passes before Gowring arrives? It can't be more than half an hour, forty minutes at most. In that time he becomes two people. One is here, sitting in the brown light that falls from the dormer window. It's raining properly now, with an insistent drone like the murmuring of bees. This self sees the pane grow liquid; the bald glint as morning hardens upon the wall. The other self seems to hear, in the noise of the rain, the voice of someone muttering in a new language. *Too late*, says the voice. *Too late now. It is finished.* The china finials on the bedstead shine. Behind the open door, he thinks he sees a dark shape passing through.

In his divided state he notices small things, ordinary things, which are, he realizes, part of the life of this room. An empty teacup haloed by stains. Two porcelain dogs with prim smiles. A chamber pot, winking its broad amber eye. They strike him as strange beyond words.

'Em,' he whispers. 'Why didn't you say something? Why didn't you give me a sign?' Laying her down on the bed he kneels, awkwardly – he, who has refused to kneel to anything for years now – on the bare floor. He bends his face to the sheet. A terrible sound is coming from the walls, from the low ceiling.

At last he raises his head and sees Dolly staring at him with her knuckles in her mouth. Dr Gowring stands behind her.

'I came as quickly as I could,' says Gowring. He is a country doctor of the old-fashioned sort, simply but reassuringly dressed in a black coat, with a high collar like a priest's.

'She won't answer me.'

'If I may,' says Gowring. He goes to the bedside and makes a few swift, probing passes over Emma's neck and breast. 'I'm sorry. She is dead. Her heart has failed.'

'How can that be? She was complaining of her back lately.'

Gowring has pulled up Emma's nightclothes and is palpating her side. It's an examination she would never have allowed in life. The skin of her belly is yellowish and sulkily puckered. 'She has suffered some internal perforation, I'm afraid. I wish she'd let me take a look at her earlier.'

Dolly begins to cry. He stares at her, with the sensation that he is seeing her for the first time. She's a child still; she is only fourteen. 'Dolly,' he asks, 'are your people from hereabouts?'

'Yes, sir. From Piddlehinton.'

'Pretty place, Piddlehinton. Some fine cottages there.'

'Yes, sir.' She starts to cry harder.

'Have you had your breakfast?'

'No, sir.'

'Well, go to the kitchen and have it. Have mine. Please tell Mrs Riggs I shan't be needing any.'

Gowring tugs Em's nightdress back over her hips. 'I will have to conduct a proper examination shortly, but I won't disturb her just now.' He hesitates. 'You have had a shock. Perhaps I should step outside for a moment.'

'That won't be necessary.'

Gowring dips his head in assent. 'What arrangements would you like to make before the funeral?'

'Before? I don't understand.'

'For the remains.'

'Oh. I see.' He takes Emma's hand. It's covered in raised veins, and is faintly warm. 'She can't stay up here. I'll have her downstairs, with me.'

'In the dining room?'

'No, in my bedroom.'

'Are you sure?'

'Perfectly. But she will need somewhere, some*thing*, to lie—'

'I'll get Hannah and Holland to bring over a coffin. And I'll have a word with your housekeeper about preparing . . . her.'

'Thank you.' Most of what Gowring has said strikes him as meaningless; he's replying automatically. He pauses. 'Does she look right to you, Doctor? She doesn't seem like herself, somehow.'

Gowring has turned away from the bed and is assessing him.

'She seems so . . . indifferent,' he persists.

'Mr Hardy. Were you planning on being alone here today?'

'I am usually alone.'

'I'll ask Miss Hardy to come. It might be better to have a woman to supervise things. How does that sound?'

'My sister hasn't been well either.' He's still holding Em's hand. 'Mary. Mary hasn't been well. It would have to be Kate.'

'I'll send your servant girl to Higher Bockhampton directly, before I make my examination. Come downstairs with me meanwhile. Come on. Let go now. That's right.'

They go down the attic steps, down the shuddering oak of the main staircase. Florence Griffin, who is the closest thing to a housekeeper Em would allow, waits at its foot, twisting her apron in her fingers.

'Oh, sir. This is a terrible day. And you've not eaten a bite. I've made up the drawing-room fire for 'ee. Will you have a cup o' tea, at least?'

'Tea would be just the thing, Griffin,' says Dr Gowring. 'May I speak to you in the kitchen for a minute about what needs to be done? Excellent. Thank you. Now sit, Mr Hardy. Sit.'

Kate

H E SITS IN THE drawing room for what might be several hours, or only one. He can hear the hissing of water in the scullery, the distant chink of china and metal, and the steady, purposeful tread of feet on the stairs. The room, in spite of the rain, is too bright. This is his armchair, where he likes to read in the afternoons while making the occasional note on a lap tray. But he never sits here in the mornings. In the mornings he stays in his study and writes. He can't imagine ever writing again. It's inconceivable that he once did. That's something that now belongs, like his early morning dream of the cliff, the shifting grey sands, to another life.

Perhaps the coal isn't catching as it should, because he's frozen all over. He's disturbed by a crawling sensation in his upper body like scabbing ice, or the grinding approach of neuralgia. He can hardly feel his fingers. One of Em's cats appears in a silent slalom and bares its belly to the flames.

He's still sitting there, chafing his wrists and watching the rain spurt down the high windows, when Kate arrives. He picks out the jangle of the bell; Florence's boots in the porch, the sliding of bolts. The two women linger in the hall for some time, speaking in low voices. He recognizes the words 'last night' and 'fearful pain'. Though the Griffins are a Dorchester family and well known to his sister, Kate has rarely been welcome in this house since it was built.

When he can't bear their murmuring any longer he gets up and goes out to them.

Beneath her upswept hair Kate's face is flushed. She's immaculately turned out, in a silk skirt with a high waist and a pleated jacket. He wonders if she always wears silk at eleven o'clock on a weekday morning. Or has she changed specially for this visit? She is younger than he is by sixteen years, but bolder and more outspoken – *and she is more resilient,* he thinks; *she's learned, as I never have, to rely only on herself.*

Kate casts her eye over the plaster reproduction of the Capitoline Venus, the cornices, the dado; the hall stand trailing Emma's jaunty hats. 'It's lovely,' she says with her usual asperity. 'Very respectable. Really very nice.'

'You know I couldn't ask you before. It was impossible. She wouldn't have it.'

'Well, Tom, I'm sorry for your loss, of course. But I daresay it's a relief also.'

'Will you come in now?'

She wavers, then walks towards him resolutely, her skirts crackling, as if into an embrace. But he doesn't open his arms. His gaze is fixed on her. She meets it without looking down.

Florence clears her throat. 'The doctor said, sir, to let Miss Hardy know when she gets here that everything's ready upstairs.'

'What is it that you and Miss Hardy are to do?'

'Sir, we're to wash – to wash Mrs Hardy ahead o' the undertaker calling. And dress her.'

'I'll do it myself, thank you, Flo,' he says.

Kate lets out an impatient *tch*. 'Really? What's this?'

'I'll wash my wife.'

'Nonsense. There's no one here to see but me.'

'It's what I want to do.'

'Well, then.' She flaps her hand angrily. 'That settles it, doesn't it? You've always done exactly as you wanted.'

As he climbs the attic stairs he has to pause and take hold of the rail. The cold is doubling in him, ripping through his chest. He wonders vaguely if he's ill; if he has, after all, caught some chill. He doesn't feel like himself at all.

The little room looks unchanged, as dreary as before. Emma is stretched out on her bed with the sheet pulled over her face. There's a bowl of soapy water on the bedside table; a sponge and flannel, and next to these, a silver-backed hairbrush.

Once the bedroom door is closed he doesn't go to her. Instead he is drawn by instinct to a small writing table under the window. It's strewn with bits of paper. He stirs them with his fingers and dislodges a pencilled note, in Em's squally handwriting.

Mrs Hardy must have Liq. Op. Sed. – which she knows to take.

He reads this prescription several times. He pushes it aside and uncovers a fragment of verse.

Oh! Would I were a dancing child!
　　Oh! Would I were again
Dancing in the grass of spring,
　　Dancing in the rain.
Leaping with the birds a-wing
Singing with the birds that sing.

It's a bad poem, like all Em's poems. Yet she thought, always, that she could write. Turning to the faceless shape on the bed he seizes the sponge, dips it in the bowl, and twitches back the sheet. Emma is completely naked, as he hasn't seen her for perhaps thirty years. He stands without moving, holding the sponge aloft. Tepid water trickles down his sleeve.

His wife's body is small and puffy, sutured with deep creases and distorted across the belly and thighs by pitted pads of fat. Her shoulders, incongruously, are slung back like a horsewoman's. He remembers her sitting at tea with the Owens two days earlier. The Americans made short work of the apple cake and cucumber sandwiches but there was a reproving stiffness about them, an undeniable tinge of dismay in the air. He'd noticed with distaste that Emma was hunched beside the pot as though whispering to it. She'd been in pain: more pain than she'd admitted.

He brings the sponge up to her breasts, but he doesn't know how to begin. He's filled with shame at his own incompetence; at his reluctance to perform this strangely lover-like act. After a moment he sets the sponge down again and draws the sheet back up over her shoulders. Now only Emma's head, with its scrawl of white, is visible. Her hair is tangled from her last night of sleep. He starts, with slow strokes, to run the brush along it, smoothing the strands on the pillow until they're arranged around her face in a blown veil.

He puts his finger to his cheek and is astonished to find that it comes away wet. He's staring at its alien sheen when there's a scuffing sound behind the door. 'Who's there?' he says, striking at his tears with the back of his wrist. 'Dolly? Is that you?'

'It's me, Tom. I'm coming in, like it or not.'

The door opens before he's able to reply. When he sees his sister something gives way inside him and he starts to sob with a chill impersonal ferocity, in long jolts that shake his whole body.

Kate takes the brush from his hand. 'You foolish boy. Enough. It's enough.' She leads him back to the drawing room, spry and teacherly, admonishing by example. Once he's seated she draws the armchair rug over his legs. 'Don't move. Rest your eyes. I'll be as quick as I can.'

He lowers his eyelids and discovers that he's exhausted. But his exhaustion is unconnected with a need for sleep, just as his tears, arriving as if from nowhere, seemed to have nothing to do with natural sorrow. Perhaps this is how it will always be from now on: this absence of any familiar feeling; this divorce from himself. The light comes and goes behind his closed lids. The blood, pounding in his head, throws indecipherable patterns against the darkness.

Presently Kate returns. He can hear her busying herself with the tea things and opens his eyes. Her sleeves are turned up to the elbow. She pours him a cup, helps herself to one. 'This tea is stewed,' she says. 'And cold.'

'Kate, did she know? *What* did she know?'

Kate regards him calmly. 'Have you informed Miss Dugdale?'

'I haven't.'

'Where is she?'

'She's staying at the Fairhaven Hotel in Weymouth. She's come down for the play. We were to go to it tonight.'

'Together?'

'Yes.'

'You can't go. You must put her off at once. Send a telegram — write it now.'

'I don't know what to say.'

Kate gives him her lean, difficult smile. 'And you the writer. Here, I'll do it.' She takes a piece of paper and the pencil from the tray beside his chair and jots down a few lines.

Mrs Hardy passed away unexpectedly this morning. Family funeral. Please go home. Letter to follow.

He sucks in his breath. 'This is unkind.'

'This is necessary. There will have to be a notice in the papers too.'

'Katie — will you?'

'Very well. But you'll have to write that letter yourself.' She starts to roll down her cuffs. 'So. James Hannah's men have come with the coffin. Everything's been seen to. I gave them a shilling tip each. I trust that was right?'

'Whatever you think best.'

'What about the play? Will you cancel it?'

He shakes his head.

'You're not troubled by how that will look?'

'Em would have wanted it to go on as planned.' He realizes that he hasn't the slightest idea what Emma would have wanted, in this regard or any other.

'Good. That's decided, then.' His sister rises, short and solid, undiminished by the morning's work. 'I'd better get home to Mary. Her chest has been very bad again. I'll stop at the post office and the theatre on my way. Would you like Henry to come and stay in the house tonight?'

'No. I'd rather be on my own with her.'

'*Plus ça change.* I'll be back tomorrow.'

'Katie, wait. The Owens are here.'

'Oh, good Lord. Where?' She glances at the ceiling, as if they might be concealed in one of the upstairs bedrooms.

'In town. They called on Monday. Miss Owen is bound to come as soon as she hears. Please hurry.'

'So I'm to have the freedom of the house at last, am I? There's to be no more creeping over to ours on Sundays, as if your own kin's a dirty secret?' Seeing his stricken face, she relents. 'I'll be here.' She hasn't touched him since she arrived, but she takes his hand now. Her grip is surprisingly strong. 'Tom, think about where you'd like to put her. Please think about a grave.' She gives his fingers an urgent shake and rams the rug around his knees. He continues to sit beneath its dead weight, rubbing his arms, for a long time after she has left.

At the close of the day he douses the lamp before entering his room. Groping for the bed, he can just make out the low shape of the open coffin at its foot. For an instant he doesn't know where he is. The dark closes over his head like water. He feels breathless panic at the finality of it and begins to undress by rote, hurriedly, discarding trousers, shirt, vest, drawers. Once they are on the floor he works his way into his nightshirt, eyes shut tight out of an instinctive modesty. He keeps his woollen socks on and is glad of them when he slips under the covers. There's no fire. It's laid out as usual, but no one has lit it. He decides to let it be. He knows that he can't set foot outside the bed again.

'Goodnight, Em,' he says.

He doesn't think he'll sleep. Instead, enclosed by clammy linen, shivering fitfully, he plays a game he used to play as a boy. He's stretched out on the heath behind Thorncombe Wood with his hat over his face. Sunlight prickles his lids between the gaps in the straw. *I am stopping here. I'll be a child forever. I won't grow up.* All around him the earth is sparsely grassed and fragrant with thyme. A treble wind calls through the thorn. Peewits rise from the low gorse, their wings phosphorescent against a trailing cope of cloud.

When he comes back to himself he finds that it's dawn. There is scattered birdsong, the calling of the wind, and beyond the glass an air so blue that it seems arterial.

Emma is in the room with him, lying in plain view. She doesn't look the way she used to. Her hair is loose about her shoulders and her heavy chins are creaseless. Even her brows have relaxed their appearance of perpetual severity. Though she no longer looks old, she doesn't look as she did in her youth either. She has become a new Em, ageless and unfamiliar.

'Emmie,' he breathes. He's filled with a simple yearning for her to be as she once was. He reaches over the blankets to touch her, but she's too far away. At the same time he's aware of the theatricality of the gesture, and that this moment – his outspread hands, the shattering light, the wind oozing thinly across the fields outside – is one that he has marked for his personal use. Getting out of bed, he approaches the coffin bare-legged. He's shaking as he kisses her left cheek, then the right. He kisses them several times, country fashion. He puts his lips to hers. 'Speak to me, Em.'

Of course she doesn't speak. His yearning gives way to relief.

Once he's dressed he starts along the passage to his study. *Like a dog going to its kennel*, he thinks. What he'll do there, he doesn't know.

'I have rarely, if ever, been so shocked as I am at this news,' says Miss Owen.

The Owens are seated at the gate-leg table in the drawing room, just as they were three days before. They are down from the Lakes on one of their regular expeditions to Dorset, having left behind their high-ceilinged house, their stables and walled garden and servant problems, and their many signed editions of his books – supposedly to see the town players perform *The Trumpet-Major*, but really, he knows, in pursuit of him. They are called Rebekah and Catharine but always refer to each other, in their silvery New York accents, as Bett and Tat. Bett has a manner so insistent that it might be considered overbearing. Tat, the elder, is mostly silent.

There's a pot of tea on the table, arranged by Kate; cups, saucers, spoons. It's the wrong pot. They are the wrong cups, the wrong saucers, the wrong spoons. Kate has used the wrong cloth.

'I simply can't rid my mind of the thought that Tat and I were the last persons to see Mrs Hardy alive,' Miss Owen adds.

'Outside of the household,' says Kate.

Miss Owen inclines her head slightly; straightens a teaspoon. 'I was almost never so shocked in my life, Miss Hardy. We called on her on Monday, you know. We were so looking forward to the play, though as you can imagine we wanted to visit dear Mrs Hardy first.' She fixes him with her alert, knowing eyes. 'The servant said she was not well and wasn't seeing anyone, but I wrote on my card, "Will you not see *us*?" And soon, and *very* slowly, she came into the drawing room, saying how glad she was to see us and that she wouldn't have seen anyone else. She *would* give us tea. She was no worse for seeing us, but better, I think. Only the pain came on now and then.'

'Yes,' he says, stroking the tablecloth. It has an ugly pattern of red roses with cruel thorns: a wedding present from Em's sister Helen. Em never used it. 'She was in some pain.'

'We begged her over and over to see a doctor,' Miss Owen says.

He looks up. 'I don't recall that.'

'It was before you joined us. She didn't think that you would come.'

He stares at Miss Owen's black fur tippet and knows that he is in the presence of one of nature's predators. It will track him down, however well he tries to hide. It will never be deflected. 'I was at work,' he says.

'Indeed.' She bares her teeth gravely. 'We did wonder if the play would be called off. But our chauffeur came with a report that he'd seen a placard in town saying that there would be no postponement of the performances. Naturally we are planning to attend on *both* nights.'

Kate gets up. 'Perhaps you'd like to pay your respects to Mrs Hardy now.'

'Why, certainly,' says Miss Owen. 'We've known her well, I may say uncommonly well, for twenty years.'

'And two months,' murmurs Tat.

The quiet once their feet have passed overhead is more complete than any he has ever known. The rain has cleared and a thin sun reaches into the room, fingering the chill old keys of the piano, like a skull's brown teeth; the terrifying roses, the mess of crockery on the table-top.

Suddenly he's angry. His rage is like a muscle, a thing so vital he can feel it labouring inside his chest. He doesn't know if he's angry with the Owens, or himself. Or with Em, for making him endure this meeting alone. *How did you manage to give me the slip again, Emmie? You were always one for abrupt exits. Whenever we had callers you didn't particularly want to see you'd be gone, just gone. You'd stay for a bit and then you'd be off, up to that attic of yours. Well, you're not leaving me now. You're not.*

'Oh, Mr Hardy. I can't believe it.' Miss Owen is back, her sister close behind. They stand there with their hands raised as if in surrender: circumspect, watchful, hungry. 'Having seen her I can believe it even less. She was so marked a personality no one could bump into her in the street without saying, "I met Mrs Hardy today." We would like to see her laid to rest.'

'Bett and I have decided to defer our return to Belmount,' says Tat.

'Where,' asks Miss Owen, 'will the interment be? Will you take her home to Cornwall?'

'This is her home,' he says. 'She'll be buried in Stinsford. In our family plot.'

Miss Owen lowers her hands solemnly. 'We shall be there.'

He laughs – a short, wild laugh. 'Come if you wish. But don't flatter yourselves that she cares. It was her favourite trick, to vanish without a word.'

He doesn't go with Kate as she sees them out to their car. When she reappears her manner is clipped. 'Whatever made you speak in that way to the Owens? Tom, please. Remember who, remember *what*, you are.'

'I don't seem to know myself, Katie.'

'Here's a reminder.' She pulls a piece of newsprint out of her pocket.

'What's this?'

'Your notice in today's *Times*.'

He takes it from her, though he scarcely wants to.

MRS THOMAS HARDY

ob. 27th November 1912

Mrs Emma Hardy, wife of Mr Thomas Hardy, the poet and novelist, died at Max Gate, Dorchester, on Wednesday after a very short illness, aged 72 years.

Born Miss Emma Lavinia Gifford, younger daughter of the late Mr John Attersoll Gifford, originally of Plymouth, she was married to Mr Hardy at St Peter's, Paddington, in 1874. Her uncle, Dr Edwin Hamilton Gifford, Canon of Worcester and afterwards Archdeacon of London, officiated at the private ceremony.

In their early years together, when Mr Hardy was establishing his career, Mrs Hardy often assisted her husband by writing to his dictation and making fair copies of his manuscripts.

Mrs Hardy had lived with Mr Hardy at Max Gate since 1885, when they first took up their residence there in what was then a new house. To the end of her life she was an energetic gardener and a lover of animals, a staunch humanitarian, and a generous sponsor to the labouring families of her parish. She is mourned by her husband, his brother and sisters, and her niece.

'A "staunch humanitarian"?'

'Show me a lady who isn't,' says Kate.

He looks over the notice again. It's more apt than anything he could, in his bewildering oscillations between numbness and fury, have composed. Kate has even swallowed her pride and put in the Giffords. 'This is very good. Thank you.'

'Do you really mean to have her next to Mother and Father?'

'It's her proper place.'

'She would have hated it.'

'Then she should have lived.'

Kate's face gives nothing away. She has their mother's hooded dark eyes and canted jaw. It is a guarded, peasant's face, like his own. 'I am glad every day that I've never married,' she says.

The Haunter

T̲HE MESSAGES OF CONDOLENCE begin to arrive in that afternoon's post. At first there are only a few, from local families and Emma's clergy friends. The Bankeses at Wolfeton House, the Wood Homers at Bardolf Manor. The Leslies at Came Rectory. The Bartelots in Fordington. He carries the letters to his desk and drops into his chair. He strokes them gently, hopelessly. He will have to reply, but he can't for the moment see how. His head is full of wind, a roaring rush, obscuring thought. He sits, feeling the truth of that noise bearing down on him. He has lost the ability to write. He's suspected this since yesterday: that in the half-hour when he knelt at Emma's deathbed, some essential part of him fled with her. Now he's sure. Language has left him.

He folds his hands, though he abandoned the habit of prayer long ago. *What am I praying to?* He presses his palms together: hard, harder, but the words won't come. At last he rests his cheek on the table-top and lets the roaring take him.

When he wakes the room is dark. The servants haven't called him. The study door is shut fast, the kitchen below utterly still. The roar in his ears has died down. There's a foreign quality to the silence, as if a familiar engine has come to a halt. It could be nine o'clock; it

23

could be midnight. It comes to him that he's forgotten, for the last two days, to wind the house clocks.

He gets to his feet. A rinsing white light pours through the window. Black bars lie over the carpet and the bookcases, where his father's violin, propped in a corner, makes a darker shape. But in that instant he feels indefinably free, as if he were an unfettered soul, let loose among the living. *So this is all I had to do*, he thinks, *to escape the world. I just had to stop attending to things.*

He knows it isn't true. He must leave this room, and make his way down the corridor to his bed. He must put on flesh.

Not yet – oh, not yet. He's a ghost, eager and expectant, as he crosses the threshold and finds himself entering the realm of the dead. Emma is lying in her coffin, her hair spread on a pillow, lapped by violet shadows.

'Emmie, I'm sorry. I was afraid last night. I thought you would still be angry with me. I've been the worst fool all day. Do you forgive me?'

The collar around her neck is stiff and ends in a fussy ruff. She would never have worn such a thing of her own free will.

He's balanced on the lip of an abyss. If he takes another step he will fall. The fall will be endless. He lowers himself onto the edge of the bed, absorbing the emptiness of the moment, in which death reverberates. This isn't the beginning of grief but something worse, an absence without form or meaning, a chaos in which everything that was once certain is cancelled. Wherever she's to be found now, it isn't here.

*

The late Friday post brings a letter from Gosse.

17 Hanover Terrace, London

28th November 1912

My dear friend,

I can't begin to tell you how sorry Nellie and I were to read your dreadful news in today's *Times*. A long marriage is an awful thing, as awe-inspiring as anything in nature, a mountain or a desert, and its extinction as unimaginable – well, what I mean to say is simply this: such a loss leaves a terrible rift in the fabric of the world. One does not know how to address it properly.

You will forgive my clumsiness of expression I hope. I know you two had your difficulties, as all married people do. I remember the afternoon Benson and I spent with you both in September when he was down from Cambridge, and how *vivid* Mrs Hardy was. She spoke, I recall, mostly of horticulture. She charmed me very much.

Nellie joins me in sending you our sincerest love, and in urging you to come and see us when you feel able.

Yours most affectionately,

Edmund Gosse

Did Emma charm Gosse? He finds this hard to believe. He sees Edmund leaning towards her during lunch, his glimmering wire spectacles and thrusting moustache: the picture of strained earnestness, like someone standing in a perpetual high wind. Arthur Benson, used to better things from the Magdalene Buttery no doubt, chewed every mouthful of his mince cake twenty times, as if it might contain shot. The meat was slightly ripe. And Emma – Emma, bafflingly, was talking about onions and roots and rose trees.

He watched her in the state of habitual terror with which he now always awaited her pronouncements. A giant paper flower, some fantastic old tea party favour, squatted at her breast. Her hair was heaped and padded like a small ploughed field. She spoke in a hurried squeak, explaining the correct way of setting a rose bush to Gosse, who kept his chin manfully uplifted. 'My,' he marvelled, and 'Oh I see,' and, 'Really, even in this cold autumn weather? Even if there's frost?'

Emma let out an elfin shriek. 'Yes, in autumn, by moonlight,' she said. 'That's the best time to do it, if a frost-wind has severed your two souls.' She laid her spotted hand on Gosse's arm.

He knew for a fact that she'd never planted roses.

'My dear Gosse,' he begins.

> This is a wretched business indeed. The suddenness of it. Emma's death was absolutely unexpected by me, the doctor, and everybody. I have reproached myself –

He breaks off, strikes out the last three words, makes another attempt.

> I reproach myself for not having guessed there might be some internal mischief at work. But I blame myself very much for something else also.

He doesn't know if he can go on. The horror of it is there, bulging behind the paper.

> It would be affectation to deny the differences between us. The day before Emma died we exchanged bitter words. It was the worst falling-out we'd ever had. In the course of this argument she said things to me which I won't easily forget. And now, you see, I can't go to her as I'd like, and ask her if she spoke from the heart. I wonder if you and Nellie have ever –

He puts his pen down. He can't ask what he wants to ask. *Was what happened to us usual? Does it happen to all husbands and wives, must we all end up as enemies to each other?* He wants to say: *Help me. Please help me, I have lost myself. I hated her, at the end. I hated her for standing in the way of my desires; simply for being there. Simply for living in the same house with me and breathing the same air I breathed. At moments I even wished her dead. But now that she's gone I feel it's not really she who's died. I am dead. How can that be?*

It's past four o'clock when he makes his way downstairs. A green light slants across the hall from the drawing room. The empty room is frigid, with the cold that recently seems to pervade everything. There's no sign of tea. He drops Gosse's letter onto his tray, intending to finish it later. The blinds are half lowered, and he goes to raise them.

From the window he has an uninterrupted view of the garden. It's sunk in an early evening mist, its lumpy grass and pines set too close together. In the distance he sees the ragged blue outline of Came Wood, and closer to home the wall of hazel he planted more than twenty years ago when the house was built, and in the lacy shadow of that wall, somebody.

Somebody is in the walk, advancing with slow, deliberate steps towards the Druid stone at the top. He can make out, quite distinctly, the deeper shadow of a head and hat above the low-lying vapour. He stops, his hand on the blind-cord, and becomes breathless, as if he's suddenly found himself treading a high rope.

When he leaves the house he is still under the spell of its strange hush. Though it's so quiet here, the far-off wood with its sycamores shouldering oak, its stout ivy-spun elms, appears to moan, as if the crowded branches were rubbing each other into wounds. But here – here there is silence; here there's no human or inhuman sound.

For centuries, before he and Emma came, no one had built or planted on this spot. Theirs was a virgin garden, they thought, a bold slash of brown and a brick perimeter in the ancient earth. Then, as the foundations of the house were dug, the builders uncovered a stone from a henge, and near it three skeletons in oval pits. The crown of each head touched the maiden chalk at one end, their tucked toes the other, like chicks in eggs. There were urns at their feet. Two of the bodies had metal circlets clasped around their skulls. One was a woman, from whom he himself had removed the bronze-gilt fibula that had fastened the fillet across her brow.

He'd erected their home on a graveyard. He'd believed that he could escape his past and build the world afresh. But he was always too alone, too remote from life. He was a person who had dwindled to a ghost in his prime, surrounded by all that unwinking newness.

To be a ghost forever – or, better, never to have been born at all. Instead of carrying this wasting flesh, to become ever more incorporeal, invisible, transparent – yes, he could imagine that. To have his intrusion into the world concluded like this, by being absorbed back into this anonymous clay, curled around a pitcher, letting the day perish in which he was born: that would be something –

He's reached the hazel walk. Nobody is waiting. Beyond it lie the old turnpike road and raw rolls of churned-up farmland; a sagging field gate, the mist condensing on its bars like silver buttons ranged in a row. He turns and is startled by the house: its savage redness, the witch's hat of its slate turret.

His wife is standing in the porch, calling his name.

'I saw her.'

He has run up to the front door, his heart thrashing. But there is no Emma; there's only Kate. She is bare-headed and carries a carpet bag. Her fingers tighten on the handles. Common sense and superstition are at war in her, as they are in him. 'You couldn't have.'

'It was just for a moment. But I did.'

'Don't be foolish. It was me you saw.'

'You, yes, but first I saw her.'

'Come inside, will you?' Kate draws him into the hall. She's arrived full of business, vigorously practical, and is unprepared for enormity. She peers over his shoulder into the dining room, takes in the dust on its surfaces, the stale, furtive smell. 'Why, there's no fire laid anywhere. Where are the maids? Have you *eaten* anything?'

He remembers now. 'They've gone to Genge's to buy clothes for the funeral. I gave them a holiday until six o'clock. I had some bread and jam this morning. I haven't been hungry.'

Kate relaxes visibly into her educated self. The drawing-room door is open wide, as it was when he rushed out. 'Jam is not food. Tomorrow, Tom. Are you ready?'

'No. I don't think I ever will be.'

'What orders have you given Jane for dinner?'

'None that I can recall. Mrs Riggs has been fixing my dinner for a good while now. I'm sure she knows what to do without being told.'

'I think you'll find she doesn't.'

'Then Flo will have given them to her.'

'I very much doubt it.' She looks him up and down, wrinkles her nose. 'When did you last bath?'

'This morning.'

'Liar. I'd like you to have a proper wash this evening. I've made up my mind. I'll be staying for a bit.'

'What about Mary?'

'Henry can look after her for a spell. They're only a few miles away and if I'm needed I can run back.' She is working herself up to the main point. 'He's all set for tomorrow, any rate. Mary won't manage it. But you know what she's like. She has no hard feelings towards Emma.'

'I'm sorry. The whole thing was uncivilized – that it went on so long. I wish it could've been mended.'

'Civilized, uncivilized. I'm really not certain what that means.' She stalls, then decides to say what she wants to say. 'Emma was jealous.'

'Jealous? Of whom? Not of you and Henry, surely. Of *Mary*?'

'Yes. You've always loved her best of all of us. Of anyone.'

'That's not true. It's just that she's nearest to me in age.'

Kate holds up an admonitory hand. 'Oh, please. Don't deny it. Now, tell me what I have to do to get the hot water going.'

The business of drawing the bath is slow and awkward. Since he didn't think to ask the servants to pump water before he gave them the day off, the roof tank is empty. When she hears this Kate rolls her eyes, hauls the copper onto the range, and sets off for the scullery with a jug.

There's no bathroom in the house. He usually washes in the hip bath in his room. But his sister draws the line at carrying jugfuls of warm water upstairs. 'I'm not your servant, Tom Hardy,' she says. 'You'll bath here in the kitchen, as you did at home. Go and fetch that tub. There's plenty of time till the girls get back.'

After a lot of toing and froing the bath is finally filled. He stands beside it, naked and alone, unable to get in. The water slants blackly, a Stygian pool. The kitchen is quiet except for the *tick-tick* of the cooling range. The air smells of fat, of old pastry and of something less comforting: rotting peelings, or drains. One of the stone flags is cracked. This is a part of his house he doesn't often see; this smut, this shabbiness. It's the back of things. He's become skilled at avoiding the back of things.

He steps into the tub and enters the water cautiously, bracing himself against the bath's tin sides. Once he's sitting he examines his partially submerged legs. He's never been robust, but this evening they seem to him particularly repugnant. They are the limbs of a working man who hasn't done a day's physical labour in his life. His shins are a narrow dull ivory, with a corded vein rumpling the surface of the left one. He begins to wash, running the bar of soap over his stomach and thighs, across the back of his neck, and under his armpits. At last he visits his testicles, cupping them in his hand, but doesn't look down.

Then he hears it: the heavy tread of a woman's foot, somewhere on the joists above. It's not Kate. It's someone slower, older.

His whole body grows rigid. He waits without breathing, listening for her. 'Why were you calling me? What do you want?' He's spoken aloud. His voice, enclosed by the gaunt walls, sounds hollow. There's no answer, only the thin slap of the water over his words.

When the bath has gone cold he raises himself out of its shallows and reaches for the towel and clean shirt Kate has left to warm in front of the range.

He dresses his pale flesh patiently, tenderly, as one might dress a child's.

That night he's woken by a dream. In his dream he is back in the cottage at Higher Bockhampton. His mother is sitting with him in his boyhood room. He's lying in bed, and he is in ferocious pain. It's his old childhood agony, the weakness that's afflicted him since birth. It fills his whole body so that he can't move or speak. Henry's bed is empty. There's no sign of either of the girls; of Mary, or Kate.

His mother crouches on a low stool by the grate, toasting bacon on a fork. Her face is bent to the fire and light leaps from her head in a feathery crown. She's singing to him in her sure alto voice, just as she did when he was little, before the others arrived to steal her away. 'What shall be my theme, when I sing to thee,' it tickles and coaxes, 'sitting by the village stream, under the chestnut tree?'

> 'Tell me, wilt thou choose
> A gay or mournful string?
> Shall love or war inspire my muse?
> Say, what shall I sing?'

She is whole, again unshattered, and the song seems to spill out of her like the promise of untold riches, like gold coin. She doesn't know that he is watching her. Shawled in flames, with her hair ablaze, she looks like and unlike herself.

He's frightened but at the same time oddly exhilarated, as if this pain and her reawakened tenderness might be the beginning of a new life.

A Ceremony

WHEN HE OPENS HIS eyes again it's morning. He's rising from the trough of darkness, not yet a body but only a point of sensation. His whole being is concentrated around the pressure of a woman's hand on his forehead. The curtains are looped back and the room is steeped in the muddy light of day. A moth hurls itself at the window, thumping against the pane with muffled beats.

'Mother.'

'Not Mother. Kate.'

'What's the time?'

'It's past ten. I've let you sleep,' says Kate. 'You were calling out in the night. But you must get up now.' She hands him a glass filled with something clouded. 'Here, drink this.'

'What is it?'

'Cider. And a drop of brandy. Make yourself decent, will you? Mr Hannah's waiting.'

He barely has time to work his legs into his trousers when Hannah arrives at the door with six black-suited men, partly shielded by a coffin lid. The men are rough and large-boned, the sort who would have been better suited to speeding a plough.

He hasn't had dealings with Hannah's firm before: old Mr Woods buried his mother eight years ago, and Kate settled everything then, too. It was Henry who informed the registrar. But he was present at her dying. He was there to hear his mother's last breath as it flicked away into silence.

In death her face was furious. Her hair, which she usually wore pinned, stood up in a huff. He stared at the array of medicine bottles on the bedside table with their Latin labels, balsams and tinctures and opiates, as if these useless things could yet contain some important truth.

Removed. Her dissatisfactions, her fiery glint, her songs, also removed – swallowed by that silence.

The world had just been stripped from him. All his sinews had been snapped. Beneath his exhaustion and regret he felt a savage sense of liberty – miserable relief that there was nothing more to be done, or feared, or hoped; that he was free to go or stay.

This feeling has never quite left him.

Now he stands there, only partly dressed, his head swimming with cider. He's aware that the bed is unmade and begins to fidget with the coverlet. 'I'm sorry,' he says. 'I haven't had a chance to straighten up.'

James Hannah himself looks unpromising. He's carrying a small hinged box and has a nose that runs to the side as if it might once have been broken.

Hannah instructs the men to lower the lid so it's resting against the bedframe, and sets his box down on the floor. There's no sense of hurry about him. The expression on his crooked features is affable, though it stops short of a smile. He nods at Em in her coffin with the apologetic friendliness of a man paying an unscheduled social call.

He's grateful for Hannah's professionalism, for his grasp of the situation, which seems to him suddenly like a form of grace. Hannah stoops and places both hands on his, bringing that broken nose close to his own. The undertaker's eyes have the mild dampness of moss.

'Nothing is required of you, Mr Hardy,' he says. 'Nothing at all. We are here to do everything.'

'Will there be time to say goodbye?'

'There will be as much time as you need. Please don't mind us.'

It appears that whatever happens next must be played out in public. The bearers jostle each other, spreading out in a respectful row. He has given up his life to a ritual that he alone, among all those in the room, doesn't understand. *Be still*, he tells himself. *Be still*.

He approaches the coffin. *Well, Emmie.* He cups her head in his hands. Her skin has a rusty tinge, like the stain on a badly washed teacup. Her lips have darkened to pewter. *So you have to go again. There's a right way to do this, though I can't for the life of me say what it is. There are rules. I know that much. I want to call you back but it isn't allowed.* He kisses her forehead. *I'll wait for you. Please wait for me.*

Two of the men step forward and shunt the coffin lid over the base until it fits snugly. Emma vanishes by degrees.

He braces himself for the moment of severing, but it doesn't come. He wants to cry out, *Stop. Something is wrong. You haven't done this properly. She hasn't gone. She's still here. She's as much here as she ever was.*

When they bring out their tools from the little box he is unprepared. He keeps very quiet, though he knows it's no use. There are four thick gimlet screws, each over an inch long, topped by cast iron slotted heads. Hannah drives them into the lid one by one, using a flat blade. The first goes in with a creak, then the second and third. But the last jars on some knot or rift in the oak.

Unperturbed, Hannah asks for an auger. A different blade is found, with a spiralling tip. Hannah gives a soft grunt as he forces it into the wood. The smell of sap darts through the air, shocking in its greenness. Minutes later the screw slips in without a sound.

Hannah wipes his tools with a cloth and packs them carefully away. At his nod the ploughmen step up to the coffin. They roll their shoulders and wedge themselves under it, three a side, lifting it to expose the plywood trestle beneath. Once the box is airborne Hannah folds up the trestle and whips it under his arm. 'Steady on the stairs, lads,' he says.

He is left behind in the bleak, sour room. All the breath has gone out of him.

'Come on,' says Kate. 'Down we go.'

'Is there more?'

'Not much more. Come, now.'

When they get to the hall the coffin has gone, but Hannah still hovers.

'Will we take the flowers now or later, ma'am?' he says.

'Later, please, Mr Hannah.'

Two wreaths, plump as life buoys, are laid out on the dining-room table. Lilies and carnations round out the smaller; the other is studded in addition to these with China asters the colour of twilight. They are exactly what the flowers presented by a grieving widower – not just any widower but an internationally celebrated English poet and novelist – and his sorrowing family should be. A card embedded in the first wreath bears the message *In loving memory – Henry, Mary and Katharine Hardy*. The card lying in front of the larger wreath is blank.

There's a bottle of ink on the table; a pen. Kate hands him the pen with a meaningful stare. He takes it from her dumbly. Its heft is unfamiliar in his hand. 'Well?' he says.

'Don't look at me like that. I'm going to stand here till you do the deed.'

He turns his back on her with an obscure sense of disgrace, bending low over the table-top. The ink gathers in a bead at the pen nib and hangs there sullenly before spurting, as if of its own volition, into words.

From her lonely husband, with the old affection.

'There,' he says. 'Are you satisfied?'

Kate raises her eyebrows. She blows on the card and tucks it behind an aster head. 'Lunch is at one. Flo has put out your clothes.' He sees her resolving to take her small revenge. 'Can you dress yourself?'

'*Katie.*'

'Fine. I'll leave you to it.'

For a moment the dressing room connecting his bedroom with what, long ago, was Emma's, appears as it always has: the ottoman drawn up to the fire, the walls solid with light. It promises routine, forgetfulness, ease; all the things that have, in the space of three days, slipped out of reach. His shirt hangs from the washstand rail, turning in the draught.

He kneels on the floor and presses his hands wonderingly along the boards. It seems to him that he can still hear the *creak, creak, creak* of the coffin screws vibrating through the house. Emma's cats have come in and lie piled before the grate, like rugs left out to dry. The air is thick with the tang of their fur.

At one o'clock he finds his way back downstairs in his black suit and town shoes that are too tight. A cold lunch has replaced the wreaths on the dining table. He and Kate help themselves to sliced tomatoes and a grudging little dish of chipped chicken, then sit and regard each other without eating. In the silence between them the hall clock ticks violently.

'You've wound it,' he says at last.

'I had to,' says Kate. 'I didn't think you were ever going to.' She smooths his cuff with a conciliatory fingertip. 'It'll be all right, Tommy. Just get through the next few hours.'

At half past one Florence arrives to clear their untouched plates. 'Dolly and Mrs Riggs have gone on ahead now, miss'ess. If you're done here I'll lay out the tea things for after and then I'll be on my way also.'

'Is it all to be cold food today?' asks Kate.

'Yes, miss'ess. There's a ham pie.'

Kate straightens her spine, considering. 'Well, let's see if the tea can be hot.'

Rain is falling as the hearse pulls into the church close at Stinsford. From here a dirt track runs past farmyards and leafless apple orchards, along pastureland and water meadows, to the banks of the Frome. At the top of the churchyard rise, sheltering under the branches of the old yew, he sees Henry. Some girls carrying chrysanthemums are blocking the church door. Kate hurries on ahead to shoo them aside, but as Hannah's men carry the coffin through the gate he hangs back.

'Hello, Hen. You look very clean.'

'So do you. I'm sorry, Tom.' Henry casts about for the right thing to say. 'She was as handsome a girl as ever I did see, back in the day.' He tries again. 'Well, I had no quarrel with her, any rate.'

'No, you didn't. How's Mary?'

'The same, thank 'ee.'

'I told Katie she shouldn't leave you both just now. But she won't be gainsaid.'

'Have her and welcome. We can manage.' Henry smiles at him. 'When the cat's away.'

He smiles back. 'Will you come to the house afterwards?'

'I'll be getting along home to Mary. But thank 'ee all the same.'

The coffin has stopped at the entrance where the children are still stamping their heavy boots, trampling petals into the mud.

'What's all this?'

'Lasses from Fordington St George Needlework Guild,' says Henry. 'They'd like to lay a tribute.'

'They can't wait out here in the wet. We'd better let them in.'

The church is cold and smells of vinegar paste and stale candles. There are two clergymen, the Reverends Cowley and Metcalfe, assisting in the service. (How pleased Emma would have been at this sign of distinction!)

Cowley appears from the vestry, chin and neck purpled by a

shaving rash, and shakes his hand. 'Blessed are those who mourn, Mr Hardy, for they shall be comforted.'

'Yes, Vicar,' he says. 'Thank you.'

While Metcalfe manipulates the lectern the coffin is stowed on a trestle in the aisle, like luggage that must be put out of the way.

Hardly anybody has come. What a solitary life he and Em led here, in spite of his fame. Man and wife are one flesh. Well, they were one flesh all right, he thinks with a shiver of anger, clinging together at first in mutual self-sufficiency – and then, later, chafing at each other in mutual resentment. Solitary – and lonely.

Behind the Owens, who are seated in the second row, he notices the Leslies and the Bartelots and the flash of Eliza Wood Homer's lorgnette, but most of the chairs are empty. He squeezes into a chair at the front between Kate and Henry and sits staring through the north window at the blank sky and the urns, glazed with rain, crowning the churchyard hatch. His anger seeps away.

Are you here, Emmie? I don't feel that you're here, after all.

The burial service begins. Metcalfe gives a cough and intones the opening line of the psalm in a scratchy quaver. 'I said, I will take heed to my ways: that I offend not in my tongue.'

'I held my tongue, and spake nothing: I kept silence, yea, even from good words; but it was pain and grief to me.

'My heart was hot within me, and while I was thus musing the fire kindled: and at the last I spake with my tongue;

'Behold, thou hast made my days as it were a span long: and mine age is even as nothing in respect of thee; and verily every man living is altogether vanity.

'For man walketh in a vain shadow, and disquieteth himself in vain: he heapeth up riches, and cannot tell who shall gather them.

'When thou with rebukes dost chasten man for sin, thou makest his beauty to consume away, like as it were a moth fretting a garment: every man therefore is but vanity.'

Vanity . . . vain . . . vain . . . vanity. The words are an impenetrable code. The wooden talons of the eagle supporting the lectern, the naked bump of Metcalfe's head: these things, too, seem freighted with a meaning which he can't understand but has no hope of evading.

Before the third lesson a hymn is announced. They start on 'O Worship the King', set to Ravenscroft's Old-Hundred-and-Fourth, unaccompanied except by the young needlewomen. His voice withers in his mouth. It's a tune he and Em never sang together, though she sometimes played it on the drawing-room piano. The sound would travel through the silent house to his study. Hearing it now is like hearing the answer to a suggestion he failed to make.

'O worship the King all-glorious above,
O gratefully sing his power and his love:
Our shield and defender, the Ancient of Days,
Pavilioned in splendour and girded with praise.'

The Fordington girls' voices are unexpectedly pure and true, dazzling motes in the dead air, both petition and fulfilment. Somewhere at the back of the nave Dolly Gale starts to cry.

As they make their way from the church to the graveside the clouds part and the late afternoon sun comes out, turning the chalk to pearl. The coffin goes down into the hole on squealing ropes.

'Earth to earth,' says Cowley, 'ashes to ashes, dust to dust.'

He's unprepared for the showmanship of the moment, its reckless public display. There's a mound of freshly dug soil lying nearby. Cowley holds out a miniature spade in his direction, handle first, and he realizes, too late, that he's being asked to cast some of this dirt into the pit. He shakes his head; stoops and drags his fingers hastily through the wet ground, flinging it from him. As the clod lands on the coffin it makes a small thud. No one else comes forward. His shoes pinch his feet.

It is unbearable, all of it, but it's almost over. At a sign from Cowley he steps with exaggerated care to the edge of the grave and places his wreath at its head. Then the girls lay theirs. He longs to thank them, but is overcome by sudden shyness.

They're about to leave the churchyard when a mud-flecked Ford crawls up to the gate. The passenger door opens slowly and a woman gets out. She's dressed in black satin, with black feathers in her hat, an onyx necklace resting on her bosom, and black gloves. There's a crinkle of reddish hair wagging at each of her temples. Her cheeks, between which a child-like nose is barely visible, are curved like butter balls. It's Em's niece. It's Lilian.

'I'm here,' she announces. 'Your roads are simply ghastly at this time of year.'

'Good afternoon, Miss Gifford,' says Kate. 'This is a surprise. The ceremony was at half past two.'

'I telegraphed ahead. I sent a *telegram*.'

'Flo?' he asks doubtfully, looking around.

'I'm sorry, sir,' says Florence Griffin. 'I don't recall anything o' that nature arriving this morning.'

'Oh, sir,' sobs Dolly. 'It was me as took en in. I forgot to say.'

'Well, never mind that now,' says Kate. She turns to Lilian with her hand outstretched. 'Tom's sister. Very glad to meet you. You'll be coming to the house, I'm sure.'

Lilian's black satin fingers remain fastidiously clasped. 'Oh, yes. My trunk is in the car.'

'*Trunk?*'

Lilian smiles. When she smiles she smiles too much, over all her face and chin, round to her ears and up into the scribble of her hair. 'I shan't be returning to London for a few nights at least. I'll be staying to take care of you, Daddy-Uncle.'

'But where is she to sleep?' asks Kate, barring his way at the door to the servants' staircase. Tremulous voices tinkle in the drawing room, punctuated from time to time by Miss Owen's sterling boom. 'You can't put her in one of the front rooms. They're not much bigger than that trunk of hers.'

He knows they aren't. He designed the rooms. He designed the whole house, which suddenly appears to him both mean and pretentious, smothered by foliage, like a house dropped into a tray of vegetation. 'Pavilioned in splendour', indeed. *Oh, Em.* Too late to do anything about it now. Too late to do anything about the boxy guest quarters, the dank discomfort of the place.

'She can have Emma's old room across from mine. I'll ask Flo to see to it.'

'That should please her. Will there be enough to eat? She looks as if she has a healthy appetite.'

'Really, Katie, I don't know. Ask Flo. Ask Mrs Riggs. I'm going upstairs for an hour.'

'Why? Why *now*?'

'Because I am tired. Because I want to rest.'

But he doesn't go up at once. Standing by the staircase door he hears splinters of female conversation coming from the kitchen; Kate's casual bargaining. A memory assembles itself, secret as a warming stone, of the old noises of home: the click of the smoke-jack, the flap of the flames on the hearth, and the light shuffle of women's slippers on the stone floor.

'Jane, will that pie stretch, d'you think?' says Kate.

How easily she talks to them, how much like herself she is. She's firm without being unkind, affable without becoming overfamiliar. You would never guess that she was born in a cob-and-lime cottage to a charity-child mother. Yet he's been ashamed half his life of her country accent, her clothes. He sees that she's always known this. She knows.

'Yes, miss'ess. Master don't eat much, and I've made an extra.'

'Good woman. Let's get it on the table.'

His room is too large, now that the coffin has gone. There are scrape marks on the boards by the bed where the trestle stood. The air is grey, the light of the November day already fading. He opens the window and looks out over the thronged pines and bumpy grass of the garden. The pines wait there as if he has summoned them to him, alert, watchful, their black sides bristling. They make their usual breathing sound, a susurration like the growth of a thousand unseen filaments. A spectral moon hangs above their tops. Except for the whispering of their boughs it is quiet. They are so dense that they seem to swallow the moonlight; threaten to open into a different dimension entirely. He stays at the window for a little while longer, watching their formlessness dissolve the visible world.

Once it's completely dark he takes up his comb, straightens his thinning hair, and goes back downstairs. On his way to the dining room he ducks into the scullery, where Dolly is heaping dirty silverware from a tray into the sink.

'Dolly, did anything else come this morning?'

'How, sir?'

'In the post.'

'Oh yes, sir. A letter.'

'May I have it?'

'Oh, certainly, sir.' The knives and forks subside with a gurgle. Dolly digs around in the pocket of her apron and pulls out an envelope, its edges bent and translucent with lard. 'Sorry, sir. I'm that joppety today.'

'Thank you. It doesn't matter.' He retreats down the passage but finds himself stopping halfway, with the greasy letter still in his hands. He's waited for this, though he hasn't known until now that he's been waiting.

He runs his finger under the flap. Inside the envelope, folded in half, there's a single typed sheet of paper.

Dearest Tom,

Because I have not written to you before that does not mean that I have not thought of you constantly. I hope, *with all my heart*, that you are well and that your silence does not mean that anything is amiss. This is, of course, a very great change for you. You have lived so long in that house in awful loneliness – with that feeling that there is no one in it who cares whether you are happy or sad. It is of all feelings the worst.

I wish that I were nearer. You know that if I had to give up the rest of my life to bring you just one half-hour of comfort or peace I would do it gladly.

With my love always,

Florence

Lilian

ON SUNDAY MORNING he keeps to his room till he's heard Kate and Lilian leaving for church. Above and below him hip baths have been filled, breakfast has been served and eaten. He hasn't had what Kate would call 'a proper meal' in days but he isn't hungry. The machine of his body seems to have stopped.

This is my house. He lies in bed and looks up at the ceiling's dim frieze, its smoke-blurred cornice. Unnoticed by anyone, a sizeable crack has begun to spread in the plaster. The building vibrates with the tread of women coming and going on the stairs and the banging of doors. *This is the house I built.* A lone pipe rumbles behind his head and he feels, all at once, as if this isn't his house after all; as if he's an interloper here, enclosed in these noisy walls that are filled with the smell of talc and frying.

At last: the shirr of car wheels on the gravel. Dropping his legs out of bed, he reaches for the lamp and unfolds Florence's letter.

You know that if I had to give up the rest of my life to bring you just one half-hour of comfort or peace I would do it gladly.

There's a terrible temptation in these words. How easy it would be to surrender to Florence's loving kindness, her need to be of service;

to hand over the burden of his sudden aimlessness and insubstantiality to her. He'd be released: from the requirement to feel, to speak, to appear in public; to be a man visibly disabled by grief, and at the same time a man who must concern himself with visitors and meals and ceiling cracks. He could succumb to nothingness. But he'd still have to appear substantial, to be present, to Florence herself, and he's by no means sure that he has it in him to do this. He'll send her a few lines and put her off for another week, or maybe even a month. He will be very gentle.

Though it's only a short distance to his study, down the shallow landing steps and along the corridor leading past the W.C., he's afraid that the sound of his movements in the quiet house might alert the servants. Once he's there and has locked the letter away in the private drawer of his desk, he knows he's behaving foolishly. Nobody comes. Somewhere else the day is gathering itself without him, as he's always insisted it should.

He turns up the lamp and is briefly dazzled by its reflection on the table-top. His things are arranged on his desk in an orderly fashion, undisturbed. The poem he was tinkering with four days ago rests beside the blotter. Securing a clean sheet of paper, he opens his ink-well and takes up his pen.

The pen's weight in the crook of his hand feels entirely natural. He breathes evenly, absorbing the stillness of the moment, in which he knows himself to be most himself and yet nothing at all, just a man in a dusty room, where the silent minutes slip past.

What should he say to Florence?

Whenever he thinks of her he sees a far-away spot, a cream spot, the colour of calico or some other unpretentious yet essential fabric, coming towards him on railway platforms, on London streets, on the steps of libraries. As he gazes at the spot he's suffused with a feeling of heat and amplitude. Of hope.

When Miss Dugdale from Enfield first wrote to him to express her admiration for his writing and to offer her services as a researcher and general 'handyman', he didn't (though that word was fresh, even bold) expect much. The invitation to tea was a mere courtesy. But then, as he was escorting her back down the drive, Florence had paused and, lifting her head – he noticed this because all afternoon she'd kept her chin tucked down – touched her nose with a small cry of pleasure to the white blooms of the bordering privet. 'Their scent is just like sherry,' she said. 'It takes you by surprise.' Until she spoke it had swum away from him, unremarked.

In those few seconds he understood that Florence had this authority: to name things, to make them appear. He turned to her in amazement and gratitude, as if she'd just given him a living piece of the world.

Since that day they've gone on meeting: at Max Gate, of course, to work – but also in tea shops and theatres and cabs and museums; at his club, at the seaside house parties of a discreet friend. Never just the two of them over a breakfast-table, never in a room, at night, alone. One evening, while walking home from the station after seeing Florence off on the train to Waterloo, he realized that he wished he could be returning to an empty house, a house without Emma in it. He simply wanted her gone. *I wish she were dead. I wish she were dead. I wish she were dead.* The thought was as spontaneous, as natural, as the action of walking itself. He realized with a stab of horror that he'd had it for some time: more years than he liked to admit.

Though Florence hasn't pressed her claim, he knows that she's waiting to be summoned to his side.

And now he must write to her.

He intends to write: *You have been endlessly good and kind. You've put up with this impossible situation where so few women would: with my demands and absences, my dark moods, with Emma's skittishness, her tempestuous friendship.*

He'll write: *You've been patient with us for so long – please be patient a little longer.*

But why? Why go on being patient, when there's finally no need? Hasn't he been called to liberty? And doesn't Florence have a right to expect something more from him?

He should write: *You don't have to give up anything. I'm here, ready to receive you – you only. You mean everything to me.*

It could happen now: the return to corporeality, to the hard outlines of the life he'd been living before Wednesday. In that life his work was real and Emma alive, and Florence existed mainly on paper. Now Florence could be real too. He could have both work and love, frank and acknowledged. He could lower his pen to the page, cast his spell, re-enter the world.

He could, but he doesn't. He realizes that he can't write to Florence at all. Whatever he says will sound forced. She's an excellent reader, one of the very best he's had; she'll be able to detect the falsity in his words at once. *You've been patient with us for so long.* That *us* has betrayed him. His wife is dead, but somehow he's still a husband. He's unable, at present, to believe in himself as a lover.

*

At ten o'clock there's a knock on the door and the handle turns abruptly. A smiling Lilian hobbles in sideways, balancing a tray against her stomach.

'How are you this morning, Daddy-Uncle?'

'Moderately well, thank you,' he says, setting his pen aside.

'Miss Hardy said that you wouldn't come to church, so we didn't wait.'

'Quite right.'

She bumps the tray down in front of him. 'I've brought you some bacon.'

He finds, to his surprise, that he's hungry. In this strange new existence he seems incapable of knowing who he is or what he wants till he's led to it by others. At this very minute he seems to be a hungry man. 'Well now, that's thoughtful,' he says. 'I'll have a little.'

There's a thick rasher speckled with melting brown sugar, exactly the way he likes it. He slices off a corner and is about to eat it when Lilian speaks. 'I wonder if I may have one or two of dear Aunt's things, to remember her by.' Her smile widens. 'Unneeded things.'

'Please take anything you like. Your aunt's bible, now. I think that must be upstairs.'

'Oh no, I couldn't take that. I was hoping for something more personal, more feminine.'

'Ah. Of course,' he says, though he doesn't begin to understand what this might mean. 'Her hairbrush?'

Lilian blinks rapidly, as if he's been guilty of an indelicacy. 'Well,' she says with a certain coolness, 'I do have *several* of my own.'

He abandons his fork. He's been drawn into a game of hide-and-seek. This is how it was latterly with Emma: this coyness with a thorn in it, this perilous beating about the bush. 'Naturally. How about – her gloves?'

Lilian glances up. He must be getting warmer. 'Gloves would be splendid. But you know, Daddy-Uncle, they won't fetch much.'

'I've been under the impression for some years that one has to buy the wretched things, not sell them.'

'Ah, but it would be such a shame to let all Auntie Emma's clothes just sit there,' says Lilian. 'Now that she's not here to wear them, I mean.' She has the grace to colour at this.

'No. She isn't.' He's mesmerized by Lilian's doughy wrists. They're soft and pale, thickly braceleted with creases. In the lamp-light their contours seem to shimmer; to become, by stealth, those of another woman. His appetite has disappeared. He longs, involuntarily, to flee. 'So. What do you propose?'

Lilian smiles again. 'If you wouldn't mind, I'd like to take some of the really good pieces back with me. Not to have for myself, but to see what they'd be worth in town. The better dressmakers are always ready to buy ladies' garments if they're nicely made.'

'Are you all right, Lilian?' he says. 'Are you in need of anything? Your aunt would have wanted me to ask.'

'Oh yes. It's not a question of *need*, merely of economy. Since I'm Auntie's closest female relative, and you've no—'

He raises his hand. *Oh, Emmie, don't. Don't say it*, he implores her silently. *Don't say the word.* 'I've no objection. I'm grateful to you.' He can feel the blood draining from his cheeks. 'You're relieving me of a considerable burden. I don't want to have to go through her things. It must be done, of course. But it will be . . . well, it will be difficult.'

Lilian is instantly, hotly voluble. 'Please let me do it for you. I'm simply here to *help*.'

'There's no hurry,' he says. She's seized his fingers and he flinches in her clutch, just as his mother used to flinch when they came bounding up to her without giving her a chance to defend herself against their love. 'Take your time. You can start on all that next week.'

'I thought I'd begin today, if it's not inconvenient.' Lilian gives his hand a squeeze. 'I'm not able to stay as long as I'd like. Once I've made sure that you're being thoroughly looked after I must dash home. But I'll be back.'

Her smile has become watery, so that her whole face is dilute with woe. She is remarkably like Em, but she isn't Em. He detaches his flesh from hers, trying for a voice that's firm yet accommodating. 'In that case, let's see if my housekeeper can lend us her keys.'

'I've taken the liberty of having a peep in the wardrobe here and I don't see much,' says Lilian, 'only a few skirts and blouses. Not even any night linen.'

They're in Emma's old bedroom, herded together in front of the dressing table. Their reflections billow and shrink in its bubbled glass like figures in a fairground mirror. Though he's passed this room daily to get to his study he hasn't set foot in it for years. Following a night's occupation by Lilian it's untidy: pillows heaped up anyhow on the counterpane, a lidless pot of Pomeroy's Skin Food, a toothbrush and packet of curling papers scattered across the table-top. There's a curious bite to the air, a lingering sweetness, that doesn't seem to belong to any of these vague and transient things.

Florence Griffin hesitates, the bundle of house keys in her hand. 'Miss'ess Hardy had her usual bed up in the attic, miss. She kept som'at o' her day clothes in this press. The things for best are in the dressing room next door.'

'I rather suspected they might be,' says Lilian. 'But the door is locked.'

'Sir?'

He meets Flo's eye. 'Open it all up.'

Flo finds the ward key to the connecting door. The lock sticks at first, but yields after a push. They're in Em's old half of the dressing room. From this side the space appears too small, too condensed. In its looking-glass world he wouldn't be surprised to see himself, dwarf-like, capering at the far end. The oak armoire that was Em's soars above them. Flo produces a smaller key.

'Here we are, miss.'

The door swings open onto a row of Emmas, headless, armless, that will spring to life at a touch.

'How exquisite!' says Lilian. 'Just feel this apricot silk. And this Irish lace. I could get at least twenty guineas for each.'

'Miss'ess Hardy always looked like a lady,' says Flo.

'She did, didn't she, Uncle? You must have given her a generous dress allowance.'

'Yes. I did.' He will go. He will go now. 'I'll be in my study, Lilian.'

'Oh, of course. You must *write*, dearest. Please put any sad thoughts out of your mind,' says Lilian, as if writing weren't done by those who are determined to court sorrow at every turn. 'I shall leave you absolutely in peace.'

He sits at his desk, his sides heaving. The bacon has curled into a fist. His nostrils are full of the odour of those clothes: camphor, and dust, and that unmistakable nectarish scent that was Emma's. The whole bedroom was pregnant with it: the room that had once been hers, and before this – in another life, when the house was newly built – theirs, as though her smell dwelled in the fabrics.

In that long-ago life the moon has risen above the pines. They're saplings still, merely the impression of trees. He is watching her sleep. The sheet has slipped back and her shoulders are white, like the shoulders of a statue. He sees, again, what he saw on countless such nights: that her lower lip has a way of thrusting the middle of her top lip upward when they close together.

Come back to me, Emmie. Just for a night. Or if not for a night, then for a minute. Come back as you were, and I'll be as I was, only better. I can be better.

'Good morning.' Kate's head arrives around the door. When he doesn't respond, she walks in. 'I thought yesterday went smoothly enough, considering that you didn't make an appearance at tea until everyone had left.'

With a great effort he gathers himself up. 'Untrue. The Owens were still here.'

'Indeed.' She turns to him, her hands clasped in mock piety. 'But I fear *they* will be with you even unto the end of the age.'

'Katie.' Taking his sister by the elbows, he rests his forehead lightly against hers. 'Thank you. How I've missed you.'

Kate tolerates the caress for a few seconds before pushing him away. 'Don't go soft on me. Where's Lilian?'

'She's sorting through Emma's clothes. She says she'll be able to secure a fair price for the better pieces in London.'

'Ah. So *that's* what the trunk is for.'

'I'm not going to begrudge her a few dresses and coats.'

'I hope she understands that's all she'll be getting from you. From the way she's taken possession I rather fear she's planning on stopping indefinitely.' Kate putters at the window, dabs a finger along the sill. 'I must say, I can't see what's so grand about these Giffords that we've had to stay hidden from them all these years.'

'None of it was Lil's doing. She may lack tact but she's a harmless enough child. She's an innocent.'

'She's hardly innocent and she's no child. She's well over thirty. Why does she call you by that preposterous name?'

'I assume it's because she misses having a father. She's been coming and going from this house since she was a girl. She's welcome to stay.'

'Tom. This isn't a time for sentimentality. Who's going to run things? You won't. Her Ladyship won't. Someone has to start giving orders to the staff if you're to eat more than leftovers and wash once in a while. You're not just a man, you're a business. I know Emma had her faults but at least she made sure you looked the part.' She wiggles a blackened fingertip at him. 'This room is dirty.'

'It's always been dirty. I don't want the servants fussing in here when I'm writing. Writing is a dirty business.'

'Clearly,' says Kate, rubbing her palms together. 'The whole place smells of cat. And what about those trees? It's so dark indoors you can't see your porridge to stir it.'

'There's a fellow who comes in three days a week to look after the garden. Trevis.'

'Doesn't Trevis own a pair of clippers?'

'I am *not* cutting back the pines, Kate. I don't like to injure them.'

'Then you'd better get somebody to do for you who can find her way about by touch.' Kate sighs, broad, iron-haired, propping her chest with her arms. She's scaffolded by a lifetime of efficiency. She has always managed to make him feel unclean; like a daydreaming fool. 'Look, I know a capable girl who needs a position. Her father is the bootmaker at Lower Bockhampton. She's been in a large house before.'

'I can't have a stranger here now. Boots! I'd prefer someone who can read to me.'

'Oh, really. How? In Braille?' A bold smile. She knows she's gone too far. 'Did Emma read to you?'

'No. But it makes no difference.'

'Then I gather it's to be Lilian, after all?'

'I've heard from Miss Dugdale.'

'Well. I did wonder.'

'I don't ask for much, Katie. I only want a little affection.'

'Literature and love aren't the same thing. Surely you of all people should know that by now.'

A Branch

ONCE THE DOOR HAS closed on Kate he goes on sitting at his writing table, arms slack on the blotter, sensing himself grow gradually more diffuse. Beyond the windows the inshore wind, laden with fresh rain, scours the fields. Watery light pools across his wrists and withdraws again.

He's a writer who isn't writing. In the domestic routine of Max Gate nothing else is expected of him; if he's not producing words he might as well not exist. Where purpose, or at any rate habit, used to be, there's the vacuum of a Sunday morning in which he has no role to play.

His new state of non-being is deeply unpleasant. Yet he's spent countless Sundays sitting just like this, without ever showing his face, practising his art – which has always been, he realizes with an inward shudder, the art of invisibility. The work of erasing himself used to seem entirely natural. Now that he isn't doing it, it appears freakish, an act of inattention wilfully disguised as its opposite.

Time itself has sagged, has become something with stretch but without shape. How he ever managed to fill it is perhaps the greatest puzzle of all. He glances at his watch. It's only eleven o'clock, yet it feels like hours since Kate left. He wouldn't be able to say, if asked, how he or anyone else in his household used to endure the day. The mystery of time's disintegration is part of the mystery of Emma's vanishing.

After a while he's roused from his torpor by a creaking sound overhead. There it is again: *creak, creak, creak*, a persistent note beneath the muffled rattle of the rain, like the tread of a sewing machine. He wonders if Dolly can be up there, sewing, on a Sunday forenoon.

Moments later he's climbing the stairs to the attic. Dolly's room is empty; there isn't a soul about. The brown corridor is as murky and threadbare as before. He stops at Emma's door. *Creak, creak, creak.* That sound, a hundred times louder and more confounding at close quarters, is coming from behind it.

His hand is strange on the lock, his body is strange. He can't be certain, as the handle turns and the door swings open, if it's yielded at his push, or pulled him in. Apart from the stripped bed, everything looks exactly as it did four days ago. The creaking, he sees at once, is being made by a blown branch from the apple orchard that's lodged itself under the dormer and is chafing at the window frame.

His disappointment arrives with such a smash that he feels light-headed.

You are gone, and not gone, Em. Was it really you I saw?

Next to the window is the desk where he sat for the very first time on Wednesday morning. He pulls out the chair and resumes his place at it diffidently, as if the self he was then isn't, perhaps, the one who's come to visit now. It's a scrawny beech-wood table, not much bigger than a school desk, with a solitary drawer. Dust has already begun to settle in a film on Emma's clutter, on her rickety poems and her prescriptions: all the rubbish of her life. How little of it there was, in the end. A few dresses, a few bits of paper.

He sits hunched over the mess, crooked and faint. Well, well. It's past mending. Soon even these things will have to go: her scribblings, her shelf of novels (which doesn't, he notices, contain a single one of his, just as there's no trace of the signed photograph of him which he gave her for her birthday last week), the painted musical box with its shaky gilt capitals, SOUVENIR DE ROUEN. There can't be much else. He'll look through it all later, once he has the house to himself again, once he's recovered himself.

Rain lashes the window, where the apple branch waves its claw. *Creak, creak, creak.* He unfastens the latch to set it free, willing the storm to strike at him. Water runs down his face.

In the plunge of his grief the wet and the cold bring a welcome clarity. There's no particular mystery here. Or rather, the mystery of Emma's absence, of her inexistence despite the survival of this trash, is everywhere. She is dead. She's utterly, irretrievably dead. She might never have lived at all.

He's about to turn away from the desk when he has an impulse to try the drawer. It won't open. He assumes it must be locked and nearly loses his footing as it jerks in his grip. The drawer isn't locked: it's merely caught, disclosing a margin of darkness. He slides his fingers into the gap. In its shadowy recess they meet with something cool and dry. After some twisting and prodding the darkness gives way to light, and he finds himself in possession of a good strong exercise book of the kind sold in town at Longman's.

The book is bent at the edges, as if it has recently been rolled up.

The cover flips back to reveal Emma's breakneck script, with the fatly looped *f*s, the *y*s like crochet hooks. Not poetry this time, but prose.

> I think possibly some people may like to know what my early life was like, & to have some account of my family; what I did with myself when I was young, how I looked, & how I met my husband.

There's a heading, underlined: <u>Some Recollections</u>. No date. He flicks through the pages. They are all filled.

It's a memoir. Emma has been – she was – writing about her youth. After the first shock of surprise he realizes that he's both moved and oddly excited. He bows his damp head, his heart jumping, balancing the book lightly in his hands. Apart from the juddering rain, no sound penetrates the deep silence of the eaves. The house might be asleep, bewitched.

He starts to read, slowly at first, and then with the lurching sensation that he's taken hold of something over which he has no control. Pictures come and go, raised by Emma's words. In his absorption he's not sure if they are her memories, or visions. A rose-covered house by the bay with a drip-stone, under which a bucket receives the slow-falling water drop by drop. A child walking on glassy rocks, her shoes and stockings off, while an older girl dodges the foam, jingling two pennies in her cupped palms. *Hurry up, Em, there won't be any left if you don't hurry up.*

A marble-streeted town, its harbour thronged with ships, its bandsmen booming a throbbing waltz in the sun. They buy buns still hot from the baker's oven and eat them, leaning against the rail, as the day broadens in slow blue strokes. Before them is the sea, a froth of silver. In the Royal Baths the stale passages echo with the high clear voice of the attendant carrying dry towels, herding the giggling bathers into dressing rooms which open on the opposite side, and there is the sea again, up close now, a great mystery that deepens at its centre – down they go, along the steps descending from the cubicles, gripping the short ropes, launching themselves onto the cork-floats, into the pool of shouting, laughing female bodies – into coolness, freshness and saltness.

A funeral, and the bustle of that place, all its stir and noise, slipping away in a torrent of farewells: the rotten rose ripped from the wall, clocks and carpets and chairs left out on the lawn all day, the brightest things from the old life exposed for the rain to mar.

A new, country home with a choked lily pond and an orchard, yellow and knobby, where mushrooms poke dumb snouts through the mud. There is an 'instrument', on which 'pieces' are played, love songs, and jigs. There are many books; *Evelina* and *Rasselas*. There's a pony for her to ride. But there are no excursions now, no guests, only a young lady with a lisp from the nearby hotel, an acquaintance of her sister's, who is once invited to tea. Together they sit and speculate about their future husbands. That is, the other two speculate. The young lady commands her to put down her 'Rathelath' and this seems so funny that she starts to hiccup. *Oh you are vile, Emma, really you are. No well-bred man will ever marry you.* She hiccups that she prefers novels and riding to husbands.

How lonely it is, among the mushrooms and lilies. How dull.

One day a gypsy comes to the door. The gypsy insists on telling her fortune, hers and her sister's; asks for two eggs, two tumblers of water. They each break an egg into the water, the white only, and watch the form it takes. Her sister begins the charm eagerly – a church with a tower arises, a pointed steeple. Her sister will marry a clergyman. Her own egg makes a very large ink-bottle and an immense quill pen, stretching across the water.

He scarcely notices that he's been turning the pages for several minutes. He has yet to reach the part where he enters her story. But now there's no escape. He can feel it drawing nearer. He can feel himself being conjured.

When I was still a young woman my sister married the Reverend Caddell Holder, of St Juliot Rectory near Boscastle in North Cornwall, & I went to live with them. To this remote spot new books rarely came, or visitors.

My sister's husband was a man much older than herself, & often unwell, & the responsibility for the upkeep of things fell mainly to her. Our parish being very poor, the church had been a long while out of repair for want of funds. The tower went on cracking from year to year & the bells lay, open-mouthed & dumb, in the north transept to which they had been removed.

Finally it was announced that the church restoration was to take place, & the whole rectory was alive with excitement. But though my sister was active in the matter, the architect, Mr Crickmay of Dorset, continued to delay sending his head man to begin operations. At last, for reasons which were mysterious to us, Mr Crickmay decided to start. His associate was on his way.

Yes, this is his life. This is what he remembers. How strange to see it from a distance, so reduced, as a mere detail of Emma's.

> It was a lovely Monday evening in March. After a wild winter we were on the qui-vive for the traveller, who would have a tedious journey, his home being two counties off, changing trains many times & waiting at stations – a sort of cross-jump journey, like a chess-knight's move. The only damper to our gladness was the sudden laying up of my brother-in-law by gout. The dinner-cloth was spread, my sister had gone to her husband, who required her constant attention. At that very moment the front door bell rang & the stranger was ushered in.

It was long ago, and yet it isn't long ago. It happened at that far-off time, and still it is always happening.

He recalls the drag of every step: waking in the cold dawn, the starlit walk to Dorchester station, the three shuffling trains, the sixteen miles by horse-and-trap crossing Bodmin Moor. He arrives at the rectory as dusk is falling. It's a flaky gingerbread house of a building, sunk in a garden matted with clover. He has come to restore the Rector's rotting church, that cracked and bell-less tower. He doesn't want to be here. He doesn't want to be the architect he is by training, but the writer he is by desire.

He'd put off this journey as long as he could, battling to finish his new book, the book on which his entire sense of himself now depends, until his mother said, 'You are nearly thirty. You can stay here at home forever and be my sick boy and try to write stories, or you can take up your place in the world. Mr Crickmay is patient but I daresay he won't be for much longer, and your father won't be either.'

His father, that veteran of missed chances, was unlikely to care one way or the other. She meant that *she* wouldn't be patient, that her indulgence of her eldest son's peculiarities had a limit. 'It's your choice, of course,' she sighed. 'I hope you will choose wisely.'

Crickmay, who wasn't so patient after all, as employers went, simply laughed. 'You must *be* someone to publish books. Are you anyone? Who is Tom Hardy? No one knows him. If you won't do this work for me there are ten others who will.'

He is no one when he leaves for Cornwall and begins his ascent of Bodmin. Fires are burning along the cliffs; funeral pyres, they seem to him, and the waves are sounding all down the coast like the slamming of locks. He is no one when he gets off the trap and starts to walk towards the house, and rings the bell.

He is still no one when a woman of around his own age opens the door. Her dress is brown – no, air blue (always, in his memory, it will be air blue). She has firm cheeks like a pink peony and squirrel-coloured hair curling over her shoulders. Behind her is a great deal of dull furniture. There's a breathless urgency about her, a shimmer of fleshly vigour, as if she's just been running or hurdling. He stares at her moist upper lip; the fort of her neck, where a radiance has begun to dart and spread.

He's gazing at her, riveted to the spot like a man under a spell, when she smiles. Though her smile is directed at him, it's so concentrated, so headlong, that he feels it passing through him to touch on some future self of which he's as yet only the ghostly emissary.

I had to receive him alone, & felt a curious uneasy embarrassment at receiving anyone, especially so necessary a person as the architect. I was immediately arrested by his familiar appearance, as if I had seen him in a dream – his slightly different accent, his soft voice; also I noticed a blue paper sticking out of his pocket.

A blue dress, a blue paper (he has a whole ream of it, stolen from Crickmay's store cupboard). How immense that coincidence will come to seem to him!

The young woman is not the parson's wife, apparently, or his daughter. Exactly who she is he can't say, because as he burbles something about the train timetable, the waiting at windy stations, she cuts across him in a high girlish voice, shaking out her curls.

He's arrived with his plans all to hand, she says, and that's good, because there isn't a moment to waste. I have no plans yet, he says. So, what's this then? she asks, brushing the blue paper with the nail of her finger. Ah no, he says, that's a poem. I write poetry. And other things, sometimes. I am trying. Well, I'm trying to place a . . . a new thing. I hope to hear back from my publisher soon. ('My publisher'! A fictitious entity, just as this version of himself, this public man of letters, is fictitious.)

'A new what? A novel? You're a *writer*?' She's serious now, no longer smiling, her lips drawn down to a fierce line.

'Yes, Mrs Holder. I suppose I am.'

'I'm not Mrs Holder. I'm Miss Gifford. Don't say "I suppose". Either you are, or you aren't. Are you?'

'Then I am, yes.'

'I'm a writer myself. May I read it? Your novel?'

'I've only known you five minutes. My own mother hasn't read it yet.'

'Probably less than that, actually. About three. Why would any man show his work to his mother?'

'I like to show her everything.'

'How wonderfully eccentric of you.'

He's still smarting from this rebuke – he thinks it's a rebuke – when a second woman appears, older and darker than the first. There's a rather nastily stained apron tied over her dinner dress. 'I'm so sorry, Mr Hardy,' says this second lady, wiping her hand on the apron with a rueful air before taking his. 'You've caught me playing nurse. My husband is indisposed and quite unable to receive you just now. He's in such pain that I can't leave his bedside. Oh dear, this is most awkward.' She glances around the room, as if seeking counsel from the sensible furniture. 'We'd hoped to give you a civilized meal after your journey.'

The peony-cheeked woman draws her back to the door. 'I'll dine with him, Helen,' she says in a loud whisper. She seems incapable of doing anything without a flourish.

'Alone? Mr Hardy will think it odd, perhaps.'

'Very well; let him.'

The dark lady turns her head a fraction to get a better view of him. 'Is he Mr Crickmay's partner, I wonder?'

'I shouldn't think so. He hardly looks like a person of business, does he? I was expecting someone quite different, some grumpy old man. He's a novelist, did you know?'

'Oh, Emma, don't. Please don't go boring him with talk of *books*.'

'Well, the poor fellow needs something to eat and drink, for heaven's sake.'

He interrupts their whispering to say that he is very sorry to hear their news, but that as far as his reception is concerned, it doesn't matter in the least, and that he'd be perfectly happy with a pot of tea. Mrs Holder hesitates. His insides wobble at the possible solecism of that *pot of tea*. Do they take their tea in pots? He should have asked for *a cup*. Then he sees that she's exhausted, even more exhausted than he is.

'If you'd be kind enough to excuse me, my sister will take my place at table this evening,' she says.

Kind enough. Caught me playing nurse. This is how they always speak, that night and afterwards, as if he were doing them a favour, instead of paid work; as if the whole of life, all the things that terrify him, were a game. They take him for one of their own. For them it's all a game. He registers a skittering sense of possibility. He can master their language. He will make it all up as he goes along.

'I'd be delighted to dine with Miss Gifford,' he says. 'I wonder, could she bear to show me over the church tomorrow – if she isn't otherwise engaged, that is? It might be rather fun.'

Mrs Holder exhales. 'Dear Mr Hardy. What a jolly idea. How *good* of you to think of Emma's amusement. I do hope being marooned in this quiet spot won't turn out to be awfully tedious for you.'

'It won't be tedious at all.' He smiles blithely at Miss Gifford, like the man of the world she already takes him to be. 'I'm certain of it.'

It was Miss Gifford, not her sister or brother-in-law, who accompanied him as he drew and measured the church; it was Miss Gifford who drove with him in the chaise to inspect the slate quarries, and walked up the hill beside him from Boscastle, and led him along Beeny Cliff – he on foot, she on horseback, directing the animal with the lightest tightening of her thighs, her cheeks pricked with spray, her hair let down almost to her elbows – while he talked about his book and dreaded the moment that she would ask him to ride, because he couldn't ride; had never sat on a horse like this one.

The horse knew what he was; he saw it quite plainly in the curl of its nostril. It was a bran-fed horse, a mare. 'She's like a sister to me,' said Miss Gifford, 'my true, wild spirit sister,' but to him the horse was just another beast of burden miraculously reprieved, a creature out of its proper place.

The spell of that week continued to grow and to bind him. They followed the line of the red-veined cliffs while the ocean hammered at its floor below. All around them lay silent farmsteads, the only sound the snuffling of cattle cropping the grass. It was all real, it wasn't imagined. The pale mews, the plunging rock, the woman cantering above, her bright hair flapping free: all real. But it seemed to spring from his secret inner life in the way that dreams do. As they stopped on the headland a cloud cloaked them and an irised rain flew down, staining the water. Then the sun burst out again, and the waves blazed indigo. He felt their power racing across the back of his hands. His thoughts were strung too thick to speak.

When he came to leave four days later, shortly before dawn on Friday morning, it was Emma (by then she was Emma) who kept waking in the night to strike a light, anxious, she explained – with a yawn that revealed the wet cavern of her mouth – to call the servants early enough to get him ready. He knew that he was going from reality to unreality; that in future, in that other place, he'd be less than himself.

He heard her go into the garden as he ate his parting meal. The room was lit by candles that made everything outdoors loom ghostly. Emma wandered on the lawn, her shawled arms raised, trailing their fringes. The hour itself was a ghost: hovering between one thing and another, either an ending or a beginning. Stirred by an emotion he didn't yet fully understand, he got up and followed her into the breaking day.

So I met my husband, or rather he met me.

He puts the open page to his lips. The ink still smells fresh. He gulps its deep notes, aware that something tremendous has happened.

He's carried from this moment in which rain agitates the window to a high slope with the pall-like sea misting the crags beneath, its purple bloom breathed from the shoreward precipices. Em's figure, phantom-like, wheels at the crest, out of his reach, waving, and shrinking as he looks back, always shrinking.

I asked for you. Here you are. Closing his eyes against the crash of the rain on the glass, he lets the book fall to his lap.

'Emma,' he says. 'Emma.' He repeats her name like an incantation. He rubs his palm over the handle of the drawer, across the dust of the table-top. All he manages to summon is the image of her corpse; its sulky belly, its shoulders braced in flight.

Somewhere in the house a clock begins to announce midday, followed by another and another. This is what's left now, this stopped-up regret, this never-ending present in which no words can come.

He's an intruder in this room. He must leave. He will fetch the keys and close it all up. He'll keep this memoir, this record of a lost time; everything else can stay. He rises heavily to his feet, stooping to shut the drawer as he does so. But it remains open, stuck fast. Giving it a shake, he realizes that there's something else jammed at the back, some shadowy thing, which his rummaging has displaced. By the light of the window he can make out a bundle, tied with string. When he eases it out he sees that it's a collection of black-spined notebooks, creased from much handling.

More reminiscences, Emmie? The thought is both gratifying and indefinably alarming. *You were quite the writer after all, my dear. Well, let's take a look.*

He sits down again with the bundle balanced on his knees and worries away at the knot in the string. As it comes loose a folded paper falls out of the topmost book and skates to the floor.

It's a letter, typed on a single sheet of onionskin. The texture is immediately familiar: he knows, even before he unfolds it, who the sender is. He has a hundred such brittle letters, locked in the secret drawer of his desk.

5 River Front, Enfield

4th October 1910

Dear Mrs Hardy,

Thank you so much for your kind note and invitation to return to Dorset soon. I would consider it the most tremendous privilege to come to you next month, if that will suit you.

I am rapidly progressing with the typewriting of your MS. I fancy that 'The Inspirer' will be your great triumph. It seems to me that this tale of a wife who is the unacknowledged source of her celebrated husband's success is set to be the most praised of your works when they are brought out, but I can quite see that it would be improper for Mr McIlvaine to publish it, since he used to be Mr Hardy's publisher. There are other – and more prestigious – publishers for your purpose. We must give the story the greatest possible chance, for it will be a *big* thing.

Everyone at home has remarked how well I look after my holiday at Max Gate. The days I spend in your delightful house are all so happy that I sometimes feel I shall be spoiled for the sterner realities of life! Thank you again, dear Mrs Hardy, so very much.

Yours most sincerely,

Florence E. Dugdale

The shame of it. The shame. This is a side of Florence he's never seen, this obsequiousness, this calculated flattery that's close to cruelty. The pile of notebooks in his lap starts to tremble. His whole body is shaking as he tries to thrust the letter back between their pages. He can't manage it; the books tumble to the ground, and as he snatches at the one on top it cracks open.

He's holding what appears to be a diary.

2nd February 1911

Tom has published a story in *The Cornhill*. Of course he's often published stories there before, but this occasion is rather un-usual as he now pretends to be a woman. It's some stale piece of local lore, seasoned like a tired old pie with his usual sprinkling

73

of rustics. He's signed it 'Florence E. Dugdale', but it's most assuredly by T.H.

How apt. My ever elusive husband, whom I barely see even when he's at home, has become a *ghost writer*.

The story must, I suppose, be excluded from the new edition of his works with its acres & acres of horny-handed prose & the poetical wool-gathering which he refers to as (I picked the lock of his study when he was away; I looked; I ensconced myself in his big chair, foraging – he now *always* keeps me out – as *never* formerly) 'the more individual part of my literary fruitage'.

His *fruitage*. As if he were some noble old apple tree. A Grindstone, perhaps. A Sour Cadbury. How can F.D. allow it? Her ambition must be greater than her pride. I can only guess at the brazen bargain she's made with him. She gets his patronage & his words & I get – why, I get *her*. I get a typist & a toady, someone who will shut the old wife up by occasionally throwing her a crumb.

If Miss D. means to replace me, then I feel sorry for the poor girl. She doesn't know that the illustrious Thomas Hardy is incapable of ordinary human affection. He has kept me his prisoner for forty years. All this time he's denied me the only thing I ever hoped for in exchange. Not the stupid literary fame they both prize so much. Oh, no.

All I wanted was a child. If I'd had a child, I could have stood it. He's made *very* sure that there was never to be a sign of one for us. He has done this with his typical narrow cunning while presenting himself to the public as a great man, a man of rare sympathies. He thinks he is someone. But I know that he is little, & commonplace. He is a common little man.

He is —

He smothers the page with his hand. With a vertiginous feeling of disbelief he claps the book shut, merely to twitch the cover back again a moment later. A title is written across the flyleaf in wayward letters.

<u>What I Think of My Husband</u>
By Emma Lavinia Gifford Hardy

It seems even now that this might all be an illusion, a trick that Em has played on him. It might be reparable, not the fatal thing it appears. The notebook is only partway filled. But this isn't just one book; there are two, three of them. There is more of this, much more.

He's shrivelling. He is falling away from himself. He sinks to his hands and knees and scrapes up the notebooks before shuffling down the attic steps like the old man he is. Once he's in his study he closes the door and leans against its panels. The lamp has gone out. A dead December gleam lies on his desk and chair. He can hear the servants' chatter, Flo's and Jane's, in the kitchen below; the banging of pans and the scrape of a knife on the whetstone, all the sounds, dreadful in their vitality, of a Sunday afternoon.

She knew. Emma knew.

She saw through his silly self-importance, his greedy feints (why did he ever think they were anything else than that?) at stage-managing Florence's career as a writer, the hunger with which he thrust the girl on her as a companion. As a friend!

Em wasn't deceived, or not for long.

Here is his room, where he has wasted so many hours in self-imposed exile. Here is his poem, with its foolish birds, its cages. *Like those in Babylon. Captive they sung.*

He pushes his papers to one side and slides his burden down. He must write to Florence. It's too late for a letter. Too late, all of it too late. He will send a telegram. He will take the message to the counter himself the minute it opens in the morning.

First he must still his fear. He quails at having to find the right words, the words that will communicate his shock and despair, but they arrive in spite of him.

I can't do without you one day more. There is something I must say. Please come at once.

Florence

H E DOESN'T KNOW, the next afternoon, if he should meet her at the station or send a man. He knows that she'll be there. Of this he's certain.

At last he decides to hire a motor car from Tilley's in town and to go himself. It arrives at the station as the 12.30 from Waterloo is drawing in. Florence emerges from the hustling crowds, a dun blur beneath the orange of the lamps, her body slim and intent. She has just one modest bag with her, and a portable typewriter. He gives her his hand instead of a kiss. They don't speak during the journey home because the driver, a lad with a nose like a blade and a chivalrous manner, is there. But she links her thumb with his under the rug, and he allows this.

When they get to the house he asks the driver to wait. He notes that Flo Griffin fails to come to the door. None of the maids appears to carry Florence's bag. He's about to ring, but thinks better of it. *I'll do it myself. Let them hide.*

'I've had to put you on the top floor at the front, next to the girls,' he says. 'It's a very small room, I'm afraid. I hope you don't mind.'

'I'm sure it will do perfectly well. I don't take up much space.'

It's true, he thinks, as he follows her up the side stairs, which are the servants' stairs. All her ways are neat and unassuming. Her shallow flanks invite only the slightest declivity in her skirt. Her shoes, fastened with the thinnest of straps, barely make a sound on the wood.

'Did you have a comfortable journey?'

'I was too anxious to be comfortable. I was anxious about you. And a little for myself, I must admit.'

'I didn't mean to frighten you.' He sets down her bag, a light thing, as self-contained as its owner. 'But there is something I want to tell you.'

He's aware of Florence's large, astonished eyes on his, and the rapidness of her breathing. She's placed her Remington on the bed and lifted her arms to unpin her hat, but stops. 'Of course.'

'Em and I had a quarrel before she died.'

'Put it out of your mind. I'm here now. That's not why you sent for me, is it – just to say this?'

Florence is standing beside her luggage with her gloves drawn off and her hand held out. He takes it. Her skin is smooth, and so febrile that he starts at the contact. She sways towards him, but he releases her. 'We didn't usually quarrel, you know,' he says.

'No, I didn't know. I don't know anything except what you've told me.' All at once she looks weary. 'Does it matter? It's not unusual for husbands and wives to quarrel.' She attempts a laugh. 'Or so I believe.'

'The sad fact, my dear, is that we didn't speak to each other at all lately. Not a word. We met in the evenings at dinner, but otherwise Em kept to her attic room.'

A tremor of irritation passes over Florence's lips. 'Then how did you manage to disagree?'

'I was in my study on Tuesday afternoon and she walked right in. I'd had my lunch brought up as usual and eaten it at my table, which could hardly have been a surprise to her. I'm not certain where Em took hers. I never asked.' Though he's staring at the braided rug beneath his feet, he senses by Florence's immobility that she's sifting every word. 'She said I was keeping her prisoner. She accused me of having married her under false pretences.'

'How cruel. And how absurd.'

'But you see, I had the queerest feeling that she never meant to say any of those things. She didn't come to attack me. I'm sure of it. She came for some other reason, and when she found me surrounded by my books and papers she couldn't stop herself. And now she's dead, and I shall never learn what it was.'

'Please forget it. It truly doesn't matter.'

'I can't. There's something else.'

Florence waits, a tumble of quick breaths. 'What is it?'

'Yesterday I went up to the attic. When I was there I discovered some diaries of hers. Not ordinary ones – all about me. They contain much more of the same thing.'

'There's more than one?'

'Yes. There are a few of them. She must have been writing them for years.'

'Are you the only . . . person they mention?'

'No. Your name appears too.'

'You must burn them.'

He nods briefly. 'Is it true? Is that what I was? A gaoler?'

'Of course it's not true. You're the most liberal man I've ever known. It's not just me. The whole world knows it.'

'I wonder now what the whole world knows.'

'We were careful, Tom. We did our best not to give her any pain.'

'You came to Edward Clodd's get-togethers in Aldeburgh with me.' He winces. 'How many times did we do that? Four? *Five?*'

He tries to remember. On the train back from Suffolk one summer after the heady freedom of a boys' weekend at Clodd's he'd dashed off a thank you note, dropping in a reference to his *amanuensis*, his *gifted young friend and assistant* with the *unerring taste in poetry*, such a *fine proof-reader* – all true! – and his hope that he might one day carry this treasure away to the seaside *for the sake of her health.*

In his reply Edward intimated regret at his and Emma's strained relations (had he even mentioned those?) and suggested that he bring his 'secretary' to stay at the house soon. Before he knew it he was sitting on a grey beach with Florence beside him, downcast in her buoyant sleeves – why, in these rare moments of leisure, was she so uneasy, so silent, when he only wanted her to notice him, to name him, as she once had the scent of the privet? – staring at the North Sea.

Thomas Hardy and his little typist.

'It was only three times,' says Florence now.

'Three too many, then.'

'I'm sorry you feel that way. Those were precious days for me.'

'Were they?' he says.

'They were precious because you were there. We could be alone.'

'But we weren't alone. Oh, God. Bill Archer was always lurking with his Kodak. And that insufferable windbag, Bury. *Professor* Bury. Bury was probably taking *notes*.'

'I doubt it.' Florence speaks patiently. 'Tom. Can't you see? You needn't worry. None of them *cared*. We weren't doing anything . . . oh, anything untoward. After all,' she says, 'there's never been any question of – we have never—'

'No. We haven't. And yet Emma suffered. I fear she may have suffered very much.'

'It's not your fault. She wasn't in her right mind. Everyone saw it. I've only ever heard people express sympathy for you, and what you've had to endure.'

'Oh, yes. I know what that sort of sympathy sounds like.' He looks up at her at last. 'Will you come with me, will you see her?'

'Now? It's nearly dark. I'm rather tired after my journey.'

'It would mean a great deal to me.'

Florence settles her hat and smiles bravely. 'In that case, of course I'll come.'

The rain of the last week has thinned to a scrim by the time they reach the churchyard. He steers Florence along the path by the elbow, skirting the shadows that are already lengthening on the grass.

He brings her to a halt in front of the row of family graves. To their left is the patch of newly turned soil with its flowers. 'My Uncle James,' he says. 'My grandmother and grandfather. My parents.' They stand around stiffly for a minute, like a couple in a receiving line negotiating an awkward social introduction. Then he bends down and removes a stray twig from the earth at their feet. 'I've a memorial stone planned for her. Not an upright one, like these old-fashioned markers here. Something more solid, to match Mother's and Father's, in the Gothic style.'

'Gothic,' says Florence. 'Most suitable.' Her head is lowered, so that only her chin is visible under her hat brim.

'This plot is deep,' he ventures. 'There will be enough room for me one day.' She's studying the cards on the wreaths, and gives no sign that she's heard him. He blunders on. 'You must know, my dear, that there's a space reserved for you in it also, should you wish it.'

Her head jerks up – whether at what he has said, or because of the gust of wind that leaps silently at them through the grass, lifting her hat away, he will never know. They duck and scramble to pin it against the base of his Uncle James's gravestone. When Florence lifts her face again she has, he sees, had a chance to recover from whatever emotion she may have felt. There are scabs of chalk on her shoes.

'I'm sorry,' she says. 'I'm so sorry.' She steadies herself, casting a look over her shoulder at the waiting car. The rain is becoming heavier, an insidious pressure, an intrusive *tap-tap*. 'Can we go back to the house? Can we go home?'

'Home, yes.' He takes hold of her arm as they turn to leave. The car engine is idling; behind the misted windscreen he can make out the profile of the driver, his nostrils flared with cold, reading the newspaper.

Water drips from the branches of the yew and trickles down his collar. Soon everything will be soaked through. Ahead of them the path winks dully, full of stones.

An Anniversary

H E HAS NO WISH to look at the diaries again, but he knows he must. With an hour still wanting till dinner he trims and lights his study lamp. The flame spits, opens its small fan. In Fordington Field a cow lows, a mournful sound bleeding into the wet air.

He arranges the three notebooks on his desk in chronological order. They seem so humdrum: stout black sixpenny notebooks, with cardboard covers. He draws a breath. On a whim he picks out the second and dives in, a man who must somehow pull himself to safety across a lethal tide.

1st January 1900

A new century has begun, but what's that to me? I feel age-old. This year I will be sixty. Sixty! Old enough to have learned a thing or two. Old enough to know better. I sit up in my eyrie, day after day. The hours shunt by. Nothing happens. Sometimes there's the scrape of a chair, or a cough or a moan, from beneath the boards of my room, where Tom is working in his study. Sometimes I can hear him speaking aloud to himself in a high, urgent voice, as if he's praying. But he's not praying. He's only writing little poems.

This morning as I bent to wash my face I knocked the tooth mug into the basin, & there it was – lying at the bottom of my memory, on the Willow Pattern – not the mug but our lost picnic tumbler of years ago. I remember walking in the Valency Valley with Tom one burning August day & coming to a place where we had to jump over stones & scale a low wall by rough steps, & get through narrow pathways. Suddenly, as if by magic, we squeezed out onto a wide grassy space where the dry earth gave way to foxgloves & campions, & a waterfall purling into a brook ten feet below.

We stayed there all afternoon, hidden from the path, listening to the long willow leaves twitching in the current, the clucking of the water. I remember that we rested our basket on the very edge of the runlet, beside its hollow boiling voice – that we drank from the same glass. Afterwards as I tried to rinse it in the fall it was dashed from my hand & sank. Down it went, into a crease of the stone. I plumbed the water with my bare arms but I couldn't discover it. It must still be there, jammed darkly. No lips have touched it since ours.

But I am still here – holding the edge of the basin, balanced on that stone ledge – looking into the leafy water. I am there, & here.

He doesn't remember that time. I am an irrelevance, a clog on his real life. He forgets that I believed in his gift when no one else did, that I saw from the very first what he might be. He forgets the Valency & St Juliot & the hot high road, the swooning day, & all our murmuring afternoons. He forgets how we picked our way up the cliff to Tintagel, & were locked in the ruins at dusk, & how he had to scramble along the wall to halloo & wave my handkerchief at the porter while I waited at the foot for him to return. I waited. The handkerchief smalled, sinking like a sail. The waves sloped like houseroofs. The shadows grew harder. When Tom got back, his trousers were torn & there was a scratch on his cheek.

'I almost didn't find the fellow,' he whispered. 'I thought we'd have to spend the night here.' He took my hair in his hands, a solid coil of it in each fist, as though he were weighing it. He was smiling & smiling.

'It's gold,' he said, '& you're a queen, aren't you? The queen of this castle.' Then he took out his pocket knife & cut off a strand. He twisted it around his fingers, unfastened a button in the breast of his coat, & carefully put it inside.

Queen of nothing.

I expect nothing from him now & that is just as well – neither gratitude nor attention, love, nor justice. He belongs to the public & all my years of devotion count for nothing.

9th March 1900

Today I felt very dejected. I was humped at my piano after breakfast, lacking the will to play a single note, when the bell rang. Bessie went to answer it & there stood a woman peddling bulbs.

Instead of calling at the kitchen door she'd come to the front like any regular visitor – a peasant in a woollen shawl, chattering about rose slips & onions.

She said she knew my husband's kin going back three generations — she referred to my mother-in-law by her first name, leaned against my door-post as if it were her own & told me with a crafty look that 'Jemima Hardy could always tell a good inon from a bad 'un'. In my confusion I bought several from her.

5th July 1900

A wife doesn't object to being ruled by her husband, so much as she does by a relative at his back. Or three of them, three witches — Hecate & her daughters — who have done all they can to make division between us. They say that I've brought nothing to this marriage, neither youth, fortune, nor children. They mock my family & call me 'Lady Emma', & think reports of their gabblings on their native heath won't travel down to the town.

Tom doesn't defend me; not a bit of it. It's Kate & Mary, Mary & Kate, & how diligently they applied themselves to teaching all their born days & how well Kate did to end up in charge of a class of infants at the girls' school in Bell Street. Oh & Mary! Mary is pure of heart, Mary is a child of nature. Mary was his near-companion in the womb. Mary with her simple-minded adoration of him has stoked his sense of his own importance, & now he is like no other man — or himself as *was*.

Lil is here for a visit & I'm giving her instruction suitable to her station in managing a house. While we were in the kitchen planning today's menu, T. came in looking for his newspaper & announced that she would do well to learn a *real skill*. I replied that, as the daughter of a gentleman by birth & the great-niece of an archdeacon, she surely has no need to train for an occupation.

'You do her a disservice if you teach her to consider work beneath her dignity,' he said.

Isn't this work? Doesn't what I do for his comfort, day in & day out, count as labour? The fact is that despite these barbs & his sisters' low insults I've always tried to love him as best I can. If only we'd had a child of our own. Then I might have done much more: taught our girl her letters (in my imagination this child is always a *she*), read to her, praised her little stories.

Lilian has no interest in books. No doubt she will marry well.

22nd August 1900

Keeping separate a good deal is a wise plan. I tend my garden & at the close of the day I come up to my boudoir, where hardly a sound – not even the dinner bell – reaches me. I see the moon rise & the birds roosting in the tree tops. A thrush has just ended his prolongings in the dusk, so loud his song in the stillness, he was almost a nightingale.

This attic has become my refuge and solace. I sit up late in my dressing gown, eavesdropping on the scuffle & flight of creatures in the wood, & wake when I please – it's a swoop from the bed to my writing desk. Tom has so much to say on paper, & the world hangs so avidly on his words, that this is my one chance to have all the say to myself. I find that I prefer sleeping here after all, away from the noise of the house. When I'm downstairs I hear its entrails grinding incessantly. There's the belch of the pump. The clink & clunk of pots in the scullery. The shuddering thump the flue makes when it's heating up.

This morning I had a rare visit from Tom. 'Are you comfortable, Em?' he asked. 'Not lonely?'

'Quite comfortable.'

'Are you free?'

'Well,' I said, 'I'm trying to finish a poem.'

'It's only that Miss Owen will keep on writing. The woman is such a drain on my time. I simply can't afford to waste another morning replying to her. She's on the prowl for an invitation to drive over from the Lakes. Would you mind very much answering for me, my dear, & putting her off? You write such good letters. Surely your poeticizing can wait?'

A drain. How his precious hours leach away. Down they go, with a gurgle gurgle glug. What must it be like, to have such slippery hours?

Perhaps you shouldn't have encouraged Miss Owen to write to you in the first place, I thought.

I have my private opinion of men in general & of T.H. in particular – grand brains – fine 'ideas' – but too often lacking in judgement of ordinary things. To those who marry authors, I would say, 'Do not help him – to the extent of extinguishing your own life – but go on with former pursuits.'

Still, I confess that I was pleased to be asked. I wrote the letter.

15th September 1900

The Gardener's Ruse

By E. L. H.

A wild rose tree from the hedge brought he,
   & planted it well in the mould,

Digging around & making a mound,
    To stand it up high & bold.

Then a hole he made, at its back in the shade,
    & an onion deep tilled in,
For the onion was bound to make roses sound,
    & a fine rich perfume to win.

Down far in the earth, hidden its worth,
    The onion, coarse & meek,
Sought the roots of the roses, to give scent to its posies,
    & brilliance in colour – a freak!

He lets the book drop, aware that his breast is beating out of tune. All of this is painful, but not yet as painful as it might be. He doesn't doubt that there's worse to come. He could still turn away and refuse to see. He could remember Emma as he intends to remember her. He could go on thinking of himself as irreproachable, without blame.

Knowing even as he entertains this hope that it's a vain one, he thumbs through the remaining entries with a hurried, fearful concentration.

3rd September 1904

Now that the warm harvest evenings are here Snowdove has wandered off & won't be persuaded to come in. He's busy paying calls up & down the lane where I hear him all night, yowling & strutting beyond the wall.

I can scarcely keep a cat, to say nothing of a man whom all

the world claims – which wouldn't matter so much if only Tom's writings were of a more honourable & truthful kind. All he produces these days are poems about how his love, like his youth, faith, &c., is dead. His lute is strewn with years-deep dust, the dingy details of his daily life loom at him, the blossom that once seemed so sweet has yielded a tart fruit, & so on. I stay out of his way up here, on high – the tart old fruit – where he shan't pluck me even if he *could*.

17th August 1908

In his sixties a man's feelings too often take a new course altogether. Eastern ideas of matrimony secretly pervade his thoughts. T. has returned from his latest trip to London in a state of high excitement. His fidelity to me is a given, of course. But there are other forms of infidelity no less wounding. I know the signs too well by now: the newest scribbling woman, the elation, the hectic letter-writing – & the inevitable disappointment till the next one.

I wonder who she is this time. He is vain & selfish & these women whom he meets in London society just increase these things. They are the poison; I, if he would but realize it, the antidote.

On. He must go on. The third and last notebook lies on the desk in front of him, its cover creased in a smile. Florence's letter juts from a corner. He slips it hastily into his pocket and steels himself for what must follow.

These final entries begin two and a half years ago, in the summer of 1910. He was in town then (in town, he recalls, to receive a rare royal honour in recognition of his life's work – an honour so longed for, and for so long frantically avoided; because what are honours, finally, but a stone rolled over one's labours, a public form of being buried alive?).

There he was, trapped and about to be exhibited for all to see. Then Emma went back to Dorset.

16th July 1910

I'm dreadfully pulled down with this cough & chill which have sent me straight home in the middle of the season, leaving Tom to preen himself at Buckingham Palace alone next Tuesday. How typical of T. to have accepted the Order of Merit though he refused a knighthood. That would have made *me* Lady Hardy, & he wants recognition for himself only. He tells me that if I send him any letters I should put O.M. *only* after his name on the envelope, and not 'Esquire', too. As if I don't know how to address a mere O.M.

But of course he won't be alone. He'll have scalp-collecting Lady St Helier to attend him, & Lady Grove of the big hair, & that girl novelist who looks like a pensive stoat, May Sinclair. Thank heavens for little Miss Dugdale, who writes that she will be visiting the flat as often as she can to type T.'s letters & see if he is all right. What a dear & useful girl! I'm much easier in my mind knowing that she'll be keeping an eye on Tom while I'm laid low here. (I have asked her to see that he is properly dressed for the investiture. It would be just like him to forget his collar stud or the right socks.)

I must thank her by having her to stay at Max Gate.

1st August 1910

Miss Dugdale has proved herself a most delightful visitor. The more she sees of my writing, she tells me, the more she admires it. In spite of her work for Tom – he keeps her tied up for *whole afternoons* with his demands – she's promised to type up a story of mine once she gets back to Enfield & to send it out to publishers. She thinks it best not to attach my name to the MS. as it would be wiser to get a perfectly *unbiased* opinion, without incurring the slightest association with T.H. She says she's quite burning with anxiety to know what the outcome will be. How clever she is, & how lucky I am to have her as a supporter. It's more than my own husband has ever done for me.

21st September 1910

Miss D. is visiting us again for most of this month, though I've barely seen either her or Tom for the last week since he works her at such a pace. I'm afraid he will wear her out. She confessed to me that she hasn't had a moment yet to start on my story – which she says is of *far* greater interest to her than T.H.'s correspondence.

I'm sure it is. Going by the time they spend in there he must be writing to half this dull county. (Miss D. is allowed into his study, while I am not – she's very efficient & quite takes him in hand, & I know that I shouldn't mind. But I can't help recalling earlier times when he liked to have me by him – when he positively *sought* my advice. No doubt I am a 'foolish fond old woman'.)

26th September 1910

Mr Strang, the artist, has been here to make a portrait of Tom for the O.M. He has exactly caught my husband's supercilious look, the ridged jaw & hawk-like eyes & sallow head with its lone outpost of hair.

But that wasn't all he caught. Once Mr Strang had finished there was a protracted kerfuffle over the chalks & Tom came down at half past four, late for tea, with Mr S. & a flushed Miss Dugdale in tow. T. murmured that our artist had seen Miss D. passing in the hall & had been so taken with her appearance that he'd *insisted* on sketching her too.

Imagine that. I wouldn't have thought her a beauty. For a young woman who has her whole life ahead of her she has a terribly gloomy face. After having her picture done she seemed more than usually woebegone.

5th October 1910

I've had the sweetest note from Miss Dugdale to tell me that she's making good progress with my story. Before she left us on Thursday she had, alas, to witness a very regrettable scene (one really couldn't blame her for looking gloomy this time).

I'd made the mistake of wondering whether Tom might send my tale to that nice Mr McIlvaine who paid so handsomely for his things in the past & who can't after all be that choosy if he took whatever T. wrote. Tom exploded in a rage – if Miss D. hadn't been there to smooth things over I fear I might have lost *my* temper in turn in a *most* unladylike way.

I believe that he is jealous of my writing. He wants to be the *only* author anyone ever reads. Thankfully Miss D. has no literary ambitions. In my experience they are a cruel curse.

11th November 1910

T. is in London for a few nights to see his publisher about the proposed édition de luxe of his work, especially vexing just now as he appears to have gone off with the study keys. I've asked Daisy to dust the room while he is away but we can't even get in. I wrote to him enquiring after the set but he says that he doesn't know what he's done with it.

He adds in a P.S. that there's no rush to clean his room in any event, as he'll be stopping in Aldeburgh this weekend with Mr Clodd.

15th November 1910

The study is open again – it turns out that the keys were in Tom's old trouser pocket all the while. What *is* one to make of such carelessness? He is back & so is Miss Dugdale. She slinks around in there. T. says that her help is essential in correcting the proofs of the new edition, since there were so many errors in the one Mr McIlvaine brought out. How fortuitous that I didn't send my story to him!

18th November 1910

I hardly know what to think. Miss D. let slip at breakfast that, with Tom's encouragement, she's been hard at work on a book of her own, a collection of animal verses for *children* – in whose amusement he has never shown the slightest interest – encomiums to baby chimpanzees & lambs & kangaroos and whatnot. It seems that at least some of the hours they spend together behind that barred door are dedicated to advancing *her* literary career & not his.

When T. proposed that Miss D. should walk with him in the garden after tea I seized my chance. In his eagerness to get her al fresco he'd left the study door unlocked & now it stood open a crack. In a heartbeat I was inside the Holy of Holies.

The room was as filthy as I remembered it, with its faint odour of old man & the crude fiddle propped against the wall, heaps of paper on the floor, yellowing in the light from the windows, & that grubby shawl draped over the back of T.'s chair. The writing table though was scrupulously neat, as has always been his habit: everything squared off on the leather just so, & batches of print lined up in rows, perfectly uniform, like fat cakes freshly out of the oven.

Poems! The proofs of hundreds of T.H.'s poems, awaiting correction for the new edition of his work – & there, in the centre of the table, sat Miss D.'s typewriter, next to two scant piles of paper, one of typescript & the other her MS. (as I thought) placed face down. A newly completed sheet stuck out of the paper bail, backed by two carbons, left as it was when she went for tea. The poem she'd been transcribing lay alongside. I glanced at it – it was called 'The Kitten'. I stopped dead & took a better look.

There were five verses, all in Tom's handwriting.

The Kitten

I like warm milk, & fires aglow
On hearths; for I am, as you know,
   A Kitten.

I like to jump at your two feet
Or clutch the inky letter sheet
   Just written.

Or something hanging from above,
A bobbin, say; or claw your glove,
   Or mitten;

Or handkerchief, or anything
That can without much damaging
   Be bitten.

While, if you enter at the door,
& stroke me, I shall like you more,
For I am, as I said before,
   A Kitten.

I turned over the upended sheaf of MS. – I scrabbled through the rest of the poems. 'The Elephant'. 'The Donkey'. 'The Squirrel'. 'The Rat'. *Every single one of them was in my husband's hand.*

   I just had time to wind the roller up, slide out the undercopy & to pocket it before rewinding everything, when I heard voices in the porch.

Well, well. What a household of writers we are turning out to be. Writers, writers, everywhere, creeping about on their velvet paws, tapping away with their little claws, forgetting, in the heat of the moment, to put in their bottom sheets.

Clickety-clack.

12th December 1910

The thin sad days drag on. I hear from F.D. that 'The Inspirer' has so far failed to attract a publisher & that she is so 'steeped in Mr Hardy's proofs' that she can't at present find a moment to send it out again. She must think me utterly obtuse. But I live too near a wood to be frightened by an owl, as they say around here.

Tom scarcely addresses a word to me. He despises *my* writing, to be sure, & it's clear that I've long since lost the power to charm him. Even so I'd hoped that I might make some dent in his indifference. I worked all this week at devising a new arrangement on the piano for one of our old airs – a peace offering, if you like. Tonight I placed it next to his napkin at dinner.

'What's this?' he asked. So he can still speak when we're tête-à-tête, without Miss Kitten purring in a corner. His voice sounded positively *rusty*.

'It's a song I've scored,' I said.

'I can see that. I seem to know the words, but not the melody.'

'The words are Bayly's "Long, Long Ago". I took the liberty of resetting them.'

'Why in the world would you do that?'

'Well, I thought perhaps that I could sing my version to you. Or that we could run through it together, after dinner.'

His head appeared to move sideways in its collar but he did not look at me. 'My mother sang this song to me when I was a boy,' he said. 'I don't like to see it altered.' He began to spoon up his soup as if he hadn't eaten in a week & refused to say another syllable for the rest of the evening.

Sometimes you try to mend a thing & it ends up more broken than before.

25th December 1910

A grim Yule. An hour ago Tom dealt me his most savage cut yet. We'd consumed a strained meal with all the trimmings – did I mention that Miss D. is here? Naturally she is, looking more & more wracked – & were slumped in the drawing room. I'd given instructions for the fire to be laid with fresh coal, but it was quite dead. When I expressed my surprise at this state of affairs T. announced that he'd told Daisy not to bother to light it as he would soon be going out. He was taking Miss Dugdale to Higher Bockhampton to visit his sisters at the cottage. Where he never takes me.

I was astounded. 'Really?' I said. 'What for?'

'To pay our respects at Christmas. To wish them well & exchange the usual greetings of the season.'

Our respects. His & hers.

'Oh yes,' I replied, '& I suppose that you will all squash into that squalid little parlour & pull out your fiddles & *sing*, too?'

'Stop, Emma,' he said.

'You'll sing, all you Hardys together. A whole bristling thicket of Hardys. You'll gobble pudding & drink cider & gossip about who built which stone barn in your father's time – & you'll attempt to poison Miss Dugdale's mind against me, though she's the only friend I've had here all these years. What do you have to say to *that*?'

He could say nothing, of course. He's scuttled off across the fields alone, leaving F. to wring her hands, & I've come upstairs to take refuge in my diary. It was very cold in that dismal room. I hope Miss Kitten has the wit to put a match to my coal, or she'll freeze.

5th January 1911

I'm a wicked woman, whose temper has always got the better of her. Helen was right. I was never meant for a well-bred man – but then, I never wanted one.

So, I thought, if his mother's version of that blessed ditty is the one Tom likes, then that's the version I will sing for him. Heaven knows I would have made a friend of his mother if only she'd let me. Though everything seems changed I'm the same now as then: the same as I ever was. So I sat at the keyboard & began to play & at last I found my courage, & my voice:

> 'Tell me the tales that to me were so dear
>> Long, long ago, long, long ago,
> Sing me the songs I delighted to hear,
>> Long, long ago, long ago.

> 'Now you are come all my grief is removed,
> Let me forget that so long you have roved.

Let me believe that you love as you loved,
　　Long, long ago, long ago.

'Do you remember the paths where we met,
　　Long, long ago, long, long ago?
Ah yes, you told me you'd never forget!
　　Long, long ago, long ago.

'Then to all others my smile you preferred,
Love, when you spoke, gave a charm to each word.
Still my heart treasures the praises I heard,
　　Long, long ago, long ago.

'Since by your kindness my fond hopes were raised,
　　Long, long ago, long, long ago,
You by more eloquent lips have been praised,
　　Long, long ago, long ago.

'Though by long absence your truth has been tried,
Still to your accents I listen with pride,
Blest as I was when I sat by your side,
　　Long, long ago, long ago.'

Within a few minutes I made out T.'s determined walk in the hall, about to pass up the stairs. It stopped for a moment, as if it would stay. But he went his way, & after a little while I heard a distant door shut.

The new edition of Tom's work is to be called the Wessex Edition, complete with an authorized *map*. T.H. has officially claimed a whole county. There's no escaping the world he has made. As I pace my attic room his web grows wider & wider. Visitors come up to the house every day, piling out of their charabancs, peering through the dining-room windows, trampling on the cyclamen. I found one today – a dewy young woman, all back-combed hair & eyes like soup plates, just the kind he prefers – scooping up earth from a flower bed in her gloved hand.

'Oh, ma'am,' she said in an elastic accent, 'please tell me: is Mr Hardy at home? I've travelled five thousand miles to see him.'

'I doubt the length of the whole of the British Isles is much greater than six hundred miles,' I observed.

'But I've come from Texas,' she mooed, as if that explained anything.

There must be a shortage of good gardening soil in Texas. While I looked on she made to slip the earth into her reticule.

'Madam,' I said, 'relinquish that dirt. This is my house. It is *my dirt!*'

My husband's books have not the same sort of interest for me as for others. I knew every word of the *first* editions – in MS., sitting by his side. So long ago, & so much endured since, in this prison he has built.

Enough. Enough. He won't read any more. The entries seem to run on almost to the day of Emma's death, though he's too mortified to trace their course to the end.

If he could he'd be swept away into oblivion. He'd throw himself into the rift between what he thought was his life with Emma, and their life as he now sees it to have been: slowly spoiled by his gracelessness and self-absorption, his blindness. Every part of him is contracted into a single point of pain. He sags against his desk, unable to move, listening to the winter wind. It whispers like the papery ruins of a human song.

He's read enough to see that his pitiful secret, his and Florence's, has been no secret after all. *But what has Florence been to me?* Her anxious eyes seem to hover behind the question. What *are* we hiding? A few wet seaside weekends, the occasional mingling of fingers in a cab. The half-formed longings of an old man for a woman forty years younger. Her tolerant, or – a terrible thought, this, but one he can't quite suppress now that he's seen the honeyed style in which she wrote to Emma – perhaps consciously calibrated, sympathy.

After so many shocks to the fabric of his existence he doesn't know, and that's almost worse. What he's most aware of is that in the wreckage of Emma's silence he has no right of reply.

His web grows wider and wider.

This prison he has built.

He turns the words over in his mind. *This prison.*

Emma's books were a ludicrous dream; a fantasy. But his had been real. They were married and life had gone on like that: the daily labour to conjure something out of nothing, to invent the world anew. She loved, while he worked. The magic of those first visits to St Juliot was diluted by this dailiness, and, with the clarifying vision of long years, disappeared. Well, that was the bargain of marriage. Em helped with his letters and copied his manuscripts and kept his house, but of course she was no writer, not really. In spite of her fondness for literature she herself had no especial gift, no power of endurance. The drive to create, he knew by then, had been his all along.

And fame came at last, wrenching, unnerving fame, with that novel which no one wanted while he was writing it, but everyone so admired once it was done.

Tess.

Was this my fault? Was it?

He's at a loss to know why Emma started keeping such a catalogue of her grievances at all. He picks up the oldest of the notebooks, feeling both exhausted and resigned to further blows. The very first entry she made was for a day over twenty years ago, in the March of 1890, when they'd been living at Max Gate for a mere five years. He doesn't recall that Em was particularly unhappy then. The uncertainty and unhappiness were, as he remembers things – as till now he's always thought them – all his.

7th March 1890

The Day of Days. In honour of it I planned a festive dinner. I ordered Tom's favourite mutton broth & veal cuts from Cook, had Molly shine the silver, & went out as the evening dew was falling to pick a bouquet of violets for the table. Then I dressed as nicely as I could, in the plum silk T. used to praise when we were first married. It's grown a little tight now, but I fancy I can still carry it off!

The dinner hour arrived. Tom didn't like the flowers. He stopped short of saying so, but I could tell that having them there annoyed him. He doesn't want anything in the house to be altered. He's forever reminding me he's not a rich man & that we must live within our means. (A minor victory though – he approves of my plan to cultivate cucumbers.)

He made no comment whatsoever on my dress. He ate well, with his usual humourless haste. He talked of work. Then I knew: *he had forgotten our anniversary.*

But he remembered Mr Gosse. Mr Gosse has been invited for the weekend.

Perhaps I'm being ungenerous. Tom's new book isn't coming on as it should & he's rather down in the mouth. I've offered my help. I think he has accepted it – it's hard to tell. His delicate irony is too easily mistaken for tenderness.

Their anniversary! They were married in September, not March. *What anniversary? What are you talking about, woman? For God's sake. If I'm to be blamed for every bloody made-up 'anniversary' that's ever slipped my mind!*

He's profoundly tired, with the sort of soul-deep weariness that follows a prolonged mental struggle, and now it's raining again, and the tank pipes are grumbling (what did Em call them? The *entrails* of the house?), the clocks striking seven. He should change for dinner, wash his face. He shuffles down the passage, hugging his side, like a man who isn't aware yet that he's sustained a fatal wound. He wishes he could climb into bed and sleep. The shabby floorboards stretch ahead, redolent of last week's polish, of feet, of mortal things.

A towel is laid out next to the ewer on the washstand in his dressing room; a fire spits in the grate. He drops Florence's letter into the flames and watches it burn before filling the basin and sluicing his hands and neck. He must find his clothes, cover his nakedness. Where is his shirt, where are his trousers? Where has she put them?

'Emma,' he says. 'Emma!' He stands there, dripping. She doesn't answer. The dressing-room lamp is unlit, but there's a smirk of light on the threshold, there's a presence behind her door. She's getting ready, brushing out her hair, whitening her teeth, sharpening her pen. She is on the cliffs, waving to him across that dark space as the spume flies up: waving or beckoning, *goodbye* or *hello*. He's filled with a sense of wrongness. How can the same woman who wrote that loving memoir have written those deadly diaries? A blast of rain shakes the panes. It seems, suddenly, as if he's stepped into a dwindling world in which water and wind are the only realities.

It's wrong. It's all wrong.

Emma

AT HALF PAST SEVEN he goes downstairs to dinner. He has no desire for food. He feels the way a ghost must feel, impatient with the habits of a discarded body, at a distance from himself. A savoury fug advances along the kitchen passage; there's the low growl of feminine conversation in the dining room. As soon as he enters it he sees with a lunge of his heart that Em is there. Emma has come.

He pulls himself up to his full height. 'So, my dear. Have you anything to say to me?'

'I'm getting on very well, Daddy-Uncle.' She plants a kiss on his cheek, enveloping him in the scent of some sickly flower. 'You don't mind me borrowing this old silk of Auntie's tonight, do you? The mourning gown I packed isn't nearly as good. How do I look?'

Not Em. Lilian. He stares at her, shaken to the depths, forgetting to breathe. How like Em she is in her deep purple dress, with her thick jowls and her hair drawn back in its tight knot – the Em of twenty years ago; Emma in middle age. She's Em in miniature, but less intelligent, and therefore less deadly. 'What?' he wheezes. 'Well now, quite presentable.'

Kate and Florence are here too. Kate gives his chair at the head of the table a rap. 'Sit down, Tom,' she says. 'You're holding us all up.'

They sit, crammed higgledy-piggledy at one end. Dolly enters with the soup and goes out, banging the door.

'Dolly doesn't do kitchen work,' he says. His heart is still jumping like a mad thing: *thump-thump-thump.* The soup is red. He dips his spoon into it. Tomato. It's the wrong soup.

'She does now,' says Kate, 'till you decide if you're going to keep her on. With four of us in the house Jane has her hands full. That girl needs to stay busy. Otherwise she'll just sit upstairs and mope.'

'Mrs Riggs,' he says. 'Not "Jane".'

Kate sighs. 'Mrs Riggs, then.'

'I'd rather we didn't discuss the servants at table,' he says.

Dolly brings in the pie. It appears sturdy enough, but closer inspection reveals that the crust is skewed. Everything is off-balance, a poor simulacrum of itself. He turns the dish around. There's a gash in the far side of the pastry. Behind it a granular interior bubbles darkly.

He gives it a jab with the serving slice. 'Have we had this pie before, Kate?'

'Well,' says Kate, 'you certainly haven't had it.' Her jaw tightens. 'It's yesterday's.'

He regards the crooked pie, his cooling soup. His new ghostly self, the self that's returned to the world after spending the last hour with the dead, doesn't feel hunger, only a baffled distaste at its previous creaturely life. *He ate well, with his usual humourless haste.* Was he, is he *humourless?* He's never thought of himself as humourless. What about Kate, what about *this* nag? He prefers Mary, he always did. But Mary isn't here; all the wrong people are here.

'Emma usually ordered fresh meat for dinner,' he says.

'Then I'll speak to *Mrs Riggs* about it,' says Kate.

'Miss Hardy has gone to so much trouble to make us all comfortable,' murmurs Florence.

'I'm sure she has,' he says. Florence. Florence is here with him, not Emma. He's standing with Florence on the churchyard path again. The rain is coming down in a slurred veil, the idling car is ticking like an oven. The driver is reading the newspaper. The columns of print tremble, black-armed. *Grief* and *love* and *removed*. So many words, exceeding his grasp.

'This soup, now,' he says. 'The soup I like is mutton broth.' He pushes his plate to one side. He feels light-headed. 'I was thinking today about that family up your way, Kate. The Debbyhouses. They were carters once, if I'm not mistaken. One of them drove us home from the station. I'm fairly positive he was a Debbyhouse. That nose.'

'Oh, are we discussing the servants?' asks Kate.

Lilian interrupts. A frizzy spiral has unpinned itself from her combed-back hair and is flapping at her ear. 'I hear that you went to visit dear Aunt's grave this afternoon, Miss Dugdale,' she says.

'I did,' says Florence. 'Mr Hardy was kind enough to take me. I found the floral remembrances very touching.'

'The splendid chrysanthemum wreath was laid by some girls from the neighbouring parish,' Lilian goes on. 'She was always giving the local children little treats. I thought the notice in *The Times* very good, didn't you, Uncle?'

He glances at Kate. There must be something wrong with his vision: in her high-backed chair she seems half her proper size. Her face has the spiteful look it often had when she was a girl. The entire room is shrinking, like a scene observed through the back end of a telescope.

'The article was quite accurate,' he manages. 'Emma was much loved for her humanitarianism.'

'Though she was herself a writer of no mean ability,' says Lilian. 'The paper did not mention this.'

'She had an original turn of phrase, it's true.'

'Daddy-Uncle, you must admit it was much more than that. You'd never have been the great novelist you are without her.'

'Is that so?' asks Kate.

From a point outside his body, his temple gives a low twinge. 'Kate,' he says warningly.

'My uncle knows better than anyone that my aunt helped write his books.'

He stares at the pie before him. It too appears stunned and small, its viscera contracted in a heap. He presses the heel of his hand into his right eye, but the room refuses to resume its normal proportions. Emma should be here. Emma would have been able to cut through this blur. 'Ha,' he says. 'The whole of Dorset helped write my books.'

'There you are, then,' says Lilian, patting her frizz. He has watched this action – so intimate and so forbidding – being performed night after night, and he's flooded by a familiar mixture of tenderness and irritation. All of a sudden he doubts himself.

Yes, here I am, Em. I think I'm here. Are you?

The woman to his right ought to be Emma; he's not entirely persuaded, on reflection, that she isn't. That's just how Em would purse her lips, how she'd wag her spoon. But her features are indistinct. He leans towards her to get a better view.

Why, he convinces himself, it *is* Emma. He's filled with an extraordinary sensation of relief. What in heaven's name though is she wearing? Her stolid expression is utterly at odds with her costume. It's a flittery, ribboned gown, bulging at the seams, that looks as if it's been stitched together entirely from suggestive scraps, like a vague recollection of some nymph in a picture by Botticelli. She tucks an escaped strand of hair behind her ear. Her lips are moving. She's saying something.

'Hmm? Yes?'

'I said, have you had a good day's writing?'

'Fairly good, thank you. And you, my dear? Have you been out?'

All at once the situation is clear to him. He's not old at all. He's a middle-aged man, and he's dining, as is his nightly habit, with a high-stomached woman in girlish silk: his wife. This costume is all that's left of the former Em — her youthful energy and high spirits; her fierce colour, her brilliant curls. He notices now that there's a bank of violets on the table, a reef of mauve, afloat in some sort of silvered ark.

'What are these? Flowers?' The violets exert a subtle pressure on his nerves. They seem to hint that there's something he must remember, that there's a gesture he should be making. 'Violets won't last a day out of the ground.'

'We've plenty more,' says the woman, giving her soup a speculative stir. 'I've been planning the new border. I'm in favour of roses — and possibly stocks.'

'Let's not have roses. They're so vulnerable to every kind of pest.'

The deformed leaf, the crippled curve; disease eating the vigour of the stalk. He tries to dispel the thought. 'Stocks are always a sensible choice.'

'I intend to set up a cold frame, you know. Then we shall have cucumbers next season.'

'Why not?' He pings the silver bowl with his fingernail. It's plate. 'We already have a piano. We'll be the complete gentleman and lady.' The woman pretends not to hear this remark, or perhaps she's heard it and dismissed it as unimportant. He must seem as full of inconsequentialities to her as she does to him. 'I forgot to say,' he adds. 'I saw Gosse in town the other day. I've asked him up for the weekend.'

'Oh, dear. You might have told me. Will Nellie come?'

'No. Only Gosse, this time.'

'Just as well. That guest room is no good.'

'I'm sure you would have drawn a much better design for the house, my dear. But mine will have to do until we can extend.'

She frowns. 'More building works.'

'Well, not for the moment. I have to be able to afford them first.'

Molly has removed the soup and brought in the veal, and they eat steadily. The meat is rather chewy, still dense with blood. The scent of the violets is overwhelming; he thinks he may be getting a headache. At last he hears Emma say, 'I was wondering, you know, if rather than going to London we could have a holiday this summer. Perhaps . . . Cornwall.'

'I'm sorry, Em. It's impossible. I'm behind on my book. I simply can't make any progress with it.'

An agonized pink creeps over her features. 'Do you know what day this is?'

'Day? No. What's the day?'

'It's the seventh of March. It's twenty years since the day we met.'

Here it is: the key to the flowers, to Em's bizarrely elaborate dress; the thing he's forgotten. 'So it is.'

'Maybe I could help you.'

'*Help* me?'

'I could be your copyist again. You've always said that I write rather a beautiful hand.'

'That's a kind offer.' Panic sluices through him. 'But my dear, can you spare the time? You're so busy outdoors right now.'

'Oh, the garden can wait. It will be just like the old days.'

Molly comes and goes with more plates, more dishes. It's like sitting on a stage, surrounded by fakery on every side. A comedy bower. When Molly is out of the room for a minute he bends confidentially from the waist. 'We must be careful. If we're to be holed up together all day like two lovebirds, the servants will talk.'

He knows, even while he's offering it to her, that this little piece of flirtation is contemptible. He's like the parody of a husband, a character from some third-rate farce, whose uxoriousness is so overwritten that it verges on condescension.

But the woman rises to the challenge. 'I won't disturb you,' she says. 'I'll find myself a wee nook somewhere. I'll be as quiet as a mouse.'

'Mice aren't very quiet.'

Her voice bubbles roguishly. 'As quiet as — as a moth, then.'

'A moth!' He's amused, in spite of himself. 'What a funny thing you are.' She's lowered her arm, and the cuff of her sleeve, its buttons straining, rests on the table. She's wiggling her fingers like the legs of an insect. There's the rub of silk against damask, a tight, dry crackle.

'Emmie.' His hand edges along the ashen surface towards hers. It's like crossing the desert. He can feel himself sinking. Why must they eat like this? Why the starched linen and the under plates, the stringy veal and the frail flowers in their imitation bowl, and this sad rhubarb now being set in front of him, rhubarb so tragically reminiscent in its ruby dissolution of a sunset that it makes him want to lower his forehead to the cloth, and howl? The pudding and the plates and the silver and the crystal fringe of the lamp, with its single dangling ball glittering like the eye of a toad – he's written them into being, made them all. He's made her: her flaccid cheek, her mouth like a sprung trap, biting back its disappointments. He's summoned this beribboned impostor who sits beside him at the dinner-table in the guise of his wife.

Emma taps the rim of her pudding bowl with her spoon. She's calling him to order, as you'd command a public meeting. 'Well, don't you think?'

'Think? What should I think?'

'That bottled rhubarb,' she says in her effervescent voice, 'has an uncanny ability to impersonate fresh fruit in the middle of winter.'

He stares at her, nonplussed. He realizes again – it's a realization that comes to him often these days – that there's a mind at work in that head about which, in spite of nearly sixteen years of marriage, he knows almost nothing. 'What on earth do you mean? It's not winter. It's March. You've just said yourself that it's the seventh of *March*.'

'By my calendar the spring equinox is still a fortnight away.'

By my calendar. The lady gardener's calendar. The hothouse calendar. She may like to garden but she is not, and never will be, a countrywoman.

'I tell 'ee it's spring!' The gurning vowel slips out before he's even aware of it. He sounds exactly like the men he grew up with, like a jumped-up builder. And isn't that what he is: a joiner, a hewer of crude fantasies that no respectable household really wants or needs? Though he's published eleven novels he's nothing more than a little man with dirty hands, knocking on the doors of the great and good, begging to be admitted to their halls. He's paralysed with rage that after all this time Emma is still able to make him feel like a supplicant, as if he's auditioning for his own life.

But Em's brow has lifted. Her whole face has cleared. She's looking at him joyfully, her eyes alight with recognition. In one of those abrupt emotional reversals of which only she's capable, his wife is smiling as if this latest betrayal of his faults has cancelled rather than raised the old, ridiculous difference between them. The poor man and the lady. Yes, how ridiculous it was! Quite how ridiculous, they alone knew. Her smile contains a dare, as if to say, *Are you the same now as you were then? I am just the same.* He has an impulse to kiss her, or shake her. He does neither.

She dissolves.

Molly – or is it another girl? They come and go so quickly, these girls, with their thin legs full of growing pains, and absent mothers, and washing he has to pay for – is already knocking the dishes about.

He pushes his chair away from the table. 'I think I may go up to bed early tonight. Since you have so kindly – since you have . . .'

He stops. Everything, the china, the cutlery, the stupid lamp, wears the aspect of a malicious joke. Emma's subservience, his apparent mastership – a joke, but at whose expense, his or hers, he can't say. 'So, my dear,' he mumbles. 'If you'll excuse me.'

He hears Kate's voice. 'For goodness' sake, Tom.'

They're blinking at him like spectators at a play. Kate's gaze is dry and hard. Her jaw goes on working silently. Did he speak out loud? Which of them was he addressing? He looks down and sees that he's on his feet, pudding spoon clenched in his fist. It's Florence who, without any perceptible hesitation, gets up; who removes the spoon from his grip and takes his wrist and tells a white-lipped Dolly – the serving girl is Dolly after all, not Molly – that there will be no need for tea in the drawing room, and not to keep back any more of the pie, but for the maids to make a supper of it.

Florence guides him to the threshold of his room. 'Pay no attention to them,' she says. 'It doesn't matter, do you hear me?'

'Dear girl. Kind girl. I knew you'd come.'

Her eyes search his face. 'What happened just then, at dinner? You were there, and then you weren't.'

'I was back in the past – with Em.' He's wavering on the brink of understanding, and he's filled with a grief so pure and dark that he feels as if he will drown. 'I seem to have lost myself, Florence.'

'Whatever you saw wasn't real,' says Florence. Her hands are folded around his. 'It's over now. You're still you – you are Thomas Hardy. You are real. *I'm* real.' She touches her lips to his knuckles.

Her constancy, her gentleness, make him feel that he, too, can be gentle and constant. Bending his head, he inhales the living heat of her hair. 'I don't know what I'd do without you,' he says.

'Are you going to be able to sleep tonight?' she asks.

'Yes, now that you're here.'

'I'm just overhead. Do you promise to call me if you need me?'

'I will,' he says. But he senses the empty room yawning behind him, the pull of it. That darkness. He's complicit with the dark and with its promise of extinction. He doesn't want to be gentle, after all. He wants to give in to his grief; he wants to give Florence a push, out into the light where she belongs.

As he closes the door he speaks roughly. 'You know I will,' he says. 'Please don't fuss. Please go to bed. Go now, Florence. *Go.*'

A Circular

IT'S NOT QUITE DAWN when he wakes. He's been dreaming of the castle on the cliff. He's still stumbling along the sands below, bevelled grey and gold as far as the eye can see, following a voice.

Hurry, calls the voice. *Hurry, now. It isn't over. Don't you see me? Here I am.* There's someone he must meet, past the furthest bank. She's waiting for him in the ruins on the cliff-top. He falters forward across that dizzying space, towards the retreating sky. A thin gleam has arrived on the horizon, faint but steady, and for a moment he's shaken by hope.

Not hope: cold. He pulls off the covers and finds that he's shivering. It's Tuesday. It's the third day of December. He's lying on his back with his dinner shirt half buttoned, alone in his bed in the widening light. No one else is up yet. His bladder is full and he has a cramp in his varicosed leg.

He retrieves his trousers and socks and limps to the W.C., urinates copiously into the pan, pulls the chain. Water thunders behind the plaster. His study is chill, but trembling with a shy radiance. The rain has stopped and a white haze rises from the ground. He sinks into his chair, still trailing the remnants of his dream, and draws his shawl about him.

Above the misty garden wall the branches of the nut walk are starred with water. A flash here and there, and then nothing. The world is as he's always known it: impervious, fixed. Absurd to think otherwise, to lose his bearings and go making such a spectacle of himself at dinner; to run here at first light like a penitent. Absurd to hope for a reprieve. Yet he does hope.

Have pity on me, Emmie. Appear to me. I'm waiting for you, why won't you show yourself?

Possibly he isn't fully awake. This is his house. He's at home. But since last night the solidity of his study strikes him as devious. He's unpersuaded by its cunning blend of old and new: Axminster rug, the bust of Dante, coral walls hung with chromolithographs of abbeys and great English poets and stately halls. The very signs of his success – the many illustrations to his novels, scene after scene of the universe he's willed into existence, mounted over the chimney-piece – seem counterfeit.

He wonders at the piercing desire he feels, his breathless sense of being in the wrong place. Somewhere in a neighbouring dimension, surely, unfolding along coordinates adjacent to these, is his real life, the life he should have been living; a well-proportioned life, equally sustained by work and love: the one that was promised when Emma opened the door to him that spring evening in St Juliot forty years ago. Not this muddle of guilt and regret.

It's a vision of such urgency that his pulse quickens. Didn't Em know as much? Didn't she feel this dislocation too? *I was immediately arrested by his familiar appearance, as if I had seen him in a dream.* A dream that came to nothing.

The house utters small groans in protest, revealing its agonized bulk as the night lifts and the shadows withdraw. *My house*, he thinks. *Our house.* Perhaps he's in the right place after all, but at the wrong time.

Was I so forgetful these last years, Em? Did you really think I no longer cared?

It takes him a moment or two to retrieve Emma's recollections from among the papers and notebooks on his desk, and to find the passage he wants. There he is, that hopeful young man with the poem sticking out of his pocket. His chrysalis.

So I met my husband, or rather he met me.

He reaches for his perpetual calendar and sets it to Monday, the seventh of March. He closes his eyes and Emma is there too, rose bright, as if drawn on the air. Not the adversary who faced him at the dinner-table down the dwindling passage of the years, but a ghost-girl-rider, galloping on the shale.

He's aware after a while that Florence has come into the room. She stands by his side noiselessly, waiting for him to notice her, making no demands. It must be mid-morning by now. She will be clean and unpowdered, chin jutting, a look of shining determination on her face. She will have come with some useful thing to do.

He opens his eyes and sees that he's right. Florence is carrying a bundle of letters in one hand and her Remington in the other.

'We missed you at breakfast,' she says.

'What time is it?'

She arranges the typewriter and letters on his book table. 'It's nearly ten o'clock.'

'I was awake early and came straight here. I haven't much of an appetite.'

'That's perfectly natural, given the strain you've been under. I hope you had a good night?'

Florence, sleepless in her narrow bed, waiting for him to call out. He can tell by her tone that she's forgiven him both for his snappishness and his unexpected ability to manage his emotions alone.

I couldn't call you. I was somewhere else, I was following someone else. 'I did, thank you, my dear,' he says. 'I even dreamed. It wasn't a bad dream.'

'I'm so glad.'

He feels a surge of gratitude towards her. She is tactful. She is patient. She is kind. She keeps no record of wrongs. Or he assumes she doesn't. She hasn't given him an answer to the offer he tried to make her in the churchyard, though, and now he daren't raise the subject again.

Florence tidies his pen tray, realigns his papers. As an apparent afterthought she begins to straighten his shawl. In the next breath her hand will touch his shoulder, and he doesn't want it to. 'Must you keep wearing this old thing?' she asks.

'It was my mother's.'

'I didn't know. I assumed Emma had made it.'

'Em didn't often knit.' He shrugs elaborately, as if he's stiff from sitting.

The fluttering hand withdraws. He is relieved. 'No, of course not. She was a *writer*.'

'Tsk. You mustn't mind anything Lilian says.'

Florence permits herself a faint smile. She picks up his paper knife and runs it under the flap of an envelope. 'You've been looking at those diabolical diaries,' she says with false lightness.

'No, no. I was merely – remembering. See, I've found rather a charming thing of Emma's about her girlhood in Cornwall. I wonder when she wrote it.' He holds the exercise book out to her. 'Did she ever show this to you?'

Florence gives the pages her full attention, as she always does when he presents her with a manuscript. There's a wrinkle of concentration between her eyebrows. 'I've never seen it before. I did type up one of her short stories some time ago. "The Inspirer". Beautiful and vivacious but sadly neglected wife, cranky little husband – a famous novelist, don't you know – who owes all his success to this gem and thankfully comes to his senses at last; tender reconciliations, moonlight and roses. Just gibberish, really.'

'This is quite different. It's rather good. In fact it quite brings her back.'

'I didn't know that you wanted to bring her back,' Florence says sharply. She goes back to slitting his envelopes. 'You seem to have forgotten how unhappy you were these last years.' A prickle of defiance. 'You seem almost to *miss* her.'

'The Emma I miss is the girl who died, oh, twenty years ago. I've mourned her for a very long time. Recalling this now makes no difference to the special regard I have for you.'

The sound of ripping paper continues for many minutes – minutes in which he discerns, dimly, that another opportunity has been lost – when Florence gives a snort.

'What's that?' he says.

'It's only a fashion circular.'

'Don't throw it away. Let me have it.'

She passes him the sheet. Pictures of women's garments are spread like pallid moths on the page. Blouses. Tea gowns. Wraps. Things waiting to be bought. Covetable things, he supposes. For a few moments he's no longer a man, but assesses them as a woman would: a pearl *crêpe de Chine* with gossamer gloves; a blue voile, the colour of skimmed milk in the pail at dawn. Why do they disturb him so? He squints at the paper. The clothes are too well drawn. They're slightly suspect imitations of the real: the idea of clothes, not clothes themselves. There are no bodies inside them; no flesh. He runs his hand over his face.

'You shouldn't be troubled with unimportant matters now – or ever,' says Florence. 'I've sorted these letters of condolence into groups. We can do them together, if you like.'

She stares at him with her perpetually bruised eyes. She's so untried, so determined to be loving and helpful. Soon, he knows, he'll begin to find her helpfulness oppressive, just as he had Emma's. 'Gosse. I must answer Gosse's letter first.' He remembers, feeling time snag, that he left it on his tray in the drawing room. 'It's downstairs, next to my armchair. Nothing is where it should be.'

'I'll fetch it.'

He opens the door for her and nearly cries out. Lilian is posted behind it, her short arms held rigidly at her sides.

'How have you been getting on this morning?' he asks.

'There's rather a lot to pack.'

'Florence will give you a hand.'

Lilian says, in a languid voice that's quite unlike her usual one,

'Florence, if I could just trouble you with a few of my own bits and pieces also.'

Florence glances at him uncertainly.

'Run down for that letter, my dear,' he says. 'And hurry back.'

She leaves the room at once.

If you stroke me, I shall like you more. The words come to him before he can check them. 'I meant Florence Griffin,' he says, 'not Miss Dugdale.'

'Oh, Daddy-Uncle.' Lilian smiles. 'It's an easy mistake to make.'

'Hardly. Miss Dugdale is here as my guest.'

'But Florence Dugdale is not a lady,' says Lilian. 'Now, my aunt – my aunt was, first and last, a lady. And I wonder,' she adds, clasping her elbows, 'what Miss Dugdale *is* to you?'

'You know what she is,' he says weakly. 'She was your aunt's devoted friend, a *literary* friend, and she's a great help to me.'

On Florence's return he surprises all three of them by tossing Gosse's letter onto the table with the rest. He takes Florence by the sleeve. 'We won't reply to these today. We'll walk in the garden instead.'

But as soon as they are in the garden he realizes that he's lost. The bushes screening his property have become a weedy hedge, through whose lank limbs he sees all too clearly the nakedness of the place. Its foliage is both overgrown and ludicrously adrift, like the hair on an old man's balding head. After the rain of the last few days the sun is shockingly bright.

He hesitates, blinking at the nubby lawn, the slack tangle of ferns bordering the path. The wet and the frail warmth have drawn out flying ants from under the flags. They scrabble into the open with a demented clockwork regularity and take off in twos, their wings vague as smoke.

'Horrible,' Florence says. 'What are they?'

'Emmets. They won't hurt you.'

She hits at her skirt to get them off. 'I don't know why such creatures have to exist.'

'Who knows why anything is born. Let them be, they don't bite.'

They're inching down the middle lawn to the straight walk, where the boughs drip and suddenly spring up, released from their weight of water. The earth is printed with the long paces of night visitors, of hares and mice. Beneath the tree canopy it's as quiet as a cathedral. Light arrives in the wooded aisle as if from another world, cleaving the misty air, uncovering forms in the formlessness.

Is this *real, Emmie? And this?* A shadow, shifting, rhythmic, falls across his feet. His breath stalls in his throat.

She's still here, in all this growth and decay, still traceable in the empty space between the leaves. She's not whole, she's not what she used to be, but in her incompleteness she seems all the more present.

When they come to the beech at the corner he stops, afraid that he's about to cry, to faint, to disgrace himself in some irrevocable way. He steadies himself against its trunk. It's as firm as bone, erupting in an astonishing feather of bronze far above the roof of the house. Its bark is as ridged as God's fingernail.

He'll wait here. He'll stand here for the rest of his days, with this tree for solace.

'Tom, are you all right?'

How has he acquired this young woman with her tensely coiled hair and her serviceable shoes? She's of an age with Lilian. She's young enough to be his daughter. He can smell the tea on her breath, the perspiration in the armpits of her dress.

'Emma used to garden here in the mornings,' he says. 'I almost expect to see her as usual, kneeling in the beds with a trowel in her hand.' The ants have vanished into the deceptive blue sky. 'I'm sorry, Florence. I'm not much use to you at the moment. I'm tired. And old.'

'It's a great change. For all of us.' She props her hand solemnly under his forearm, as if to support him.

He wants to shout, *I may be old but I am not an invalid. I am not ill, I am not infirm. I am the same as I was before.* But *before* – what was that?

The Calendar

TEN TO FOUR. THE CURTAINS are drawn against the encroaching dark, the lamp is lit. Since his funny turn in the garden this morning he's been made to have complete rest. He's had mutton broth on a tray, a hot brick for his feet. He's been undisturbed. His study calendar is displayed beside his tinderbox on the bedside table, where he put it when he came up to his room several hours ago. It's still set to the seventh of March.

He should be sleeping, but he can't. *I've been asleep for twenty years,* he thinks. *Nothing in my life was what it seemed.* He understands, now, that the past hasn't ended. It lies all around him, of a piece with the present, concealed behind the most innocent things.

Before. At last he has an unobstructed view of it.

In this *before* life rings and thuds with spades and bricks and buckets of mortar in a bare field that's whipped by the winds from every direction. Builders' braziers are lit at dawn and smoke into the night. The soil churns, hammers deal their blows. Until there arises, as if by a convulsion of his brain, of the earth itself, a house. His house, abutting the Wareham road and within earshot of the railway, commanding views of Fordington Field across to Came

Wood and the downs that run, Janus-faced, to the sea. From its upper windows he's able to gaze northward over the Frome Valley to Stinsford churchyard, all the way to the woodland and heath gird-ling the stone-floored cottage where he was born, his home for as long as he can remember.

He has returned. He has come home.

But this brand-new house: this, now, is home. In middle age he finds himself back on his native soil with the wife his mother has always disliked, living a bare three miles from his mother's hearth, in possession of a kitchen with a stove, a place to hang the laundry, a well and a pump and a cess pit. He has a hall and a drawing room and a dining room; he has three bedrooms and a dressing room; he even has a water-closet. He has Portland stone window sills and oak window frames, corbelled chimneys and lead flashings, a porch of Flemish bond, and – no mere decorative feature, this, since he's reached the halfway point of his life and has never doubted his own mortality – a staircase wide enough to carry a coffined corpse down.

On the night of their arrival he and Emma cower in the dining room that reeks of varnish, as wary of each other as newlyweds, eating bread and cheese. There's space in the attic of the house for three or four servants, never less than two. They've yet to hire one. Outside, the violated ground; the dream, still unrealized, of a garden. A wall – a six-foot wall, and within it two thickly planted rows of hazel, sufficiently far apart to allow for a pathway in between. The other trees will come soon: the beeches, a screen around the house of three thousand pines. But also yew, double-blossom elder, apple grafted onto quince stock, wych elm, walnut, holly, spindle.

His trees.

Em is in charge of the flowers and vegetables, the herbs and salad greens. Things growing low to the earth. She lays out a kitchen plot and a lawn; she quizzes the girls who begin to come in search of positions as cook, as parlour maid – local girls, the daughters of the county's cottagers and day-labourers, the sort of girls he might once have courted. Low girls, like his sisters.

He's married above himself. He's been removed for many years now from the life Kate and Mary have been living in their cottage on the heath and at their training college, from their country squabbles and schoolmistresses' gossip. From a distance he's observed their patient gaining of qualifications and their grappling at respectability. And Henry – well, Hen is the son his father had hoped for, and at last got: steady on his feet, square-handed, imperturbable. A proper builder.

He loves his siblings and he's pained by them, by their countrified ways, their studied consonants. He's pained by Emma too, by her hats and her garden parties, her condescending philanthropy to their neighbours, and her resentment of this old love. On Sundays he creeps across the fields to his mother. She says that it will all end badly, but that's what she says about everything. (And hasn't it already begun to end badly? Doesn't he set off daily on a journey, longer each time, on which he knows Em can't accompany him, and from which he'll have to return alone?)

He's working harder than he ever has in his life. Work is what there is for him, work is what he does. He gleams and glistens with work. He begins writing immediately after breakfast and remains indoors till he's finished for the day. He's always been abstemious, as his mother taught him to be, and this doesn't change. He eats lightly, doesn't smoke, drinks seldom. He writes and writes.

The irony is that he could be anywhere. He could still be in any one of the succession of lodging-houses and rented terraces where he and Em spent their early married years. Having an entire house of his own to write in is irrelevant to the feat of the imagination he must perform. When he works he pays no attention to his surroundings; he might as well be writing in a cell. He might as well be writing on his knees. He writes because this is what he does, and because there is nothing else he can do.

The other irony (how the ironies pile up!) is that his books aren't fit for purpose. He's trying to write books in which the world can shelter, books that have the same red-brick solidity as his house, but all he seems to manage is a lean-to or a hut. His words don't contain things in the way he wants them to. Instead of becoming clearer to him as he goes on, the connection between his words and the world gets ever more tentative, more provisional. He's made a landscape, but it appears to have a life of its own that bears scant relation to the one he set out to make. This landscape is where he lives, this is where he has his being. None of it is real. The real world ebbs a little further from him every year. Sometimes he steps out of the house after the day's writing and hardly recognizes what he sees: the stubby trees, the guttering hills. Everything looks reduced and mean. At these times he feels as if the material world isn't the real one after all, merely the one that's visible.

Does he deserve this house, brash as it is; does he deserve his gradually increasing comfort, the gratifying if never totally unqualified praise that's starting to come his way? Probably not. Thomas the Doubter. Thomas the Unworthy. Does he deserve Mary's pity, Kate's envy? Are these things any more real; do they exist at all, outside his imagination?

The house, though – the house exists. The house is always hungry, always needing another sack of coal here, another layer of paint there. He wonders if he's wasted his energies in bringing it into being, and the thought is like a small death. Still, there's a reprieve, a stay of execution: Emma seems happy enough. Em is occupied with her rhubarb, her violets.

Except that now, twenty years later, he knows this was as much an illusion as anything else. Here, in her diaries, risen from the abyss of *before* with a shriek of furious disruption, is the truth. All that time, as he wrote in this house, Emma was writing too.

Emma was never happy.

8th March 1890

Mr Gosse has arrived. He's come to stay till Monday. He is a poet, of course. Even so – I can't help longing for something less *prosy* from the visits of T.'s literary friends.

Mr Gosse is principally interested in his stomach.

He's attentive, nevertheless. He knows exactly what to say. He leaves Tom in the dust. I'd half hoped that my husband would yet surprise me with some way of marking our special anniversary, but no. He's going off à deux with Mr Gosse tomorrow. T. understands only the women he invents – the others not at all.

A step. Someone is coming. He raises himself higher in bed, sending the diary in his lap tumbling between his knees.

There's the step again, on the landing. As the clock starts to strike four the door opens a crack. Florence. He pulls the coverlet up to his waist.

'Did I wake you?' she says.

'Oh, no.'

'Do you feel better now?'

He tries for a smile. 'Much.'

Florence enters on tiptoe and goes over to stir the fire. A long tongue of light darts across the carpet to the bed. She's busy with the coals for a while, riddling and prodding, and then sits beside him, resting her arm along the back of his pillow. 'Will you come down for tea?' she asks.

'Not just yet.'

'In a little while, perhaps?'

'Yes. Perhaps.'

Her eyes skim the room, searching for something to fix. 'Your calendar is wrong.'

'No, no. Let it be.'

She touches her hand to the nape of his neck and he flinches, though he doesn't mean to. He's grateful for her efficiency, for her willingness to efface herself. All day, things – the brick, the broth – have been managed with a discretion foreign to Kate. Since his collapse in the garden this morning Florence appears happier too.

They sit quietly, companionably, watching the yellow shadows of the lamp parry the blue firelight shadows on the chimney corner.

'I must go,' Florence says by and by, 'or your sister will have eaten Miss Gifford.'

'In one gulp.'

'Between two pieces of bread and butter.' She kisses the top of his head. He flinches again. 'I'll save a cake for you.'

He doesn't move. Getting up is impossible. He's stupefied by the hall clock's heavy tick. It's as if he's being drawn down to the bottom of the sea. He has no choice but to sink. He wants to sink. He hasn't been able to admit to Florence how powerful this urge is: the desire to slide from himself. He follows the smatter of her footsteps as she crosses the landing to the staircase, the creak of the oak under her weight. There's a swirl of voices, distant as dry leaves, and then a door clicks, and save for the ticking of the clock there's silence.

The figures of his calendar ripple in the blaze of the fire. He should stay here, in the present, he should follow Florence downstairs. But at every moment, it seems, he can glimpse that other time rising up behind the hour, occluded but increasingly distinct, as if from the trackless ocean floor. It beckons to him, its shires and towns and rivers spread on ash-gold sands: the territory of the dead.

He waits on the shore, alert to the chuckling of the waves, and feels a gathering of the waters which may, after all, simply be the motion of his heart.

A beat. Another beat. The minutes dissolve in the space between each contraction. He touches his face for reassurance, to tether himself to the familiar, but he knows that he's already lost. He is following a ghost. He's poised on the margins, on the verge of the solid world. When he can't feel his body any more he turns away and looks down, from his haunted height, into the depths.

Lyonnesse

HE'S STILL IN THIS room, but it's no longer a bedroom: it's again the room where he works, directly across the landing from the one he occupies with Em.

It's 1890. It's Saturday the eighth of March. Four o'clock. Gosse will be arriving within the hour, and must be collected from the station. The trap has already come; old Debbyhouse, girt in the livery of his trade, his magnificent nose offset by the visor of his wideawake, has gone round the back for a cup of ale and a quick bite of bread.

The manuscript he's been staring at since breakfast is spread on his writing table. He abandons it and staggers to the window, rubbing his knees.

Afternoon light sifts down over the bare fields. After a cold dry winter the weather's been unseasonably warm and fine all week. Below him the garden appears tenuous, a patchwork of thirsty grass and chalky soil. Only his young pines – slender as spears, full of purpose – seem capable of sustained life. His own head, with its secretive lip and spade-shaped beard, floats above them in an eerie transparency.

All day he's been trying and failing to write. Not just today: it was the same yesterday, and the day prior to that; every day, in fact, for the past few months. He's reached the midpoint of his new book and he has no idea – really, not the slightest idea in the world – how to go on. Turning back to his table with a spasm of self-loathing, he opens the drawer where he keeps his correspondence. Before he fetches Gosse he'll allow himself a single moment of undiluted despair.

Lying face up on the heap of letters is the one that's stopped him dead. He removes it gingerly, holding it between his forefinger and thumb as if he's handling a snake. In spite of everything, in spite of the good reviews and the money and his house, monument to his competence, this letter has the power to paralyse him whenever he looks at it.

Macmillan & Co., London
25th November 1889

Dear Mr Hardy,

I have now read your manuscript, representing the first half of your book in progress – read it always with interest and often with pleasure. The rural scenes seem to me especially good, once again demonstrating the happy facility in catching and fixing the phases of peasant life, in reproducing for us not just the manners and language, but the tone of thought and the simple wisdom of village rustics, that we have come to expect from your pen.

More patronizing guff.

But there are other things that strike me as less happy. Of course you will understand that I write only of the fitness of the story for serialization in my magazine, beyond which I have neither the right nor wish to go. It is not easy for me to frame my discomfort in precise words, as it is general rather than particular, so let me try to sum it up in a single objection.

It is too obvious from the first page what is to be your heroine's fate. The whole of this first part of the tale is a sort of circling around and back to her seduction (or is it something worse than that?) which is hardly ever, and can hardly ever be out of the reader's mind; even her husband-to-be, who is inclined to 'make an honest woman' of her, seems unable to get past a purely sensuous admiration of her person. Her capacity for stirring and by implication for gratifying these feelings is pressed rather more frequently and elaborately than strikes me as altogether convenient, at any rate for a family magazine which will be read by the daughters of respectable men.

You use the word 'succulent' more than once to describe the general appearance and condition of the Frome Valley. Perhaps I might say that the overall impression left on me by reading your story – so far as it has gone – is one of rather too much succulence.

And then, the *coup de grâce*:

All this, I know, makes the book 'entirely modern', and will therefore, I have no doubt, bring it plenty of praise. I must confess, however, to being rather too old-fashioned – as I suppose I must call it – to quite relish the entirely modern style of fiction.

You asked for my frank opinion at this point. I must therefore tell you, with regret, that though I remain a profound admirer of your work, *Macmillan's Magazine* does not propose to publish your story.

Yours very sincerely,

Mowbray Morris

So far as it has gone. He's that laughable thing, a writer stranded in the wreck of his illusion.

This is the third rejection of the manuscript he's had, and it's by far the worst. He may have to accept that the book is unsellable. He wants to reply, to give an account of himself, but when faced with this letter he's unable to think straight, and anyway, what account can there be? Outside of his writing he lacks any sort of real agency. The habit of writing has made him deaf and dumb.

Tossing the letter back into the drawer he walks up and down, raking his scalp, clawing at his beard. The latest issue of *Macmillan's* is lying on the whatnot with the rest of his periodicals. In a fit of pique he seizes the volume and hurls it at the wall. Immediately he's ashamed, and stoops to pick it up.

He's bent over, smoothing pages, when Emma opens the door. 'I heard a noise,' she says.

'Oh, it's nothing – I dropped this. So clumsy of me.'

A sceptical wince. 'Everything's ready. There are clean towels in Mr Gosse's room. I hope you won't be late getting back from the station.' Em screws up her eyes. 'You look like a scarecrow. What's happened to your hair? Why aren't you wearing your jacket?'

'I've a little while yet. The driver's just having his bit, and then I'll be off.'

Emma's hand flits to her breast. She's dressed in haste; she's missed one of the buttons on her bodice. 'I did wonder, Tom,' she says.

'Yes?'

'That thing we spoke of yesterday.'

'We can't manage Cornwall, Emmie.'

'Not that – my helping you. I wonder if you've given it any further thought.'

'There'll be plenty of time to talk about it later. May I?' He leans over and captures the dangling button, which is covered in a slippery fabric; tucks it back into its buttonhole. They stand together in brief, flustered proximity. 'Look,' he says, 'are you on your way to the kitchen? Could you give Debbyhouse a nudge?'

Em's breathing is effortful. He's aware, suddenly, of how simply and neatly put together she is: lungs, heart, beating blood. His being gives a throb of recognition.

'If you promise,' she says, 'not to get distracted with – well, with books.'

'Who, me?'

'Yes. *You.*' She licks her finger and tweaks his beard into a point. 'I'll just see to the kettle, then.'

As Em hurries down the stairs he has an urge to call after her, to beg her to come back so that he can tell her the truth: that it's too late for her help. He's failed to become whatever he and she once hoped he might be. He's managed to get so far, and no further. Too late, he's realized that writing isn't a support or a comfort. It isn't a friend. It's always been his master, dismissive of his moments of weakness, asking for more than he can give.

137

In their bedroom he flattens his hair before going into the dressing room to change his trousers. He's barely got downstairs, and is shrugging on his jacket in the hall, when there's a churning of gravel outside and a yowling of cats. Stepping into the porch, he unbolts the door to see Gosse striding up the drive.

'Edmund!' he shouts. 'How the devil did you get here?'

'I walked,' says Gosse. Indeed he's still walking, with great seriousness and energy, scattering cats to the left and right of him and swinging a portmanteau and a furled umbrella as he goes. He treads lightly, throwing his weight on the forward part of his feet, his long torso held erect, his gait curiously suggestive of both eagerness and discrimination.

'I was on my way to fetch you.'

'Oh dear. I should've told you there was no need.' With a final stride Gosse has reached the porch, his fringe bobbing like the crest of a cockatoo. In spite of the Cambridge lectureship and the poetry and all those opinion-shaping literary reviews, there is something faintly comical about him. 'I walk everywhere these days. Keeps me fit.'

'What a dynamo you are.' He takes Gosse's bag, his umbrella, his spring overcoat. Gosse's jacket and tie are the last word in correctness. 'How's Nellie?'

'Oh, you know how it is. She's a trifle worn. The children are very demanding.'

He doesn't know. 'It's good to have you. Welcome to Porta Maxima. You're our first real visitor.'

Gosse surveys the half-hipped roof, with its brick and slate protrusions poking into the blue. 'Great heavens – you've a *turret*. It's just like Camelot. Did you really design it all yourself?'

'I did.'

'It looks awfully grand.'

'Still smells of paint in places. We rattle about, rather. But the pines are doing well.'

'Are you sure Mrs Hardy won't mind?'

'Why, no. She was set on 'em. Said she was tired of living on a public turnpike.'

'Ha, I meant – are you sure she won't object to my intruding on your weekend?'

'Why ever should she? If you can bear to keep an old married couple company you're at liberty to intrude as much as you like.'

The guest room is next door to the bedroom he shares with Emma. Its window faces the dark yard and horseless stable where Trot, the tabby, littered a few weeks ago. To brighten up the room he had the walls painted a holly red, though he's not persuaded now, faced with their glare on this immoderately sunny March afternoon, that plain white wouldn't have been better. But red was the correct colour to have. There's always a correct colour, even if it turns your life into a perpetual Christmas.

Em is right: the room is a disaster. The fashionable red walls make it appear even smaller and more squashed than it is. Sleeping here must be like sleeping inside an intestine. He has further misgivings about the scalloped gilt bedside table, which wouldn't look out of place in the palazzo of an Italian poisoner. But he's proud of the walnut bedstead, bought in Dorchester for next to nothing; the quilted cover and matching pillowcases, sprigged with forget-me-nots, sewn by Mary for their homecoming. These things seem to speak of simpler nights, of a dreamless sleep under open windows, of an existence in which everything is still possible.

Gosse has kicked his portmanteau into a corner and is perched on the bed. 'So,' he says with an exploratory bounce. 'This is rather all right.'

'Not too small? It's a bachelor's room, really.'

'My dear friend. That's what makes it so perfect.' Gosse lies back with his arms folded behind his head, glancing around. 'What a charming table. And just listen to that quiet. I haven't heard quiet like that in a decade.' He smiles with slow relish. 'I feel about twenty.'

'I don't.'

'Well, of course you don't. It's easier for me. I'm not nearly as decrepit as you.'

Is he old? He's nearly fifty, young enough yet to feel older than his years. 'Oh, shut up. Perhaps your twenty-year-old self would like some tea.'

'Will there be jam?'

'Rhubarb, probably.'

Gosse sits up like a pressed spring. 'Rhubarb is my favourite.'

'Mrs Hardy, this is, frankly, the best jam I've ever tasted.' Gosse pauses, spoon, charged with jelly, aimed at Emma over the pot. 'Did you make it? I defy anyone to suggest an improvement. It's the very Platonic *ideal* of jam.'

He knows that Gosse is being sincere. He's achingly sincere, and the fact that he might praise the work of your hands to your face, and claim later that parts of it were in fact indigestible, makes no difference to the truth of his feeling now. Everything is as it should be. There's jam, there are thin rectangles of bread and butter, still unmarred by a single bloody cucumber; the blinds are up, the ugly furniture shining in the March sun, and Gosse is thoroughly delighted with the depth of his own response to what had only ever promised to be an ordinary event.

He's unable, though, to summon up even an answering flicker of rapture in himself. When he looks at his friend he sees how unscintillating he must appear by contrast, how hobbled by doubt. There are the Gosses of this world, striding forwards, and then there's him.

'I did,' says Em. 'It's the very last of my winter preserves.'

The spoon sheds its load smartly on the rim of Gosse's plate. 'Then I must savour every precious mouthful,' he says.

How like Edmund, the consummate critic, to sack you while maintaining the outward conventions of civility. Men like Morris and Gosse – the publishers, the reviewers – understand how life works. How to get exactly what you want, how to finesse things so that the world rewards you for being outspoken; for being yourself. Though he's merely a teller of stories, maybe he could still learn how to do it.

But Gosse has raised his head, the jam forgotten. He's listening, caught off guard by the fugal boom of the winds rolling down the fields of Came. 'What's that? It sounds like the guns of Trafalgar. Or a particularly unhappy ghost.'

'It's just the wind,' he says. 'This house is too young to have ghosts.'

'The wind! It's so dry here, and I've always thought of Dorset as a wet county.'

'Well, it is wet when it's raining.' Surely no poet was ever quite so literal-minded. 'Come on, eat up. You'll be needing your strength. I want you to help me with some research tomorrow.'

'Mrs Hardy,' says Gosse. 'What *can* your husband be planning?'

'Your guess is as good as mine,' says Em. Trot, stretched on her lap like Cybele the Many-Breasted, regards the interloper with a baleful eye.

'Since you're such a keen walker,' he says, 'I'm taking you to Portland tomorrow to look at the cottages. When I'm constructing a book I like to see how other fellows have managed their materials.'

Gosse laughs. 'Ever the architect, Tom.'

'I am. How do you write your poetry? By stabbing a pin in the dictionary?'

'Yes, that's precisely how.' Gosse dispatches a rectangle of bread without resorting to anything as venal as chewing. 'Will you come too, Mrs Hardy? While we're inspecting buildings we could visit that pretty castle on the cliff. What's it called?'

'Sandsfoot,' he says.

'Oh, goodness me, no.' Em smiles flatly. She's shifting the empty teacups around with the concentration of a chess player, intent on not unseating the now dozing cat. She appears cool and remote again, a person of lines and surfaces, no more. *What a mystery she is*, he thinks. *How little I know about her.*

The cups have all been returned to their tray. Emma strokes the button above her heart: the lightest touch. 'My days of chasing castles in the air are over.'

*

Since his youth a railway has been built on the pebble bank to Portland so that, except when the rails are flooded by the tides, the peninsula is quickly accessible. Late on Sunday afternoon they're jolted along under the familiar line of bran-coloured stones, and soon arrive at the station. Gosse emerges as if freshly hatched among the isle's white cubes of oolite that have recently been exposed by human hands after being buried for unreckonable geologic years. His town finery is only slightly crushed.

'You did well to bring your umbrella, Edmund,' he says. 'That's forestalled any chance of rain.'

Gosse pretends to prod him in the ribs with it and he plays along by shying away. They climb the steep incline of Fortune's Well to within sound of the stonemasons' yards across the common, where eternal saws, regardless of the day of rest, are grinding on eternal blocks of stone. The cottages and their heavy stone features look the same as always. The gardens, each surrounded by a wall of dry-jointed sprawl, are the same. It seems to him – he wants to ask Gosse if he feels this too – that the whole world has turned to stone.

'Well-made, aren't they?' he says instead.

'Rather crude.' Gosse studies a sagging lintel. 'You know, I'm not convinced that writing is much like masonry, after all. *Ars longa*, and all that.'

'*Ars* nothing. No book of mine or yours is going to last as long as a single one of these walls.'

As they set off to explore the stony lanes, he's awed, as always, by the towering rock, the houses suspended over houses, one man's doorstep rising above his neighbour's chimney, the gardens hung up by an edge to the sky: the unity of the entire island as a solid four-mile block of limestone. *Why do I bother with my silly stories?* he thinks. *Why do I try at all?*

Once they've been wandering around for a few hours and the sun is starting to dip into the bay, he points to the north-east. 'Shall we walk to the castle now?'

Gosse's glance is quizzical. 'If you like.'

They make their way over the plateau and down to the path leading along the beach. To windward lies a long, monotonous bank of stones, on the other side of which they can hear the churning of pebbles by the sea. They follow the coastal track, braving the battery of wind-blown spume flying across Chesil Bank. On their right stretches the inner bay, the distant riding lights just beginning to come up, bleak and vinegary. Behind them a faint spark here and there in the lower sky indicates a rise in the land. Before, there is nothing definite, and can be nothing, till they reach the bridge a little further on, and see the ruin of Sandsfoot Castle beyond that.

He has stopped walking. A thin veil of sand blows up at them, stinging their faces.

'Why are we here?' says Gosse quietly. 'We're not really here to look at cottages, are we?'

'I don't know what I'm doing, Edmund.'

He rubs his sandy eyes. Life is often so colourless to him, so depthless, and the writing about it so real. He's like a man who sleeps and dreams and prefers his dreams to being awake. Sometimes he thinks that he can't feel what he should feel about his waking experiences until he has dreamed them again in words. If he loves Gosse it's because Gosse, in spite of his talent for living, understands this.

'Isn't your new book coming on?' Gosse asks.

He shakes his head. 'Tillotson expected me to slash it to pieces. I've got nowhere with *Murray's*, or with Morris at *Macmillan's*.'

'What about *The Graphic*?'

'Locker's prepared to buy it, but I daren't offer him the thing as it is. D'you know that Morris took exception to my style? Apparently I'm too modern. Too . . . too *succulent*, the expression was. Would you believe, he threw my own word back at me!'

'Those magazine editors are all stupid.'

'I can't afford to lose the magazines. That damned house of mine *gobbles* money.'

'Why not do as they ask and cut out the offending parts? The – the succulence?'

'You want me to mutilate my novel.'

'I want you to get every ounce of the recognition you deserve,' says Gosse. 'You know what I think of your work. But perhaps it's a question of proportion. You've become so *lopsided*.' He frowns at his gritty shoes. 'I didn't like to say this before.'

'Proportion, eh. Who's the bloody architect now? Gosse, all art is a throwing-out of proportion. If I distort, then it's only to show what matters, to make people see what they'd overlook otherwise.'

'Yes, but you distort too much. Your books are uncomfortable to dwell in. They frighten me. All those traps and shadows – it's not *real*.'

'Realism is not art.'

'Your readers want to be instructed. They want to be told that things can get better if they do such and such. There it is.'

'What if I don't want to instruct them?'

'Then you deny them hope – and you deny them pleasure. Be

careful, Tom. Be careful that you don't just become a looker-on at life.'

'Oh, pleasure. So much weight is put on pleasure. As if this life were a simple comedy, and not the fatal thing it is.'

'What's Mrs Hardy's view of the book?'

'I haven't consulted her. She doesn't hear a word I say.'

'You're lucky. Nellie hears absolutely everything I say at all times. She even hears things that I am thinking about saying but haven't said yet.' Gosse fixes him with a shining eye. 'You should ask her.' He smiles his gradual, candid smile. 'You really should.'

The last of the daylight has disappeared and a sea-fog has come up, smelling like laundry in the wash-house.

'Would you like to know what I think?' he asks.

'Of course.'

'I'm not in a position to instruct anyone. Art is just the secret of knowing how to use a false thing to create the effect of a true one. It's *all* false, Edmund. We're not real builders, we merely put up façades. I'm a fraud and so are you. Ow. Don't hit me.' He wrests Gosse's umbrella from his grasp. It's an expensive one: bone handle, taupe silk. 'Come on,' he says. 'It's getting too dark to see. Let's go back.'

Gosse leaves on Monday morning, taking his conversation and his umbrella and the fine weather with him. Gosse has flown home to Nellie, disappearing again into his variegated life. Meanwhile he's left glum and hungry, having eaten too little bacon at breakfast, with several hours lying ahead till the next meal and nothing to sustain him now but sheer will. At ten o'clock, as he's sitting down to work, it promptly starts to drizzle.

The book must be faced. Trot swerves in with a low warbling purr and begins to weave around his legs. He tickles her side with his foot. 'Go away,' he says, giving her a push. 'Stop being like us, can't you? Stop all this skulking and *insinuating*. Go away and be a proper animal.'

He looks at what he wrote last – how many months ago now? Three – three whole months. Three and a half. Here's a man; here's a woman, married that very day. It should all be so simple; if only human affairs, or writing about them, were the slightest bit simple.

They sat over the tea-table waiting for their luggage.

He feels as if he might never go on, might leave his hero languishing forever, on what should be his wedding-night, in the parlour of the manor he has rented for himself and his new wife; sharing her bread-and-butter plate, brushing the crumbs from her lips with his own, ignorant of the blow that is to fall on them both.

Dinner-tables. Tea-tables. All the stuff of married life. And behind that, something more, something worse, a vast carelessness in the way the very fabric of the world is stitched together, against which these totems have no power.

He reaches for his pen, wets it, turns the full stop into a comma. *This at least*, he thinks, *I can manage. It's just a comma.* And finds, to his surprise, that he's finished a sentence and begun another.

> They sat over the tea-table waiting for their luggage, which
> the dairyman had promised to send before it grew dark. But
> evening began to close in and the luggage did not arrive.

Yes, that's it. He dips his pen into his inkwell again. Two just-joined souls embarking on their doomed journey without any of the usual defences of civilization. Not even a brush and comb. And each about to be exposed to the judgement of the other, on this bride-night. Does she, the woman, know how much hope he's sunk in her? She does, yes. Does he, the man, realize how utterly she is the creature of his good or bad faith? Hardly. Perhaps no husband ever has.

The house is quiet, his door shut. He's a writer with a failing book on his hands. What else can he do, except go on?

> But evening began to close in and the luggage did not arrive,
> and they had brought nothing more than they stood in. With the
> departure of the sun the calm mood of the winter day changed.
> Out of doors there began noises as of silk smartly rubbed; the
> restful dead leaves of the preceding autumn were stirred to
> irritated resurrection, and whirled about unwillingly, and tapped
> against the shutters. It soon began to rain.

An hour later he is again a middle-aged man surrounded by bad furniture. He's covered three or four pages. He looks it over – the whole bag of tricks – and listens to the rain falling on the roof like corn thrown in handfuls by a colossal sower.

Turning back to the earlier portion of his story, he rubs his eyes with his knuckles. Very well, then. In the version he must write for a quick sale there will be no seduction – no rape.

His pen hovers above the page. Here is his villain, entering the darkening wood of the Close where his heroine lies asleep. Night is coming. He calls out to her. Does he know how utterly she is in his power, the victim of his good or bad faith? Of course. The villain always does. Self-knowledge seems mostly to be what distinguishes bad men from good ones.

> There was no answer. The obscurity was now so intense that he could see absolutely nothing. The red rug, and the white muslin figure he had left upon it, were ~~now~~ all blackness alike. ~~Alec?~~ He stooped, and heard a regular breathing. ~~Rose-Mary~~ ~~Sue~~ ?? was sleeping soundly. He knelt, and bent lower, and her breath ~~touched~~ warmed his face, and in a moment his cheek was in contact with hers.^ and with her hair, and her eyes A ~~damp~~ wetness accompanied the touch of her ~~eye~~ lashes on his ~~face~~ skin, as if she had wept.

He draws a bracket around the passage, and in the margin he writes: *Omit.* If ripping out the keystone of his book for the moment is the price of continuing, he'll pay it. What there'll be instead he doesn't yet know, but he's sure that he can come up with some temporary bodge of straw and plaster to hide the damage.

Throwing down his pen he goes out onto the landing, calling.

'Em,' he calls. 'Emmie!' She won't be in the garden today, now that it's raining. She hates the rain.

He discovers her huddled on the drawing-room sofa with Trot and the young tabbies. She's a crumpled silhouette against the wet window, shoulders limp, chins sagging. She's sitting as if she is to sit there forever.

'My dear, did you mean what you said a couple of days ago? I find that I'm in need of an assistant with my new book after all.'

Em jumps up. The cats open their eyes and dart off noiselessly, like a shoal of minnows. 'Oh! This is unbearably thrilling,' she says. '*Unbearably.*'

'Come, Emmie. It's only a story.'

'Yes, but I haven't seen any part of it yet. You once used to show me your novels as you wrote them, you know.'

'I'm sorry,' he says. 'It's no fault of yours. A man's working habits can change. You were a good copyist and I was happy to have your help. I would be, again.'

Em speaks with a strange unsteady emphasis. 'I mean to make you happy, Tom.'

'Why, my dear.' On impulse he sits down, patting the sofa cushion beside him. He's unexpectedly moved. He wonders what he dares say to her. Now that he's about to approach the edges of the silence in which he writes, his heart is shaking.

Em resumes her seat, back straight, fingers tightening on an invisible pair of reins. 'Does your book have a title?' she breathes.

'Right now it's called "Too Late, Beloved!" Or possibly "Too Late, Beloved".'

'What's the difference?'

'The exclamation mark, of course. With, or without? I haven't decided yet.'

'Ah, yes,' Emma says cautiously. 'That does require some thought.'

'Morris has let me down.' A nervous laugh. 'I intend to send it to Arthur Locker at *The Graphic*. In the run-up I'll be making some modifications to the story as I go along, here and there. Perhaps you could use a black pen as you work. But the modified passages need to be copied out in coloured ink, see?'

'Why?'

'Well, so that the originals might be easily restored later.'

'Restored how?'

'I've decided to put them back in their places when it's printed as a book.'

'I wonder what your Mr Locker will say about that.'

'I won't be asking him for his opinion on the matter. I'm tired of being made to tiptoe around the imaginary sensitivities of the imaginary heads of imaginary households of daughters when there is nothing – no, *nothing* – in these pages that isn't moral and to spare.'

Em gives him a bemused look. 'What's in them, then? Is it so very bad?'

'Oh. Well, a violation. Illegitimacy. Murder, eventually, I think.'

Her mouth turns up. 'Just your average family reading, then.'

'It's all in the execution.'

'Ah.' She flings back her shoulders, as if she's about to break into a canter. The droop has gone out of her. Her eyes, her hips, her jaunty elbows, are full of mirth. 'I'm ready if you are.'

*

On going to bed that night he can't shake off the dread that he's recklessly exposed himself. The room he shares with Em is too warm, its air heavy with the sweetness of her toilet water. He opens the window and starts to shed his clothing, dropping first his socks, then his trousers on the floor. He tosses his drawers across the back of the dressing-table chair and, nightshirt on, gets between the covers and waits for sleep.

But sleep escapes him. To the many indignities and casual humiliations of marriage he's now added another: giving his wife free access to his latest creative blunders. Emma has been shut away in the drawing room for the better part of the day, working on his manuscript. He wonders what she'll have made of his scrappy paragraphs, his cancellations and suppressions and revisions.

She's seen them before, he tells himself, and groans. *Yes, but not like this!* He pulls his shirt down hard over his knees.

After what seems like an age he hears Em coming in. He follows her movements around the room while she tuts at the mess he's left; the smack of the latch as she closes the window, the prolonged rattle of the wardrobe. She climbs into bed and shifts her hips about for a few moments, but doesn't settle. He can feel her coming nearer. The mattress yaws under his buttocks: she's bending over him. She lays her hand on his shoulder. There's a competence to her touch, an impersonal hopefulness, like a cook trying pastry.

'Are you awake, Tom?'

He doesn't answer. It's like being in the presence of someone he hasn't yet met. He's aware of being naked beneath his night things, a middle-aged bridegroom stripped bare.

'Your book is *glorious*,' Em says. 'It's the best thing you've ever done.'

She lies down. Ten minutes more of burrowing and twitching, and then her feathery snores tell him that she's drifted off. Once he's certain he turns around. By the light of the moon Emma looks as serene as a ship in harbour. She's stretched out on her back, fingers laced over her breasts. There's a long blue smear on her thumb.

He thinks of the women he's met in London, the wives, young and old. He thinks of Gosse's Nellie, with her sharp angles and agile tongue and her red hair wrapped across her head like a sultan's turban. He's known Gosse for sixteen years, but he still doesn't truly know Nellie. He remembers Edmund telling him that she used to be an artist, before their marriage. He imagines her as a mother, waxing and waning; he tries to imagine her digging in the dirt of a flower bed, or stained with paint. Which is the real Nellie? None of these, perhaps.

In bed Em doesn't smell of scent; she smells of soap and flannel, and onions, the daily smells of their married life. He puts his lips to her ear, careful not to disturb her with the current of his breath. 'Thank you,' he whispers.

She mumbles, but doesn't wake. He crawls into her shadow and falls asleep.

Jam

H<small>E'S DISTURBED IN THE</small> middle of the night by the backwards and forwards switch of the sea. He is walking along the shore towards the castle. He can see it quite plainly: the pitted walls, the westward plunge of the rock. It's a clear spring night, full of stars, the rime still on the spray. How short the distance from here to there seems in the starlight. It would be simple, he suddenly sees, to cross the murmuring miles and gain the far bank. If he hurried he wouldn't have to wait. He could start climbing, and the rest of his life would follow.

It takes him several moments to realize that the crumpling of the waves on the sand is the rise and fall of his own breath.

'Em,' he says. 'Let's have our holiday in Cornwall. Let's not wait till summer. Let's go now, while the weather's so mild.' He rolls over to face her. 'With your help I can write as well there as here. What do you think?'

She doesn't answer. He sits up, gasping. A chill breeze blows across his nerves, though the window is shut fast. There's an owl calling from the wood, each of its cries amplified by the silence before and after it. It's the silence, unpunctuated by any answering breath, which he's been used to for twenty years: the deep silence of solitary sleep. He clutches at the dark beside him and finds his fingers closing on emptiness. He's alone in his bed. It's December, not March. It's now, not then.

Emma is dead.

'Tom, are you awake? I heard your voice.'

His door is ajar. A woman in a nightgown, candle in hand, approaches the bed on bare feet.

'Florence,' he says. It's all slipping from him: the sea, the stars, the whispering sands. 'You're here.'

'Of course I am.'

'Am I too late?'

'For what?'

For everything. 'For tea,' he says.

Setting the candlestick down, Florence lays her palm against his face. 'It's past midnight. You've been in bed since this afternoon. When you didn't join us I decided to let you be.'

'I'm sorry.' He draws aside the coverlet to reveal the spectral glimmer of the sheet. 'Sit here with me for a little while.' He's shivering as if he's been pulled out of a flood. He didn't think such desolation was possible. If he looks back, he will lose himself entirely. 'I keep coming adrift.'

Florence sits by his side and smooths his bedclothes. 'You were dreaming again,' she says firmly.

'No, no. I was with Em, the Em of twenty years ago. She was as real as you are now.' He touches Florence's arm. 'Which of you is the dream?'

'You tell me,' she says with a stony smile. In the glow of the candle her cheek is like marble, its curve at once fine and resilient. Her hair is still fastened in its daytime roll. He reaches up and pulls away a pin, releasing a treaclish strand.

Florence's surprise shows in the raised tendons of her neck. After a few seconds' hesitation she puts out her hand and rests it on his chest. 'Shall I stay with you?'

'Oh, my dear. The others. Better not.'

They lean together, their gestures courtly, their words rationed, like two people in a mummers' play. Her fingers are light on his body; such small fingers for a grown woman. 'Lilian's going in the morning,' she says.

'Is she?'

'I thought you'd be pleased.'

'I am, of course.'

'It'll be just the three of us then.'

When he wakes again he knows by the smell of stale ashes on the hearth that he's still here, in the present. He edges out of bed, thrusting his feet into slippers scratchy with cold, finds his dressing gown and clumps out onto the landing. He waits with caught breath in the early morning silence. It's so thick that it suggests something tangible, rather than the absence of sound.

An unearthly light embrowns the stairs and the lower regions of the house. For a minute he's giddy with the promise of a revelation, as if this ghost-light might be the source of his sense of dissolution, the double exposure that's erased the order of things. But the hall below has a determined daytime look, brassy clouds massed behind the porch window, the dial of the barometer hovering at the word *change*. In the clouds' burnish he recognizes the aura of coming snow.

December snow. Somewhere beyond his roof time goes on running in the right direction. The weather, relentless, indifferent, continues to happen.

The kitchen, with its ranks of copper and china-ware, is deserted. The range is unlit. There's a bald shine, as of sweat or ice, on the flags. It's the very picture of cheerlessness, like a kitchen in a nightmare.

He longs, with his whole being, to reject this version of his life. He stops in the middle of the room paralysed by suspense, seeing himself as if from above, a drab little man who must creep from his solitary bed at dawn to haunt his own house. There was a life to be escaped, the life of his father and brother, the life of ordinary men. Instead he's ended up with this shadow-life; neither one thing nor the other, in nor out of the world. Who is Tom Hardy? He is a man who dreams while he's awake. He's a man without children or grandchildren, and now without a wife. He has a mistress he hardly wants. He's a man who has no power, only words.

My Emmie. What a poor excuse for a husband I was. You were loyal and true. But you're gone, and our very last conversation was a quarrel. He wishes he could change it now, but it's all past changing. *I don't care any more*, he thinks. *Let it all go cold; let snow cover everything. Let it all be buried.* He's ready to kneel down in the snow, to be erased.

After a while he goes to the window and pulls back the kitchen curtains. There's that strange naked light again, like the glare of a fresh page. His sight is soaked in it.

Perhaps this life, which suddenly appears so makeshift, can still be rewritten. Or at least revised. He's aware of a prickling ache, a famished defiance – so old as to have become part of the bedrock of him – stirring at his core.

To his amazement he finds he's ravenous, with a crude and childish hunger that seems to insult every subtler feeling. Jam. He craves jam.

The pantry is unlocked. He can't see a candle anywhere and has to grope among the gargoyled forms on the whitewashed shelves in search of the right-shaped pot. There are unfamiliar twists of metal, curved skins of enamel and glass, things that rattle when they're picked up and shaken. Em's preserves are at the bottom, recognizable by their rubber collars and wire jaws. He runs his hands over a nest of jars, coaxes off a lid.

At once the smell of blackberries fills his nostrils. Inserting a forefinger into the jelly he wiggles it about until, with a soft kissing noise, a clot pops to the surface. His stomach clenches as its weight meets his opened mouth and melts on his tongue.

In the dark he remembers the builder's yard in front of the cottage, beyond the parlour casement, where his father brings down the hammer onto the stone in steady circles, down, up, down, up, the snow just beginning to fall. Jam is a daily treat he's allowed because he is *not strong*. He licks his finger slowly, trying to delay the disappointing moment when he will taste himself. His mother is feeding Mary her porridge in the chimney corner. Kate doesn't exist yet, Henry doesn't exist. Mary is alive; he is alive. He is three years old. He was born dead, but he lived. He is the smallest and feeblest of boys, still weak from his baptism of pain. And now he's given jam but must stay inside.

While his mother is busy with Mary he slips out. He watches his father, the sweat patches on his shirt, arms liquid in the dense air. His father stops his swinging.

'Hello, Tommy,' he says. 'Look here, my lad. This is no place for 'ee. You'll catch your death. Get on indoors with your mother.'

He doesn't go: he wants to touch the stone, to inhale its dust, to see the steam rising from his father's body.

'Jemima,' his father shouts. 'Get your son out of my yard.'

There's a scuffle of boots in the kitchen. When he emerges from the pantry Jane Riggs is leaning against the stove, strapping on her apron. She has an implacable face, wide and undistinguished, with a mole above the lip. He's at home among such faces.

'Good morning, Mrs Riggs,' he says.

'Oh, sir.' She notes the spoiled jar like a general on a long campaign assessing the fatalities on the field of battle. 'Stealing jam like a boy. You'll have a sup o' bread with that.' It's an order, not a question. She picks through a hill of polished cutlery. 'Or a spoon, leastways.'

'I'm sorry, Mrs Riggs, thank you,' he says, reaching for the spoon.

'Hands,' she says, snapping at his wrist with a cloth.

He goes out to the scullery to wash his sticky fingers, dashing the water over his mouth for good measure. When he comes back he sees that there's a place set for him at the table: napkin, butter dish, plate.

'That's better,' Mrs Riggs says. The loaf is as yellow as the edge of a bible. She cuts off the heel, then presses the knife down again, the whitened slice falling away cleanly from the crust. 'Butter?'

'Yes, please.'

He feels the bread arriving in his belly. After a few bites he can't eat any more. 'This is excellent,' he says.

'I should hope so, sir.'

'I may go upstairs again presently.'

'Sir, if I might make an observation.' She stares at him, arms cocked, mole like a bullet. 'You ought to show some sense.'

'Am I not being sensible?'

'No. You are not.'

Jane Riggs has attended to his most basic needs for several years. If anyone is allowed to lecture him, surely she is.

'Jane, I must know.' This woman, with her scoop-eyed stare and her quick way with a knife, will tell him the truth. 'Did Mrs Hardy suffer very much these past few months?'

'I can't say, sir. You'd have to ask Dolly.'

'I don't want to frighten her. I'm asking you. You talked to her every day.'

'Well, I don't know about death.'

'What do you know about?'

'I only know 'bout cooking.'

'I only know about words. Maybe not even those.' He bows his head. 'I'm not sure why I'm here. Not just in your kitchen. I mean, here at all.'

'We're all born into the world for som'at. We all have our place.' Her expression says: *And we should know what it is. And* you *should have known what it was.*

He wants to shout, *Is that so?* He's a child again. He wants to beat off the knowledge, to run out of the dark house into the breathing day. *No*, he will say. *No, you're wrong. I still have a choice. I can still be someone else.*

'Mrs Hardy is in God's care, sir. And so are you.'

'I've been looking for God for more than seventy years. I think, if He existed, that I would have found Him by now.'

'Well, sir, you've found the jam, anyhow,' says Mrs Riggs. Giving the jar and spoon a wipe, she nods at him to take them. He laughs and clutches the jam to his chest.

Up the stairs he goes, trailing his fingers along the posts.

As he steps into his dressing room, the trace of sweetness still on his tongue, he's feeling small but mutinous. He can hear Lilian stirring in Em's room. He slips the jar into his dressing-gown pocket, tightens the cord, and knocks on the connecting door before turning the handle.

Lilian is seated at Emma's dressing table with her head bent over Em's open jewel case, a morning wrapper tied slackly about her waist. The room is in an even worse state of disorder than when he saw it last. There are shoes and unidentifiable elasticated things strewn across the floor. A plaid travelling costume is spreadeagled on the bed. Lilian's trunk stands at its foot, cords straining.

'All packed, my dear?' he says.

'Oh, Daddy-Uncle, you're up!' Lilian rises to her stockinged feet. He has a vague impression of unbrushed hair and swaying flesh. Without her clothing she looks unformed, like a woman of clay. She regards him warily. 'You gave us a fright yesterday, falling ill like that.'

'It was nothing. Just a slight chill. I must have caught it in the rain on Saturday. Miss Dugdale nursed me most capably.'

He can sense Lilian making up her mind to understand him. 'She is a very capable . . . person,' she says. 'I'm sorry if I spoke out of turn, yesterday morning.'

'I don't recall you doing anything of the kind.' He gestures at the jewel case. 'My goodness, what a collection of trinkets your aunt had. I hope you've had a chance to choose something from it for yourself.'

'I didn't want to presume.'

He's amazed that he could ever have mistaken her for Em. Em was never this crude, never this flat-footed. 'Allow me.' He goes over to the dressing table and hooks out the largest of the pieces in the case, a bracelet strung with opals the size of boiled sweets. 'This would suit you. Emma used to wear it when we were in town for the season. Give me your wrist.' He clips the cuff around Lilian's arm. There. Done.

She is so clayish, her hair so draggled, her smile so fixed in the exposed folds of her face, that he longs to give her something else. Beneath the lamp there's a square velvet box that's been tossed aside in the onslaught of Lilian's packing. He lifts the lid and is dazzled by a diminutive landscape of winks and flashes. 'Lilian, look,' he says. The box contains a diamond necklace with a matching brooch and long drop earrings. 'These are rather impressive. Wouldn't you like them?'

'Ah, no. They're only paste.'

The necklace, a doubled chain of brilliants, is paper-light. 'Yes. I remember now.' And he does: Emma standing at the mantel in his room, the red-coaled glow of the fire peeping into the loose hair about her forehead, firing the skin underneath. The spark of the stones at her neck. His heart leaps up, but plummets again as quickly. False jewels, false fire.

'Not these, then,' he says, dropping the counterfeit diamonds back onto their bed. 'But I'd like you to have the rest. I'd like you to have all of it.'

Lilian's mouth sags in astonishment. 'I couldn't possibly.'

He pushes the jewellery case towards her. 'Please take it away with you, Lil. Please.'

Her eyes find his: grey eyes with sad pupils, like Emma's. 'You should keep this, though.' She reaches into a drawer in the bottom of the case and removes an oval locket. 'This should be yours,' she says, sliding it into his hand.

He recognizes the little casket at once. Em gave it to him as a lover's gift forty years ago, during one of his visits to St Juliot. The clasp is loose and the locket wobbles like an insect poised for flight. He runs his thumb down the middle, stroking its tarnished wings until they lie splayed under the lamp. Here she is, risen from the dark behind her sliver of glass: a miniature painted Emma of pink and brown and cream. There's a piece of her hair in the facing oval, curled in a glossy parenthesis.

The blood slows in his chest.

He hasn't seen this locket in – how long? Not since they moved to Max Gate, certainly. Maybe even before that. He can't recall when or why he stopped carrying it with him, except that it's not the sort of thing a husband, once in possession of the original, would need.

He gazes at the picture in wonder. Emma is looking, not at him, but at something a short way off. Her expression is rapt and a trifle stubborn. Her hair is clustered above her forehead in a heavy crown. She's all aglow, this reckless, handsome girl in her lace collar, a girl who is determined to love and to be loved, to rush in and make a writer of him, and who is sublimely ignorant – as ignorant as he himself is – of what that will mean.

She is still the woman who sees him where no one else does. He is still the man who wants to blaze forth in her eyes.

While life has come and gone in his house, this uncorrupted Em has lain deep in a box, unnoticed by anyone.

He doesn't know what to say at this unlooked-for gift. He stands with the open locket balanced on his palm, remembering Lilian's terrifying changes of mood, thinking that behind her shifting flesh and her relentless grin there's a younger, less petrified Lilian, who once wanted to sit on his lap after dinner and dutifully went with him to picture galleries and who tried to read the improving books he pressed on her. What a disappointment he must have been, as a father. What a bore.

'Thank you,' he says. 'I'm feeling rather tired again, so won't come to the car to see you off. But you must know, my dear, that I'm sorry you're leaving.' He leans over unsteadily and kisses Lil on the cheek. She's too taken aback to smile. All her energies are being marshalled into trying to look unshocked.

'I'll be back in a week,' she says.

'I'm not going anywhere,' he replies.

Mother

HE'S TOO AGITATED TO return to his room. He needs fresh air. In spite of the cold and the threatened snow he steals downstairs, still in his dressing gown, and slips out of the side door.

The garden is furred with crystals, unrecognizable from two days ago when he walked here with Florence. The ants have all flown. At the edge of the fern border, back scrolled like a sleigh's, is the bench where Emma used to rest while gardening. He hugs his dressing gown to him and sits down. Hanging the locket around his neck, he raises the picture to his lips. Em swims up at him with her sunlit hair streaming out over her shoulders.

I'm sorry I never took you back to Cornwall when you asked me to, Emmie. I was far too busy writing. I thought we'd have plenty of time. Every day, our life together was running out, but I didn't hear — I didn't see. Too late, he sees it all. An icy breeze wheezes through the skeleton hedge from the north. Frost has combed the grass into a silver path. Surely if he began now, if he set out now on that road to the west, he'd find Emma waiting on the shore. He could take her hand, he could touch her living brow. Isn't that how it always was? He went home after their first meeting, but he always returned, and each time he found her there. All the grey years he was working in London, only his visits to that margin of blue sea with its cliffs and surf-fringed shore seemed real.

He knows what he wants. *I want to hold you in my arms, Em. I just want that moment. Where can it exist? Nowhere. Outside time.*

He closes his eyes and sees himself and Em, two tiny figures, walking up the hill from Boscastle at the close of a spring day. They've jumped down from their chaise to ease the pony's load. Primaeval rocks form the road's steep border: pinkish stones, lung-like, delicately veined, plumped by the declining sun so that they appear like animate things, part of the breathing body of the world.

They're so young, he and she, so full of heat, talking and talking – what do they talk about? Books, probably. Love and books. Books and love. It hardly matters. Their heads are close together. Her hair brushes and clings to his face. The sky is a thickening gold gauze; knapweeds wave their pennants in the salt-edged air. They're the only two people in the story of Creation who have ever walked, or read a word. They're the only two people who have ever loved.

He writes to her every day from his office in Bedford Street. *I think I'm ready to begin the true work of my life, Emmie. And that is, being an author – and being your husband.* Does he mean it? He's scarcely touched her. He's only kissed her mouth twice. Is twice enough? He has no idea. He wants to own her, not exactly as a wife, but as a being superior to himself, in the way a servant might be said to own a master. In their world there's no language for such a desire.

Emma never questions that writing is what he should do, that everything is still before them. Her letters are unchilled by doubt. *Nothing is as important as this dream of my life,* she writes back. *No,*

not dream, for what is actually going on around me seems a dream rather.
You'll make a great name for yourself, Tom, I know it. You're like the
tree in the psalm: you will bring forth your fruit in due season. Whatever
you do will prosper.

They're too innocent, this Tom and Em, these tiny people, talking about 'life' as if they were life-sized. Their knowledge is just a digest of other people's words. They are too simple.

After one of his visits to St Juliot he goes back to Dorset with his mind made up. A week passes, and then another. Coming downstairs on a Sunday morning he discovers his father on the settle, waistcoat unbuttoned, smoking his pipe. His mother is snipping dead leaves from the window plants. He can hear the merciless blades of her scissors before he gets to the bottom step, *snick-snack-snick.* She looks at him as if she doesn't understand the meaning of his long stay with her. Her face has worn this expression for several days.

'Will you be sending your boxes along to town by the carrier on Monday, Tommy?'

'I'm not going back to London again,' he says. 'Not in my old position, anyway. I've given up architecture.'

His mother puts down her scissors. 'I thought something was amiss. Have you been let go? I wonder you didn't tell us sooner.'

'You've been a while in the West Country this last time, certainly,' says his father. 'If the boss man's displeased with 'ee, then you'd best go and explain yourself to him directly.'

'It's not that, Father,' he says. 'There's more in this recent visit of mine than you think – a good deal more.'

'Not more than *I* think,' says his mother, gazing doomily at him. He blushes. His father looks from one to the other.

'It's Miss Gifford. I knew she was after 'ee, Tom – I knew it,' his mother says.

'After me!' He laughs. 'Good Lord, what next!'

His father waggles his eyebrows. 'That's the way the wind blows, is it?' he says, with his easy tolerance of human folly.

'She's a pretty piece enough,' his mother continues, 'and very lady-like and clever too, I'll be bound. But you ought not to be in such a hurry, and wait for a few years. You might go higher than a penniless pa'son's chit then.'

'You don't know anything about it, Mother,' he says impatiently. 'Why, to marry her would be the greatest blessing of my life – socially and practically, and in any other respect you'd care to name. No such luck as that, I'm afraid; she's too far above me. Her family doesn't want a country lad like me in it.'

'Then if they don't want you, I'd see them dead corpses before I'd want them, and go to families who do want you. Isn't that so, Thomas?'

'I'm afraid I don't understand the matter well enough to offer my opinion,' his father hedges.

'And giving up your position!' says his mother. 'I'm astonished, Tom. What would you live on, if you married? How can you want to do better than you've been doing?'

Dead corpses. That's just like her: grimly over-emphatic, shovelling it on. He struggles against his ancient, nerve-fraying terror of her bad opinion, her bottomless capacity for dismay. 'Well, I won't do better in the way you mean,' he says. 'I suppose you'd call it doing worse. I'm going to earn my living by writing books.'

'What crazy twist of thinking will enter your head next? Does

Miss Gifford know how you intend to support her if she's fool enough to hitch her cart to yours?'

'She does, and she's all in favour of it. She doesn't think it's foolishness. Just the opposite.' Prideful Tom, greedy and impractical. Tom the Dreamer. Scornful Tom.

His mother speaks calmly now, but he knows her too well to miss the force of feeling behind her words. 'I hadn't the least idea that you meant to go backwards in the world by your own free choice. I've always supposed you were going to push straight on, as other men do – all who deserve the name – when they've been put in a good way of doing well.' She squeezes out a thin smile. 'I suppose you will be like your father: like him, you are getting tired of doing well.'

'Now, little woman,' says his father, and says not a word more.

For several minutes nothing is heard but the ticking of the blank-faced clock on the mantel.

'I can't, Mother,' he says at last. 'I've had enough of what you call doing well. I can't manage it any longer.'

'But *why*? Why can't you do as others do? Why can't you be like other men?'

I don't know.

Forty years later there's no escaping it: the fully bared thing, grinning there. He's never managed to be like other men. Oh, he's pretended to be, but he's been playing a part. His marriage to Emma, so fruitful for his work, was in almost every other way – every way that mattered – entirely barren. He's written about love and suffering, but

169

he knows that his mother was right. He's never felt any of those emotions very deeply, beyond the urge to write about them.

Two kisses. Two! Suddenly those kisses seem like the seal set on his failure. He never gave himself up to life, remained a deliberate observer, at a remove from the world. Wasn't that what Emma said when she came to his study on the day before she died?

You know it was. The dark outline of her shape on the wall; the ashes under the grate lit up by the fire in a torrid waste. Her words, like burning coals, heaped on his head. *No proper husband. Uprooted me. This gaol of a house. A lie.*

All of it, *a lie.*

As Em spoke he felt himself becoming invisible, vanishing into the coral walls of his room: surly, resentful, a boy again. He was finally unable to answer her. He was frantic to turn back to the shelter of his work. Behind the window he could see the old beech rooted to the earth, his pines; their crazy shock-haired filaments.

These trees knew, they still know, what staying alive requires: the ruthlessness, the inflexible will to grow, to become ever more like themselves. All his life he's done whatever he needed to do to survive, to write. But that wasn't quite the same as living a human life. He wonders if he can claim to have written at all if he hasn't lived.

A twig cracks underfoot, followed by an ambush of skirts. Kate subsides heavily beside him. 'Pff. That's that. Lilian's gone.' She hitches up her hem and rubs her calf. 'Penny for 'em.'

'I was thinking about Mother,' he says, hiding the locket in the breast of his dressing gown. 'I was imagining what she'd say to me now.'

'"I told you so", probably. That's all she ever did say.'

'We should have had it engraved on her headstone.'

Kate's mouth twitches. She steals a sideways look at him. 'Well, I'm willing to get the mason in, if you are. Poor Father. Still, he managed to keep silent around her when it suited him, didn't he?'

'Yes. That man's silence was wonderful to listen to.' He shakes his head. 'I'm an idiot, Katie. I wanted to please her, but I only seemed to disappoint her. I've managed to disappoint everyone.'

'Nonsense,' says Kate. Their arms are touching; he can feel her solidity, the muscle of her flesh, through the sleeve of her blouse. 'You're a miracle, that's what you are. Didn't even know how to breathe when you were born, and see how well you've got the knack of it since.' She utters a low laugh.

'Very funny. Did I ever tell you I once overheard Mother and Father saying that they didn't expect to rear me? They spoke quite loudly. They probably thought I was asleep.'

'Well, you showed everyone, Tommy. You've always done whatever you set your mind to. All those certificates of completion you were given. French. Latin.'

'I was good at Latin. Better than at living, possibly.'

'You certainly were.' She nudges him. 'Go on. Do "table" for me.'

'*Mensa, mensa, mensam. Mensae, mensae, mensa.* You try it.'

'*Mensa, mensa. Mens*— Mercy, Tom, it's not natural. I give up.'

'That's the vocative, you know, *mensa.* It means "O table". I forget the rest.'

'Why would anyone want to address a table?'

'I have absolutely no idea.'

Kate pats his hand. 'It's marvellous, anyhow.'

They sit without speaking. There's a robin advancing on the

lawn. Every once in a while it stops and presents its breast to them gravely, like an actor striking a pose. It's the Henry Irving of robins. As he looks on, the robin drives its beak into the turf and conjures some stretched, bloodless thing. A mealworm. In a *snip-snap* of bone blades the worm is gone.

He feels hollow, as if he hasn't eaten in years. Taking the jam jar out of his dressing-gown pocket, he sets about attacking its innards with the spoon.

Kate bites her bottom lip. 'Is that jam?'

'Yes. Would you like some?'

'No, thank you.' She drops an envelope into his lap with a suppressed sigh. 'Here, Mary's sent you this. She'll be wanting to see you, I'm sure. A walk will do you good.'

'I'm too tired.'

'How can you be tired? You're not using any energy. You're not even writing.'

'I find that not writing is as tiring as writing. More so, maybe.' He takes a lick of jam. 'You sounded just like Mother then.'

Kate gets up. 'I've not come to argue with you,' she says. 'I only meant to give you Mary's letter.' She begins to walk away, but pivots on her heel. 'Before I forget, we've run out of sugar.'

'We can't have. I never take sugar.'

'Yes you do.' Kate ticks off the occasions on her fingers. 'On your rashers, in your tea, in that jam that appears to have become your staple food, in the sago pudding you're to eat for your dinner, if you do eat it.'

'Mrs Riggs will buy some more.'

'Mrs Riggs has asked me to ask you for the money, or no one will be buying anything.'

'She should have said so. I'll see to it. How much sugar do we need?'

'Two pound bags will do for now.'

'And that will be . . .?'

'Sixpence. When did you last go to a shop?'

'I can't remember. Does it matter?'

'Oh, Tom. You don't wash, you hardly stir from the house. You're eating out of a *jar*. You don't know the first thing about running Max Gate. You've got to pull yourself together. I can't be your keeper forever.'

'I haven't the will. I've tried, but I don't want to.'

'Then what *do* you want?'

'I want her here, Katie. I want her back. I hate this place without her in it. I want to hold her to me. I want to touch her hair and smell her breath and kiss her lips.'

Kate looks bewildered. 'Who? *Mother?* Miss Dugdale?'

'No. Emma.'

'Well, that's not possible.'

'It must be. It must!'

'Why must it? Because you say so? Because you've written books? *Poetry?* Are you the only person who's ever suffered loss? You, you, you. An old fool with his scribbling. With his stupid words!'

'My words built this house.'

'But you've made – your *words* have made – nothing living. How do you think it was for me, when Mother and Father died? You think they only cared for you, their miraculous boy. But they cared for me a little, too. For Mary. For Hen. Oh, for you more, to be sure. But they cared for us a *little*. And now they're gone, that's gone too.' Her throat is making an awful clicking noise. 'So I'm not minded to pity you beyond a certain point. You've had your own way your whole life, you've had every advantage. Fancy schooling. A perfectly good profession which you threw over. Yes, yes, I know –' she gives a derisory flick of her fingers – 'I sound *just like Mother*. Let me finish. A chance – a chance at marriage. And if this ugly, empty old house is the best you've got to show for it all, then . . .'

'Then what?'

'Well, then I suppose you'll simply have to find a way of existing in it.'

Off she goes, her boots gouging black darts in the frosted lawn. What she's said is so close to the burden of his own recent thoughts and to Emma's accusations that he wants to lie down on the bench and never get up. He feels as heavy as iron, as cold and as lifeless, choked with an emptiness that's close to overflowing. *I'm nothing*, he thinks. *I'm no one.*

He sits without moving, shouldering the weight of his despair. He's holding Mary's letter tightly to his chest. It takes him a while to summon up the courage to open it.

My dearest Tommy,

You are feeling sorry for yourself, and I wish you wouldn't. It's either a downpour or a drought with you and never anything in between. Well perhaps I will allow you a little dryness since Kate is there. It's a hardy plant that can withstand her. (See, I'm quite as clever at words as you.)

I am sad for you that Emma is gone, much sadder than you

can know. We weren't always kind to her. Please don't tell Katie I said this.

Tommy my love, you will grow green again, I promise. Come and visit me soon.

Your Mary

He's roused from his misery by a loud trilling near his slippered foot. He looks down and sees the robin. It's drawing nearer, its coat fantastically puffed, beak flashing. It hops up to the bed where a caterpillar is making its way along the frozen earth and spits it with a single lunge. A minute later he sees its scarlet form disappear into the ferns, like a brand swiftly waved.

A Hairpin

THE CLOUDS HAVE BALLOONED and the sky is beginning to splutter grey sleet. Mrs Riggs and Kate are both right. It's folly to behave like this: like a dotard, a drowning man, a man on the edge of extinction. He will speak to Florence. Florence will know what to do.

There's a smell of baked fur coming from the drawing room, where Em's cats are stretched in front of the fender. Florence is wedged in his armchair, head tilted at an unlikely angle. For a chilling moment it looks as if her neck were broken. He goes closer. She's fast asleep. Her mouth is distended in an O of surrender, her breathing raspy. In sleep she seems older, less self-possessed than when she's awake. She has a redness about her nostrils and, lower down, the beginnings of a double chin.

He kneels beside her, marvelling at her expression. Florence's sleeping face is full of suffering and hope – the hope a child has, on slipping into unconsciousness, that everything will be better in the morning. He's wrenched with pity for her. He wishes he could cradle her head on his shoulder, that he could find it in himself to release her. But he doesn't know how to manage the suffering in himself, that's the difficulty. 'My dear,' he says. 'I hate to disturb you.'

Florence opens her eyes. Their rims are a hectic crimson. 'Tom. No one told me you were awake.'

'Have you been crying?'

'It's the cats. I think they're making me ill. I've the most peculiar tightness in my chest. Do I look hideous?' She scrabbles in her sleeve for her handkerchief and blows her nose. 'What's the matter, what's wrong? You should be resting.'

'I'm well enough. You look beautiful.' It's true: she's never appeared quite as lovely to him as she does now, in her spoiled state. 'Florence, listen. I scarcely dare ask you this.'

'Ask me. You may ask me anything.'

'Will you stay?'

'Stay . . .?'

'Will you stay and take care of me, when Kate goes?'

'She hasn't mentioned that she's going.'

'No, but she'll have to eventually.'

Florence gives him a look of such fierce pride and helplessness that he feels he has struck her a direct blow. 'Would it be right?'

'I can't manage this house. I can't manage my days.' He's sunk down to the bottom of himself and is gazing up at the surface. There he lies, a thing of iron. 'Can you believe that I don't know what a bag of sugar costs? Of course you can. It seems there's not much I *do* know. Apparently I'm an old fool whose entire life's work is useless. But the worst of it is that I don't seem to know how to write any more, either. I doubt I ever will again.'

'Oh, Tom. You're far too hard on yourself. It'll all come back if you give it time. I'll deal with your editors in the meanwhile, if someone must.'

'I shouldn't expect you to be my gatekeeper, dear girl.'

'Why not?' She sticks out her chin. 'They won't get past me.'

He smiles wanly at her. 'Well, I don't doubt *that*.'

Florence returns his smile. His heart goes round to her in a rush. They're all right after all, they're in cahoots, as they've been for the last four years. 'Just let them try,' she says.

How out of his element he is. He's aware that the question between them has shifted, but he can barely keep his head up. 'You're too good to me,' he murmurs, laying it on Florence's knee. Her fingers settle in his hair and start a tentative progress back and forth over his crown. After a while his paralysis begins to lift. Maybe he can believe in this version of himself. He can enter into it fully, he can turn the page. His eyes close. This isn't so difficult, after all, being carried along in the current of Florence's will.

He's almost asleep when she speaks. 'I'm a little puzzled by something you said on Monday, while we were in the churchyard. I'm not sure what you wanted me to understand by it.'

'You'll have to remind me, dearest. My thoughts are so addled right now.'

'But how *could* you forget? You said . . .'

When she doesn't continue, he raises his head. Florence's hand is clamped to her mouth. At first he thinks that she's about to sneeze or cry. Then he sees that she's staring at his chest, where Em's locket has fallen out of the neck of his dressing gown and dangles in the firelight, its two halves still splayed. 'What's that?' she says.

'Merely an old keepsake. Lil found it in Emma's jewellery case.'

'It's Mrs Hardy, isn't it?' Florence falls back in the chair. '"The girl who died twenty years ago".'

'My dear, if I didn't know what a level-headed person you are, I'd almost believe you were jealous of a poor ghost.'

Florence makes a whickering sound in her nose. She is so pale that he's afraid she's going to faint. Her left eyelid is starting to swell. 'It's so difficult to breathe in this house,' she says. 'I don't feel quite myself.'

'Let me run to the kitchen for a glass of water.'

'No, don't,' she snaps. 'You'll only make yourself ill.'

'Then I'll ring for one,' he says.

'I haven't come here to be waited on. But perhaps you can tell me why I *am* here? Oh, good God.' She tugs at her collar. 'Enough. This is all rather upsetting, Tom. Upsetting, and – and frankly – mystifying. You're unwell – you're behaving irrationally. All this talk of ghosts. Skulking around in your night things.'

'What would you like me to do?'

'I'd like you to go straight back to bed.'

'Of course, if you say so.'

'I do.'

'Don't leave me, Florrie,' he says, capturing her hands. 'Please stay. I can't manage without you. There'll be no more skulking, I promise.'

He can see her striving to master herself. He rubs his thumbs along the soft skin of her wrists and feels the pulse jumping there.

'Yes, then. For the present, yes,' she says. 'Running a house is no trouble, anyone can do it. But I'll have to consider what this means – and so will you.'

He prises her fingers apart, brushes his lips lightly over each palm in turn. 'My darling girl,' he says. 'Without you I don't think there is a present.'

On his way up the stairs he meets Flo Griffin coming down them with a bellows and a caddy stuffed with rags.

'Are you back off to bed, sir?' she says. 'I've set your room to rights and seen to your fire. Shall I bring 'ee a mo'sel o' breakfast?'

'I've breakfasted, thank you.' He reaches into his dressing gown for the jam jar and spoon. 'You might return these to Mrs Riggs, with my apologies.'

Flo gives the jar an incredulous glance. She places first it, then the spoon, on the rag pile in her caddy. 'Yes, sir,' she says.

'Flo, will you be turning out Miss Gifford's room today?'

'Yes, sir.'

'Then please make up the bed with fresh linen. Miss Dugdale will be moving downstairs.'

'When, sir?'

'Straight away.'

She's taking in his dressing gown, his unshaved chin. 'Is Miss Dugdale going to be staying on longer than she first reckoned?'

'That's entirely up to her. But she's kindly agreed to oversee the housekeeping while she is here. I would like you and Dolly and Mrs Riggs to take your orders from her for now.' Flo still hesitates. 'What is it?' he says. 'Do you have a question?'

'Dolly's parents won't like it. She's been brought up in a strict home.'

'I'm quite sure that there is nothing in this visit by an old friend of Mrs Hardy's to cause Dolly Gale's parents the least alarm.'

'There's som'at I've been meaning to return to you, sir,' Flo says. 'I would ha' returned it to Miss Dugdale, but I didn't know how best to do it.'

'What are you talking about?'

'This, sir.' She puts her hand in her skirt and pulls out a hairpin. 'Dolly and me came across it when we were tidying your room. Here you are.'

She drops the pin onto his palm. He holds it, regarding her, this daughter of generations of Dorset field-folk, with her dogged gaze and red complexion, her hair crimped in obeisance to fashion: no beauty, but a sinewy, sensible young woman. A clever one, too.

He can feel shame scorching him from the feet up. 'You could perfectly easily have put this back among Miss Dugdale's things, instead of annoying me with it,' he says, flushing.

'Yes, sir,' she says. 'I will next time. Will that be all, sir?'

'You're a good girl, Flo, and I've always relied on you. So did Mrs Hardy. I hope you're still happy at Max Gate?'

'I try to do my work as well as I can.' Flo looks at the basket in her hand, looks at him. In a flood of feeling she brings out, 'Miss'ess Hardy was a good mistress.'

He stands with his head slightly averted. 'If there is anything you need,' he says, 'I hope you will let me know.'

'Perhaps you could let Miss Dugdale have this month's house-keeping money, sir. We're running short. I haven't wanted to trouble you.'

'It's no trouble. How much did Mrs Hardy allow for?'

'She made twenty pounds go a long way, sir. She could make a neck o' mutton do for five.'

'Then we'll continue to follow her excellent example.' He smiles stiffly and thrusts the hairpin into Flo's caddy. 'That'll be all, thank you, Flo,' he says.

Diamonds

*O*H GOD, *I* AM *an old fool,* he thinks as he continues up the stairs. *Oh God, dear God. I've lost myself. With every day that passes it only gets worse.*

The sleet has turned to slashes of rain and the leaded panes of the stairwell window are already dulled by the spreading wet. On the first floor he stops at the open door of Emma's old room. He takes in the dent in the pillow, the loose threads in the rug pulled up by the heel of a boot or shoe. There's a rectangle in the dust on the dressing table where the jewel case was. The velvet box with its pretend treasure is still there. He wavers on the threshold for a moment, pulse skipping like a thief's, and darts forward to snatch it up.

In his bedroom the lamp is lit and the comforter turned back, ready to receive him. Emma's diary is lying on the rosewood night stand. He sets the box down beside it and lifts the lid. The diamonds look as real as before.

He removes the locket from his neck with a groan. *What am I to do with Florence, Emmie? I never meant for life to be like this. The story I told myself about our future was never like this.* But he knows the truth isn't that simple. He's always managed things through sleight of hand: it's what he does. He's summoned Florence as surely as he conjured Emma, all those years ago. When he glances back at the ghost-days of delight in St Juliot, those meteor days of falling in love, he can't understand how their train of sparks led here: to this dark morning blotted by rain, the smallness and finality of it all, the monotonous thump of his heart which doesn't mean anything other than despair. He's wandering on the bank of a river that he fears will sweep him away and then run on without him, all the way to the sea.

I tried for a real life, only to end up sitting in a room, alone. I believe that I meant it, that my efforts were sincere. What if I'm mistaken? What if the past I recall is just another story, whose details I've invented? Help me, Em. How did it all go so wrong, where did I fail? He fumbles at the pages of the diary, searching for the place where he left off.

Gosse came to see them that spring of 1890, and then – what? He's afraid, shaken by great thuds of self-doubt, without any of his usual instincts to guide him. Wherever he looks, Emma's handwriting surges from margin to margin. He's not in control of this story.

It takes him a few minutes to find the next entry. Drawing in a lungful of air, he steadies himself for the plunge.

2nd April 1890

Spring! Even Tom & I can agree that it really is spring at last, the most brilliant spring we've had in years. The long dry winter is over & everything is on the brink of flowering, reaching & spreading forth as if it were an undiscovered country.

T. has returned to his book & I am doing my best to help him. He is less unhappy than before, I think. He is always writing. His new novel is so lifelike, the emotions of the men & women in it so much like the feelings of real people (more real!) that I can't help feeling he *knows* them all – & if that is the case, then he might – mightn't he? – still be able to know me.

Tom has a rare gift. In spite of his many faults & his sheer ordinariness as a person, this *must* mean something. What's the use of being a great writer if it doesn't also make you a great man?

He lets out a low hiss. Yes, he remembers this. This at least is familiar. He remembers sitting in this very spot where there was once a writing table instead of a night stand, when that distant time still had breadth, colour, smell, voice.

He is less unhappy than before. At nearly fifty it wasn't a simple thing to strike a fresh note from the dull metal of himself, to become whatever he is now. *Yet I did it, Emmie. After so many years of trying, I finally wrote the book that was meant to set me free. Surely that wasn't wrong?*

The past whispers to him, its contours flittering, imperfectly glimpsed. He waits on the shore and stares into the seaward haze. Along the cliffs there are lights, scattered but distinct, burning like a pharos-fire. Perhaps this waiting isn't despair, or even death – not yet. He's waiting for the word from Emma that will return him to life.

He brings the diary up to his face – close, closer – until the words become a world, then mere shapes, scratches on a white sky, the shadows of rocks, ripples in water. She isn't here but she is every-where, facing round and about him, a thin ghost rising from the page.

What are you doing, Em? Where are you leading me?

But he can't see or hear clearly any more. Somewhere above him the skies have opened. Rain slams against the window. The flame of his lamp gulps and smokes, disturbed by a freak in the atmosphere. Here is the cough of a clock, the slap of a wave. The lost world calls out, heavy as iron, in a voice that's at once deep and bright. Here, it says. Look down, now. Here.

Is this what you want, Em – to drown me? Then let me drown.

It's Wednesday the second of April, 1890. Spring! It's nine o'clock on a spring day and he's ready to start work. The mornings are still cool enough to make a study fire acceptable, but there's a change in the air, a new moisture. Following the dryness of March, the hills beyond his window are just greening, as yet unembarrassed by the weight and brilliancy to come. The apple trees have budded but not bloomed. Soon the roads and orchard-grass will be spotted with fallen petals, the heads of the clover darkened by the honey-bees that hang from them in summer, humming, in long veils of sound; when the cuckoo, blackbird and sparrow will drown out the insistent call of the nightjar, at present lingering over its tune of one note. Right now though the world makes no claims on him. He inhales its promise before turning from it to pick up his pen.

For weeks he's been writing steadily. With Emma to copy out his changes to the first half of the book, he's pressed on with the second. *Emma*. The hinged syllables of her name dart briefly through his thoughts. The arrangement is going better than he'd dared hope. She's quick, and rarely disturbs him. She seems untroubled by his revisions and uncertainties. And after the initial anxiety of that self-exposure he's found that he's been able to exclude her again. If she'd been a different woman, alive to his dream, still the girl he'd courted so many years ago on Beeny Cliff, it might have been otherwise. Or if he'd been a different man, perhaps.

He casts his eye back on the beginning of the new phase of his story. The awful moment of revelation is over; his heroine has confessed her guilty secret, the birth and death of her illegitimate child, to the young man she's married. She's not the woman her husband took her for. Within hours of their wedding, the two have started to face each other without illusions.

> The fire in the grate looked impish, demoniacally funny, as if it did not care in the least about her strait. The fender grinned idly, as if it, too, did not care. The light from the water-bottle was merely engaged in a chromatic problem. All material objects around announced their irresponsibility with terrible iteration. And yet nothing had changed since the moments when he had been kissing her.

He pauses, inserts a qualification: *or rather nothing in the substance of things.* What is it that changes when you realize that you've been in love with someone who has never in fact existed? They'll accuse him of being fantastical – his editors, the critics – yet isn't he simply describing, in dramatic form, what every married couple must at some point experience? What's lost when your idea of the other dies? He knows the answer: only the entire world. In brisk, tight letters he adds, *But the essence of things had changed.*

The wife, poor ghost, doesn't understand that she's now just the spectre of who she once was. She goes on uttering her faint cries of love, as ghosts will. This passage needs work – he hasn't yet caught the high plaintive note of the lost, the one who is left behind. *I meant to make you happy*, she says. It's not enough; it's too much like life: scrappy and unconvincing. He crosses this out, produces the words that, though entirely invented, will sound real.

'I have been hoping, longing, praying, to make you happy. I have thought, what joy it will be to do it, what an unworthy wife I shall be if I do not!'

On he goes, confident at last, expanding and reshaping. He's forgotten the paralysis that stopped him from writing all winter. This desire, this purposeful extension of himself – this is what he was designed for. How long will he feel this way? Half an hour, an hour? Half a day, possibly. And the same again tomorrow, if he's lucky.

Drawing a glistening caret mark in the margin, he puts his pen to the page. In the charged light of this spring, he sees that one of the hardest things for the human heart is to accept that its love is no longer welcome.

'I thought that you loved me – me, my very self! If it is I you do love, O how can it be that you look and speak so? It frightens me! Having begun to love 'ee, I love 'ee for ever – in all changes, in all disgraces, because you are yourself. I ask no more. Then how can you, O my own husband, stop loving me?'
    'I repeat, the woman I have been loving is not you.'
    'But who?'
    'Another woman in your shape.'

The door jerks open. 'Tom.'

He glances up. 'Em,' he says.

'Oh my, you've already begun. I didn't mean to interrupt you – I just wanted to give you these pages.' Emma lays a bundle of manuscript on the table. 'You know,' she says carefully, 'even with all you've had to cut out, this is good. It's *so* good.'

'Thank you, Emmie.' He flexes his fingers, dips his pen into the inkwell, fiddles with the blotting paper. 'Is there anything else?'

'Tom, I've had an idea. For – for our book.'

'*Our* book?'

'Why, yes,' says Em. 'It makes me happy to think of it as ours, as we're both working on it. Is that wrong?'

'I suppose not.' She shifts her weight from one foot to the other, but makes no move to go. 'What's this idea, then?' he asks.

'Well – when your couple, Angel and – and . . . What name have you settled on for her? You've crossed it out so many times that I wasn't sure. Is it still to be Rose-Mary? Or Sue?'

'Tess. Tess Troublefield.'

'Hmm. I wonder if that isn't a little too – too . . .'

'A little too what?'

'A little too plain.'

'She's a plain woman. She's a *dairymaid*, Em.'

'Ah, I don't mean that sort of plain – and in any case that's not plain at all; to call a working woman with her many sorrows Troublefield is downright poetic, wouldn't you say? No. I meant plain as in *obvious*.'

'Well, what would you call her, since this is apparently now our book?'

'Didn't you tell me that your father is descended from the Jersey le Hardys?'

'Yes, but what's that to my – I mean *our* – story?'

'Lots of Dorset labouring families have names that sound as if they might once have had a fair bit of poetry to them. The Goulds. The Quintins. And those handsome carters at Lower Bockhampton, the what-are-they-calleds. The ones who all look as if they should be striding around in chain mail.'

'You mean the Debbyhouses. They used to be the De Bayeux family. That's what they tell people, anyway.'

'Exactly. You could do that with the name.'

'Do what, my dear?'

'You know, take a real one and smudge it a bit.'

'*Smudge* it?'

'Blur the edges. Blend it in.'

He smiles. 'I'll think about it. Thank you.'

Though he nods at Em encouragingly, she doesn't appear inclined to leave. He notices now that she's holding a square velvet box of some sort. 'We haven't got to my idea yet,' she says.

'Haven't we?' He lays down his pen, resigned to playing his part. The sooner they perform this scene, the sooner he can get back to his couple and to the revelation he's just had of the illusory nature of the beloved – a truth that seems all too close to home as his eyes meet the expectant eyes of his wife. He says, 'What else did you have in mind?'

'This Tess of ours. When she and Angel have had their bridal supper you go straight to the poor man's confession, and then of course to hers—'

'What d'you mean by "poor man"? Are we writing the same book, my love? His unhappiness is all his own choosing.'

'He can't choose any differently,' says Emma. 'He doesn't have it in him to be happy, you see. He would be unhappy whatever he did.'

He rubs his hand over his beard as he lets this sink in. Despite his irritation he feels a sideways, dislocating jolt. 'Goodness, Emmie. I think you may be right.'

'Yes, dear. I'm often right. Now, my idea is this. Perhaps, before we come to her confession, Angel could make Tess a present.'

'What sort of present?'

Em places the box solemnly on the pile of manuscript copy and lifts the catch. Inside there's a double *rivière* of brilliants, pooled around a shower of smaller ornaments. 'One like this,' she says.

He stares at her in amazement. 'Good Lord. Those are the biggest diamonds I've ever seen. Did you rob the Tower of London?'

'Don't they look like the real thing?'

'Well, aren't they?'

'Of course not. They're glass. I bought them from Dudley's in Portsmouth for a few bob when I was a girl.' She laughs, flirting the necklace in front of her collar. 'I wore them everywhere.'

'*Did* you? What did your sister think?'

'She thought they were vulgar. What a vain thing I was.' Her face grows serious again. 'Tom, Angel's must be real.'

'But where would he have got his hands on a treasure like this?'

'It could be a bequest. A legacy, from a relative – held in trust for his wife, whoever she might be, on his marriage.'

'And now he's married a milkmaid, and the jewels are hers. And she'll look better in 'em than any woman of fashion. I like the irony of it.' Suddenly he says, 'Em, put the necklace on; put it on!' He helps her with the clasp. 'Your dress isn't right. It ought to be a low-cut one for a string like that.'

'Ought it?'

'Yes,' he says. 'Here, tuck in the upper edge of your bodice, like this. That's better.' He steps back to survey her. 'My heavens,' he says. 'Don't you look fine.'

Em is standing by the fire. Its high-coloured light spills over the stones on the bared skin of her breast, so that she is, for the space of a breath, no more than a constellation of white, red, and green flashes.

'But you know, Em, Tess is a simple girl. Why are we dressing her in diamonds?'

'So that she looks her very best when the worst happens. So that she looks like a lady. It's the least thing you can do for her.'

Even though she's so near she seems indefinably remote. He takes a step towards her and raises a finger to her cheek. 'I'm sorry I haven't been able to buy you jewellery, Em,' he says.

Emma shakes him off. 'I don't want jewellery from you. I've never wanted it.' She's turning away. She keeps her back to him while she unfastens the necklace. As she slides it into the box she murmurs, 'Must you give her a child?'

Her head is bowed over his papers, her shoulders bent. He puts his hand on the nape of her neck. 'Let me hold you, Emmie.' She faces him sadly. He encircles her with his arms, pulling her as close as he dares. He can feel her heart struggling against his. The ashy glow of the fire picks out the purple veins of her temple, the valleys of her neck, the depths of her greying hair, throwing the outline of their bodies onto the wall and ceiling as a single shape.

Though he tightens his embrace until it feels as if he and Emma are one person, it's the writer – whose job is to name things as they are without ducking or hiding from the truth, to preserve the integrity of the world – who replies.

'Without a child the story makes no sense,' he says.

The Voice

THERE'S A SPATTER OF noise from across the landing, above the drip-drip of the rain. He raises his head, peering into the wet half-light. Shivers come and go along the floor. The air is trembling with the furious beating of wings. He's about to call out when he realizes that it's the sound of a sheet being shaken and drawn tight. *It's nothing*, he tells himself, *it's no one. It's just Flo and Dolly, getting Emma's room ready for Florence.* Far off, as if it's being swung in a bottomless well, a bucket starts to clank.

His mouth is dry and his heart jerks painfully against his ribs. *The day before you died you said I was to blame, Emmie, that we'd never had a child.* That long-ago spring was the last time he and Emma shared a bedroom. But they were already middle-aged by then; what difference could his decision to sleep alone have made? Her hope of children was long gone.

He turns the diary face down on his night stand and studies its spine in the frail halo of the bedside lamp. He doesn't think that he can go on with whatever this is, this trial by water, this fording or drowning. He's too old, and too afraid. He thinks of the violent ocean, the rocks on the Boscastle road all those years ago, pink and alive; the heat of a bygone day. The brown stones of Portland with their egg-shaped hearts of white. *World without end.* But not a world without change: it's a world that raises cliffs and rivers and trees, and men and women, and has no scruples about extinguishing them again. In earthquake, wind and fire. In silent disease and sudden death. In the blink of an eye.

I can't continue your story, Em. I don't have the strength.

Emma's voice – small and firm, commanding as the voice of a bell – speaks to him as distinctly as if she's sitting in his ear. Yes you can, she says. I know you do. My story started with a woman on a shore. It began with a castle on a cliff. It began with magic. Now go on.

There was no magic.

Raising mountains *is* magic. You made a world, and you brought me to live in it. Then you changed it all. You moved everything around. You rebuilt it.

Did I?

Yes, you did.

Perhaps I did. This house; later I changed the house. But I thought you wanted those changes too.

I didn't want you to change the whole foundation of our life together. Oh, why did you?

I didn't mean anything by it, Emmie. I was sleeping so little. I was so unprepared for what was happening to me – I was merely trying to contain it somehow.

And then?

Well – and then. Things changed. The weather changed. It was uncanny.

You see. Magic.

At first it was only his study he intended to move. He remembers the coming of summer that year; the sweating passages of the place when they got back from the London season, as if Max Gate lay under a spell. Em's large-leaved rhubarb and cabbage-plants were bewitched too, their broad limp surfaces hanging in the heat like half-closed umbrellas. He'd given himself up entirely to his work, to the painstaking, persistent toil of it.

Not magic, Em.

But your heart turned to stone.

Was it stone? It felt like fire. In the evening he stepped outside, looking at the sunset over the adjoining fields. He was awake to it all, alive to it all, in a way he had never been yet and never would be again. In the direction of the sun's rays there was a glistening ripple of gossamer-webs, like the track of moonlight on the sea. Gnats, knowing nothing of their brief glorification, wandered across the shimmer of this pathway, lit up as though carrying an inner flame, before passing out of its line to become quite extinct.

That's how it was — wasn't it?

When she doesn't reply he sighs and reaches for her diary. *Then tell me how it was.*

2nd August 1890

It's so hot now that even the bees & butterflies are drowsy. The air is weighted down with the smell of yellowing grass & stung apples & baked earth. On the edges of the feverish town sheep dot the meads like specks of flame. There isn't a human being to be seen out of doors.

Tom is moving his study out of the large room over the landing to the guest room next to ours. He goes bit by bit, & book by book. His *Aeneid*, his Aeschylus & Ovid & his Latin Grammar have all flown. He's working like a man under an enchantment. He sits up after dinner & comes to bed past midnight & is back at his desk before breakfast. He says that the best room he ever had for writing was his boyhood one, & that he prefers composing in a smaller room after all.

Then why build this house, I wonder? Why insist on bricking us both up here & on having half a dozen useless bedrooms & attics & reception rooms? Why haven't we filled them, why do we tiptoe about as if we're at a funeral, why is there only *us*?

I finished copying today's chapters as the afternoon was fading. While Molly lit the lamps I went upstairs to deliver my pages to Tom. Usually I can hear him muttering & chuckling like a man wrestling with devils, but this evening not a sound came from behind that door. I knocked. He never does reply, & so I went in.

Tom was asleep with his cheek on one arm, his beard squashed sideways over his MS. I put my hand to his forehead. It was dry. At my touch his lips moved a little, still shaping words. Not ill or possessed, then, just himself.

'Tom,' I said, 'you shouldn't be sleeping at a table.'

He opened his eyes. 'Is that you, Em?'

'Who else should it be?' I asked.

'The Queen of Cornwall, perhaps. You're rather queenly, you know, even without your diamonds.'

'You're gabbling,' I said. 'You aren't sleeping enough.'

'Sleep is irrelevant, Your Majesty.'

'You know very well it's not,' I said.

'I'm afraid that I won't be able to dream if I let myself sleep, Emmie.'

'You really are talking absolute nonsense.'

'I'm dreaming as hard as I can.' He yawned. 'In my dream I'm putting together a story, but it so rarely seems to be the story I set out to tell.'

'If you mean this novel of yours,' I said, 'it's quite solid. Safe as houses.'

'Do you really think so? Nobody else does.'

'Yes,' I said, '& once you're able to put back the parts you've left out, it will be stronger still.'

'Will it?'

'Of course. It won't merely be a dream then. It will be real.'

'Em,' he whispered after a moment's hesitation, 'do you find what I do . . . respectable?'

'What an odd question,' I said.

'It's just – so often I feel like an interloper at the parties we go to in Town. Everyone likes to read novels, but I doubt they quite know what to think about novelists. They want what I make but they don't like to see it as labour. There I am, clumping all over their drawing rooms like a yokel, a backwoods Hodge, trying not to stare, hoping I haven't left dirt on the carpet. I feel as if I'm only in that world through some terrible error.'

'I'm not sure that respectability has ever been very high up on the list of necessary qualities for an author,' I replied.

'Oh, my dear.' He took my hand. 'I meant to do much better by you than I have.'

'Don't be silly.' He looked so forlorn & out of kilter, with his flattened beard sticking up on one side, that I couldn't help smiling. 'Do you remember when we climbed the hill from Boscastle to St Juliot, long ago?'

'I do. I remember your hair. I remember that it was windy & that your hair blew in my mouth.'

'I was waiting all afternoon for you to kiss me.'

'Well, did I?'

I shook my head.

'I suppose I talked about some book or other,' he said. 'Probably the one I wasn't quite managing to finish.'

'It didn't matter. I knew by the time we'd got to the top that you'd finish it, & that I'd marry you.'

'Dearest Emmie,' he said shyly. 'May I kiss you now?'

'You're full of strange questions this evening.'

'I won't if you don't want me to, you know.'

'Come here, Tom.' I bent down to him where he sat & pressed my lips to his. I'd forgotten how small & slight he is, & how afraid his mouth is behind that beard.

'I was such a boy then,' he said.

'Such a frightened boy.'

'I wonder where that boy went.'

'He hasn't gone anywhere,' I said.

5th August 1890

The guest bed has vanished into what used to be Tom's study, & is now – I don't know what. Since Sunday he has begun spending the night there. I woke at half past seven yesterday to find his place next to mine undisturbed & my husband already in his new study, writing. The same again today. Poor Tom. Better than sleeping at a table, I suppose.

31st August 1890

It's like sharing a house with a restless spirit. Tom didn't come down for lunch this afternoon. At two o'clock I had a tray sent up, which presently came back untouched.

'But surely even dreamers have to eat,' I protested. 'You'll do yourself damage.'

'Don't grumble at me, Em,' he said. 'I've never felt better.'

This is a strange sort of dreaming that needs no sleep, & a strange sort of being alive that has no physical wants. At night I can't rest & lie awake thinking of that eager pen scratching away on the other side of the wall, listening to the occasional ghostly murmur.

It's a very grave fallacy that novelists understand the personal application of their own novels. I suspect in fact that it is generally the last face of them that they decipher.

Very well. I'll admit it, Emmie. He didn't realize it then, but that spring and summer idyll of writing was really an elegy. It was no more than every other book had demanded of him: that he should sacrifice human comforts and diversions; that he should turn away from the world, from Emma, and work. He was doing what a writer must do. He was sticking to his story. *How could I have known? I was just doing my job.*

Was that all?

Yes.

Really all?

Yes. She doesn't speak. She's unconvinced. *No,* he thinks. *No, then . . . No! It was much more than that. I was happy. I was fully myself. I was Tom Hardy. After fifty years of trying and almost succeeding, I finally knew who I was, and what I was for. Why couldn't you be happy for me too?*

For the first time in his life he felt that the business of authorship was a substantial experience, not just an imitation of what's real. Every evening he raised his eyes from the page and saw the waning light on the red wall before him, signalling the end of another day of work that didn't seem like work, but like a miraculous reconstruction of himself.

At night, behind that wall, there was a dense silence. In the mornings as he hurried from his new bedroom to go to his writing table Emma was always there, waiting on the landing.

He can see her quite clearly, broad and rustling, planted in his path like a vine. Her face with its puzzled brows, the brows of a middle-aged woman who has got the life she wished for and has found it wanting, is wearing a wounded frown. 'Tom, you've slept in that room for more than a month now. Can you be comfortable?'

'Oh, entirely. What's the matter, Em? You look cross.'

'I'm not cross,' she says. 'I'm surprised.'

'Then your eyebrows should be going up, not down.'

'Don't be vexatious. I'm trying to talk to you.'

'I'm sorry, Emmie. Please tell me you're glad at least that we're making use of all our rooms. The smaller study suits me perfectly. You said yourself that it was quite hopeless as a guest room.'

'I thought you disliked the colour.'

'I've rather taken to it. It's like writing in a heart, or a womb.'

'I wonder how you come up with such peculiar notions.'

'Years of practice.'

'But I don't see why you should have moved yourself into a different bedroom too.'

'It's the sensible decision. It's so hot just now and I wake so early. I'd like to stay up late to write sometimes, without disturbing you when I retire.'

Em is silent for a moment. 'Are we then never – never to have . . .?'

'Oh, I'm sure we'll have visitors,' he says. 'Maybe not overnight ones, for the time being. But that would have been out of the question in any case, with my book going on as well it is. If it sells, we can extend this house. You can add whatever extra rooms you like. We'll erect an entire conservatory for your cucumbers.'

'Cucumbers.'

'Yes.'

'You hate cucumbers.'

'I intend to develop a taste for them.'

Em twitches her skirts, shadowy among the shadows. 'Then I wonder what's preventing you from sending your story off?' she asks.

'I'm nearly there. Before I can, I still have to get rid of the . . . well, the seduction in the Close.'

'The rape.'

'The rape. Quite.'

'I don't see how you're going to do that.'

'All of this is exactly like building a house, Emmie. In my original plan I've put in a ballroom next to the entrance lobby, only now I find that it's not needed. My reader doesn't want to dance.' He laughs curtly. 'In fact, he's violently opposed to dancing. The room has to go.'

'But you can't pull out a ballroom. If you do, the whole house will collapse.'

'Precisely. I have to repurpose it somehow. Make it into something more acceptable. A chapel, perhaps,' he adds with a grimace.

'That would have to be a very queer sort of chapel.'

'Now you're getting the idea.'

'Well, then,' Em says, just above her breath, 'I think you may have your answer right there.'

'I do?'

'Yes. Alec could trap Tess in a sham marriage.'

'Sham – how?'

'He could pretend that he means honestly by her. He could persuade her into a private ceremony – not in a chapel or church, in a room somewhere – that resembles a real marriage in every way, except that everything to do with it is a lie – the ring, the registrar. And by the time she realizes the lie she's already given herself to him, and it's too late.'

'Heavens, Emma,' he says. 'How do you know about this sort of thing?'

'Oh, Tom. From novels, of course. I may not be an architect, but I do *read*.'

'It's certainly an ingenious solution, if a little far-fetched.'

'Really?' She gives him a cold look. 'I don't think it's far-fetched at all.'

Why did you begin to resent me so after I wrote that damned book, Em? What was my crime? Following your advice? Using the gift you loved me for? Being rewarded for it? When the story appeared the following year in three spanking new volumes, bound in sandy-coloured cloth and with its hacked-out passages restored, neither of them guessed what was about to happen.

Everyone talked about it. Everyone wanted to buy it. Within months he was lifted from lukewarm distinction as an English novelist to a position of world fame. The strangest part of it all was that a fiction built from the materials of his hidden self should have turned him overnight into a public property to which everybody felt entitled to lay a claim.

He accepted, as Em couldn't, the split between his two lives. There was the life people thought he was living, shiny and on view, and there was this other. The other life was the true one, not in the least rarefied: a stony life, plodding and intractable, erected block by block, a self-enclosure that was made to endure. To his dismay he found that he was married to a woman who didn't grasp this. She was jealous; she was suspicious. *Did you really think that I did all this, bore that tedious trampling crowd, because I wanted to? Just to keep you out? It was never about you. I simply don't understand what my crime was. You gave up on me. Why, Emmie?*

He riffles through the later entries in the notebook with a mounting sense of desperation.

13th November 1894

Fearful disruption this entire autumn as we have workmen in, altering the house. T. has designed a larger kitchen & scullery with a new study for himself above them, & two extra attic rooms above that.

These are going to be mine.

We are of course obliged to stay through it all because of T.'s writing. His self-involvement is total – half the time he is only thinking about this place & how to improve it – & for the other half he is thinking exactly the same thing about his books.

25th April 1895

My eminent partner is in London en garçon. He writes that he went to dinner at Mrs Crackanthorpe's a couple of evenings ago & that while there he met Mrs Patrick Campbell, who is very eager that he should turn *Tess* into a play & give her the starring role. He has lunched with Lady Pembroke – he has been to the theatre with Mrs Henniker.

He's rather tired, but won't be returning home on Friday after all. He is going to a 'crush' hosted by Lady Jeune purely because he doesn't want to seem disagreeable.

He says it is very wet & raw in Town & that I'm not to come down for a week as he doesn't think I could stand it there right now. Most thoughtful, I'm sure.

27th July 1896

Another novel, another succès de scandale. Or perhaps just a scandale, plain & simple. The whole county is in a stir about

Jude. Eliza Wood Homer called today & as I poured our tea I could see that she was itching to address me in italics.

'Oh, Mrs Hardy,' she panted, ignoring the cup I'd put before her & grabbing my hand instead. 'I am so very sorry for you.' She drew closer. 'That last book, the one with the milkmaid! – & now *this*. This filthy *stonemason*. All those – *carnal doings*. I hear that the Bishop of Wakefield has thrown his copy into the fire.'

'Really?' I said. 'The Bishop has a fire going in summer large enough to burn a five-hundred-page novel?'

'You must be as appalled as any of us that Mr Hardy has seen fit to describe marriage as a *hopelessly vulgar institution*,' she persisted. 'You have challenged him, I trust.'

'What good do you think that does? I didn't see the manuscript before it was published. These days he keeps his work quite hidden from me.'

'But you should *say* something. You are his *wife*.'

I could hardly tell her that since he's become so visible to the public T. behaves as if neither of us were quite real. He works alone in his new study directly beneath my feet, while I curl myself into the attic space above his head. This is how we exist now: two people in their coffins, two ghosts, stacked one on top of the other.

I merely smiled. 'My dear Mrs Wood Homer,' I said, 'if my husband set any store by that hopelessly vulgar fact, you & I wouldn't be having this conversation.'

So many ghostly afternoons, spent in silent rooms. I came up to the attic at midday with a new book from the library, but I couldn't open it.

Here it all was. The narrow corridor, the low door, the dark floor with a gleam of sunlight on it from the dormer. Yes, I thought. This is the place. Something must happen now.

I sat at the table & waited. My feet grew hot in the sun & after some time I removed my shoes & stockings. A pleasant breeze blew through the window. I sat, looking at the little toes crumpled under. All at once the light seemed to me like an alley of brightness down which I could dance if only I tried.

I got up & attempted to perform a leap. It was remarkably easy, almost like flying. This is how being at one with the air feels, I thought. The air. We fret about it being too cold or moist or too rushing, buffeting us on land or water. It has all sorts of life-giving qualities yet it seldom quite suits us, or not for long anywhere. Finally, being unable to use it, we die for want of it.

I leaped again, & again & again, with my limbs spread out. The breeze blew over & around me & the sun shone on.

A rat-a-tat-tat came at the door. It was Tom. 'Emma,' he said. 'What are you doing? I can hear you, you know. I can hear every movement you make.'

The sound of his voice brought me back to myself. 'I am stretching,' I said. 'I am thinking.'

'Thinking. While making all that noise.'

'Yes. I am stretching my mind.'

Though truthfully I wasn't sure any more.

Tom's first volume of poetry is out this week. He tells me that from now on he is going to be a poet only. I admit that I felt no small relief, till I picked up the copy sent by the printer & came across 'The Ivy-Wife'. The creature in these verses (is she a creeper? Some sort of *parasite*?) tries to attach herself first to a tall beech tree, then to a plane tree, but is rebuffed. Finally she manages to trap an ash by weaving her green claw around him, & in gaining his strength & height so cramps & binds him that she fells them both.

'Tom, what's this?' I asked.

'It's a poem about plants,' he said.

'I think not.'

'Come, Em. It mentions three particular species of tree.'

'Yes, & one particular species of misery. You seem determined these days to make some sort of point about – well, about marriage. About *me*.'

'Why must everything I write be about you?'

'I don't know!' I cried. 'Why do you insist on slighting me? Why, now that you are so admired, must you tear down our life together?'

'I've never insisted on anything, Emmie. I've only ever tried to provide for you as a husband should. My whole thought has been to make you comfortable & happy.'

'So you don't mean to tell the world that I hobble & choke you?'

'You're being unreasonable,' he said, keeping his eyes firmly fixed on his waistcoat buttons. 'People notice, Em. My sisters have heard reports about the town, & are concerned about you.'

His sisters! That cut-price coven on the heath! That clump of nettles, goading & stinging him with gossip! I was so angry I couldn't speak.

I fear I am prejudiced against authors. Too often they wear out the lives of others with their moanings if unsuccessful – & if they do become successful they throw their aider over the parapets.

14th February 1899

T. wrote all morning. This afternoon, as the setting sun drew a violet bow along the hilltops, he started off on a walk up Conygar. On seeing that I was unoccupied, he asked me with a great show of solicitude if I wanted to join him. 'No, thank you,' I said, 'I think I shall go back to my attic & read.'

It was a lie. Novels & poetry do not appeal to me as they once did. I no longer believe that literature can tell us anything true about this world, or that love proper, & enduring, is in the nature of men. I have learned that from my husband.

Year after year of resentment, of dissatisfaction, of complaint. He didn't understand it at the time. He gave Emma everything she asked for, every comfort she wanted. Her own kingdom upstairs. Bracelets and necklaces too, eventually.

He gave her things, oh yes – all the wrong things.

The upheaval across the landing has long since stopped, and the house sunk back into its rain-swept trance. He's nearly come to the end of this first diary of Emma's. There's a single entry left.

So often I am told that it's my privilege to be married to a man of genius. Well, if it is my privilege it is also my misfortune. I dare anyone to spread evil reports of me – such as that I have failed in my wifely obligation to Tom, which Kate has actually said to my face, or that I have 'errors' in my mind, which she has also said to me, & I hear she repeats to others. What right does she have to accuse me of being unloving? Of his many failures as a husband she knows nothing.

I've asked the servants to move a bed into the attic for me. I no longer want to sleep in our old room alone.

Next year I will be sixty. I am a dry old woman, a desert. I have lived so long without Tom's affection now that I doubt I'd know it if he offered it to me again. I can't bear having Kate or Mary to visit. The shame of having them see us here, bricked up alive in our make-believe marriage, is too much.

Today I walked out of the house. I went onto the road, thinking I might follow the Winterborne Came path up to the skirt of the woods on Conygar Hill, from which the place would look distant, its red walls like the wings of a butterfly or a blot on the sky. I am so unused to walking that simply getting into the fields took half an hour. A few steps past the turn-off to Came Rectory I stopped & glanced around. There was the wretched town of Dorchester, the railway line, the mean, useful buildings, & the bruise-coloured roof of Max Gate rising above them all. I tried to pretend that I'd sunk to the bottom of the ocean & that this was a phantom city, or that I was merely dreaming; & I tried to go on.

My knee hurt. Somewhere inside those walls he was writing. I went back.

Up here in my attic I watch the sky pinking & paling, day in & day out. Tom's pine saplings surround me from every side. How thirsty they are. How cunning. They're the only things flourishing in this chalky ground. Though they may appear humble now they will soon grow taller than the house.

I can climb as high as I like, but I know I can never escape.

Sometimes I think the whole of literature is a prison, erected on vanity & illusion. It has a thousand gaudy rooms & a million turrets & a grand front to lure the gullible, but it's a prison all the same, a prison that takes constant shoring up & tending. If you are married to one of the keepers then there will only ever be a Little Ease in it for you, & as to your real life – well, you can say goodbye to *that*.

Tom's sisters say I am mad & perhaps I am. Mad to have let myself be caught. Mad to hope still for the word of love from my husband that will set me free. If I could, I'd fly out of the cage he has made for me. But where would I go?

He never knew why Emma banished his family from Max Gate. She was ashamed – not of Kate and Mary, but of herself. Of Tom and Em. Of him.

He lets his chin sink slowly onto his breastbone. Somewhere above his head the rain is driving at the roof, coursing down the slates, but he's scarcely aware of it. He's drenched in misery. He's crossed the river and reached the far bank and he hasn't drowned, but he may as well have.

I'm alive, he thinks. *Alive, and unequipped to do whatever I'm supposed to do next.* He must speak, though he doesn't know how.

Emma . . . He falters. *The shame wasn't yours. You were a good woman. You were a good wife. I'm sorry I was always so occupied, so preoccupied. I'm sorry that I forgot our anniversary. No — our* anniversaries. *I didn't even realize there was more than one. That's how bad at marriage I was. I'm sorry that I never took you back to Cornwall. I'm sorry that I didn't manage to find the right words for you. I'm terrible at words, actually. Who would ever have guessed?*

'I'm sorry for all of it,' he says out loud, straining to see into the bleak space separating that time from the present. 'It wasn't your fault. Do you hear me?'

But it's too late, he knows. She doesn't hear him. She's past love, praise, blame. She isn't standing on the shore, or on the cliff. She isn't waiting in the ruin of the castle as he hurries over the sand, old and lame, with his heart in his hands. She isn't there at all. She's out of his reach, curled under the clay, shut in the cell of her grave.

The river has run on. The rain she hated is beating down on her. Whatever he didn't say will never turn into words now.

Ashes

ON THURSDAY MORNING he goes straight to his study with Emma's diary. He reunites it with its fellows and lines the three notebooks up on his desk. He's already seen enough of the later two not to want to read them through to the end. Unlocking the bottom drawer of the pedestal he gets out the tin box where he keeps his cash and begins, methodically, to count out bank notes: one, two, three, four, five. Five White Notes, each with a blank reverse. Twenty pounds. The letter he started to Gosse is lying face up on the blotter. When he's done he puts it in his dressing-gown pocket with the money.

Before he leaves he places his palm against the grain of his table. He's spent a lifetime sitting at tables. Eating at tables. Writing at tables. Eating as he writes at tables. Sleeping at tables – it's true. 'O table,' he says. The words are a swindle. Like all words, they're counterfeit, without substance or colour. 'Useless,' he says to the silence.

In the dining room Kate is finishing her breakfast. 'Good morning,' she hazards.

'Am I in your way?'

'Don't be such a stunpoll.' She wipes her lips with her napkin. 'This is your house. Sit down. Have some toast and jam.'

He sits and appraises the chafing dishes on the sideboard. He will try – he will. 'I think I'd prefer eggs if there are any, thank you, Katie,' he says.

Kate's eyes narrow. 'We've a whole bucketful of poached eggs. And no Lady Lilian to eat them.' Seeing he's in earnest, she arms herself with a serving spoon and lifts a domed cover. The eggs twinkle at him improvidently. 'One or two?'

'Two,' he says, feeling reckless.

She helps him to three. 'Eat up, Tommy, or they'll go to waste.' Once he's almost cleaned his plate she gives a difficult cough. 'Look,' she mumbles. 'I was rude yesterday. I didn't mean to offend you. I'm a contrary old cow.'

'No, you're not. I'd have been lost this last week without having you here to run everything. I don't know how you keep it all straight in your head.'

'Oh well,' Kate says. 'I imagine it's because I don't have more important things to think about.'

'Katie, pax. You're right. I should give some thought to how I'm to manage. I'm no good at change.'

'You'll want to have a long talk with Miss Dugdale, I expect.'

He puts down his knife and fork. 'As a matter of fact I was just on my way to speak to her.'

'She's out back. She's been up with the lark.' Kate starts to clear, brisk as always, stacking their plates with the silverware bundled on top. 'You've moved her into Emma's room, I see.'

'Yes.'

'I mentioned to Flo Griffin that you felt it best to lock the door to the dressing room, as of old.'

'Thank you. That was tactful. The matter of the door never even crossed my mind.'

Kate softens. 'I can be tactful if it's called for.' She flattens her napkin with a conclusive air, but he knows she's not done. She's making an effort to be generous in victory. 'Tom,' she says, 'I'm sorry for what I said about this house, about it being so empty. There's still time, you know. This could be a second chance for you.'

He finds Florence sitting at the kitchen table with Jane Riggs, drinking tea from a saucerless cup. The two are talking together but stop when he comes in.

'Miss Dugdale,' he says, 'may I borrow you in the drawing room for a moment?'

Florence gets up. If she disapproves of his being out of bed, she doesn't show it. 'Of course,' she says, in a voice that's a little too loud.

She follows him wordlessly along the corridor. When they get to the drawing room he sees that it's been coaxed into a state of extreme order. The shutters are pinned back, the blinds raised. The hearth is swept and the grate is heaped with fresh coal. His lap rug lies in a triangle across the back of his armchair. He notices that the tray bearing his pen and ink has been placed at the precise point towards which a person seated there might be expected, from long use, to stretch his hand.

'My dear, what were you doing just now?' he asks.

'I was settling the butcher's order with Mrs Riggs,' Florence says.

'Over tea?'

'Was that wrong of me?'

'Well – I don't know. Emma never drank tea with her.'

'I won't do it again if you'd prefer me not to.'

He feels his mouth shaping a vague smile. This is not his province. So many things aren't his province. 'Do as you think right,' he says. 'I just wanted to be certain that you had enough money for the housekeeping.' He hands Florence the notes he's counted out.

'But this is only twenty pounds,' she says. 'What ought it to cover?'

'Why, everything.'

'Everything? Food, servants' wages, cleaning materials, coal, oil, candles – everything?'

'Emma always managed quite well on twenty pounds. We're a very small household, after all.'

'Are we?'

'Oh, yes.'

'A household. Is that what we are?' Florence gives him a perplexed glance. She's at sea, handicapped by her desire to please. 'Will you dress today? Should I lay out your clothes?' She fingers the lapel of his dressing gown. 'Shall I read to you?'

'No, no. Thank you, my dear. I haven't forgotten the conversation we had yesterday. I intend to behave so much better to you, Florrie. But there's something I must do. I must finish my letter to Gosse.'

'Look at me, Tom.' She holds his eye. She's trying very hard to communicate that she's still here, that she's prepared to forgive his behaviour, that she believes there'll be nothing further to forgive. 'I'll type it up for you.'

'There's no need.' He feels a rush of admiration for her survivor's instinct; for her willingness to expend herself, her fastidious refusal to bargain. He kisses her hand and puts it away before she has a chance to object. Before he's made to relent. 'He's used to my scrawl. I've delayed enough – I'll do it directly.'

'Then I'll see to it that you aren't disturbed,' Florence says, in the tone of a woman who means: I can take a hint, if I have to.

Once he's alone he sits down in his chair and rearranges the rug over his knees. He stares vacantly at the cold hearth with its scuttle and brushes, its spade and tongs, the vases on the mantel and the pictures to either side of the chimney: water-colours of Tintagel Castle and Boscastle, prints of Tess on her knees before Angel Clare and of her lying asleep among the stones of the Great Plain. He won't trouble to light the fire. He wants, more than anything, more than warmth or company, to share with Gosse his new understanding of – well, of what? Prisons. Trees. This house. He isn't entirely sure, nor is he at all sure yet how to say something that might lie beyond speech. But it's right that he should try to do it here, surrounded by the relics of his marriage – the nubby cushions, the rubbed tea-table, the dead piano – the whole dismal tomb of his life with Emma.

He settles his tray on his lap, unscrews his ink bottle and lays the letter out in front of him. It's been nearly a week since he began it. Eight days since Em went. Haltingly, he rereads the last few lines.

The day before Emma died we exchanged bitter words. It was the worst falling-out we'd ever had. In the course of this argument she said things to me which I won't easily forget. And now, you see, I can't go to her as I'd like, and ask her if she spoke from the heart. I wonder if you and Nellie have ever –

He crosses out the last half-sentence. *If Emma was unhappy, if she felt trapped by our life together, then I was to blame. The fault was mine.* Instead, he writes:

When you and Benson were here in September I may, I fear, have seemed rather distant towards her, and towards you. There were many things I could not see at the time.

There they are, Emma, Gosse and Benson, lunch eaten, strolling across the lawn in the wan September sunlight. They look out of place in that wilderness, Gosse in his pressed suit, Benson artfully rumpled, the lace train of Em's dress snagging on the scrappy turf, and he trailing behind in his plus fours: an unassuming country gentleman, or a retired half-pay officer, perhaps, from a not very smart regiment, courteous enough but knowing all the while that he lacks openness, that he's waiting for the afternoon to pass and for them all, even Gosse – especially Gosse, who is keeping up his usual stream of exaggerated gallantry – to go away. It's too much. Today, it is all too much. He follows them mutely.

'Let me tell you a story about a rose that grew in the night, Mr Gosse,' says Emma with a breathy giggle, 'if you would like to hear it.'

'I'd like that above all things,' says Gosse.

'She was planted on a fair day, and called to life by the kiss of the sun. Before long a cloud passed over the sun's face and his rays grew dim. The rose was sad, but she made up her mind to wait patiently for the skies to clear and for the light and warmth of the sun to return.'

'A wise rose,' Benson observes.

'I think this may be an allegory,' says Gosse.

'Well done, Gosse,' says Benson.

'The sun grew larger and ever brighter behind his cloud, which glowed like an ember, but he refused to come out. Now the rose felt very unhappy. She unfurled her best petals, longing for him to notice them and to show her his face.'

'Did he oblige?' asks Benson.

Gosse murmurs, 'Of course he did.'

'No,' Em says. 'He did *not*. He stayed hidden in his cloud, blazing triumphantly in the sky, but never condescended to shine on her again. At first the rose bent her head and shed her finery and drooped right to the ground. Then, as the years passed, she learned how to grow in the dark. She budded by the light of the moon. She realized that without the sun to disturb her there was no difference between night and day, and that she could flower whenever she pleased. She put out bloom after bloom, even though no one ever saw the fruit of her labours.'

'That required great courage,' says Gosse.

'Bet she grew a few thorns too,' says Benson.

'Oh, enormous ones,' says Em.

She wasn't in her right mind. That's what the world thought. Em's unstrung chatter, the high, huffing talk about moonlight and thorns and roses when there wasn't a rose to be seen in the whole garden: yes, this is how a woman would sound who was mad. Only she wasn't mad. That fool, Benson, leading her on in his chirpy aesthete's voice that produced such unnerving effects in ordinary conversation. Thinking her as great a fool as he.

'Ah, it's a case of Ovid's *saepe creat molles aspera spina rosas*,' says Benson. '"Often the prickly thorn produces tender roses." A charming parable.'

'It's no such thing,' says Em. 'It's just a story about plants, like my husband's poem "The Ivy-Wife".' After a moment she adds, 'Are you married, Mr Benson?'

'Alas, no. I've never been lucky enough to meet the right companion. Our young Cambridge women are so worldly. So energetic. So, well – *female*.' He bends adroitly, mischievously, kisses her hand. 'I envy Mr Hardy his domestic happiness. You understand that an uneventful home life is essential to the work of creation.'

'I don't know about that. He gives me no credit for my part in it.'

'Naturally he couldn't have achieved greatness without you. It must be a tremendous source of pride to you to know that you have ministered to his daily comfort all these years. You have allowed him to write, free from any distractions. You have been the handmaid to genius.'

'Handmaid.' Emma exhales long and hard on the word. 'We women have been sacrificed for ages to men. The absurd idea kept up by you all, which has so far been humbly accepted by us, is that your manhood is a much higher state than a woman's womanhood.'

Benson seems to snigger. 'Then I hope you will be quick to correct us, Mr Hardy included.'

'Oh, I am,' says Emma. 'I always beat my husband in the mornings.'

'Beat him!' titters Benson.

'Yes. But only with a rolled-up copy of *The Times*. It's very suitable for the purpose. That paper also spouts a great deal of nonsense, don't you think?' She taps Benson playfully on the shoulder. 'Be careful, or I'll be coming after you with it.'

'My dear Mrs Hardy,' Benson chuckles, 'you are a person with quite, ah, singular ideas.'

'Well, I write myself, you know. Poetry and reflective prose, mostly. In fact I have been working on a little thing this last year. Some recollections.'

'In that case you could be Mr Hardy's biographer. You must know him better than anyone.'

'I scarcely think so. I'm not much of a fiction writer. And most biographies are fiction, I find.'

Some recollections. He puts his hands over his eyes, dazed by a flash of pain. All those silent hours, those days and nights while he worked in his study and avoided Emma and they managed not to speak, she was busy writing her memoir in the attic above him.

Oh, but she was writing well before that, he thinks. *She'd been setting down her version of our marriage in those damned diaries of hers for the last twenty years.*

Try as he might, he can't reconcile this thorny, diary-writing Emma with the writer of the memoir. That writer remembered – with impersonal tenderness, with sure-footed rapture! – opening the door of his life to him. *That* writer was aware of the warring versions of Tom and Em. But she'd accepted all that had gone wrong, the man he'd failed to become, and cherished the rest. In the very act of writing she'd managed to escape to a place where such generosity was possible.

How these two Emmas could exist in the same person is a mystery to him.

Yet isn't he also made up of two people, one suffering and experiencing, the other observing, distanced – capable, when he's able to maintain that distance, of being something more than himself?

Why, yes. Yes, of course. He's a writer. In his marriage to Em he was *the* writer. He never took her little forays into poetry or prose seriously, never thought for a minute that she could travel that stony road, or perform the same magic. The journey was his to make.

In the end she'd got there by herself.

He glares at the pen in his hand. *What did you really want, Em? Did you want me* not *to write?* The idea is so outrageous that he thrusts his letter aside in a blur of confusion. *You might as well ask me not to exist.*

He's too troubled by the thought to stay seated. Pulling on his overcoat and boots in the hall he wanders out of the front door, turning impulsively at the corner of the house towards the nut walk. Behind the boundary wall he can see the hilltop trees of Conygar outlined against a fading moon, still visible between gusts of morning cloud. There's a quick wind blowing, a speckle of rain. All that life, continuing.

He faces into the wind, breathing deeply. He doesn't know why he was born, or, having been thought a stillbirth, why he lived. *But at least writing has given me a reason to inhabit my patch of earth. I could never have given it up. If that's what you were hoping for, my dear wife, you may as well have asked me to pluck that moon from the sky.*

Shadows chase across the face of the Druid stone at the far edge of the lawn. It's mired at the foot in wet leaves that cling to it like black kisses. The hazel in the alley whistles as it battles with itself; the ash hisses amid its quiverings; the beech rustles while its boughs rise and fall. He can hear a thrush singing, two thrushes. These are brand-new birds, sprung from nowhere. Twelve months ago they were only particles of grain, and earth, and air – and rain. It's always raining.

Why do you call me out here? I've said I'm sorry. I can't undo what's done. His frantic strides have taken him around the perimeter of the wall to the brink of Emma's vegetable garden. In its wintry dissolution it looks more like a spoil-pit or some abominable workshop, a dark disfigurement in the earth, than a prized feature. The verges of the beds are littered with parts of things that once thrived and now lie cut down, cylindrical, hollow, their vegetal tubes exposed in sagging heaps. Smoke, drawn by the breeze, spirals from the remains of a fire. *I'm nothing. You've had your say. I've admitted my part in it all. Leave me alone. I'm a pinch of dust, of mud, of ash.*

'Hello, mister.' There's a child squatting in one of the ragged beds, turning the clods over with a stick. In spite of the cold he is wearing short trousers. He's a small lad, all bones, his skin pearled with the pressure of the skeleton within. His nose is running. 'Hello,' says the boy again, rubbing it on the back of his hand.

'Hello.' He pulls himself up. He's never seen this child before. 'What are you working at?' he asks.

'I'm making a garden.'

'Well, now,' he says, striving for calm, for the proper note of authority. 'It may be too late in the year for planting.'

'I be'n't planting. I'm making.'

'I thought in gardens planting *was* making.'

'Nah. Grandfer says we's to dig us a proper bed first, or things won't grow's they should.' The child holds out a spare stick. He has several, collected for the purpose. 'Yer, 'ee can take a turn.'

He balances on his haunches. 'What do we do?'

'We chuck it over.'

They jab at the mud for a while. The cold earth falls away in shapeless folds. The boy, he notes, is abstracted. He sits in the dirt primly, almost fastidiously. He's scarcely even in the world. His stooped shoulders, his legs, his thin grey hands, his face, long to be out of it. Only his brain, concealed behind that gleaming forehead, continues to conspire against him, to plot for life. His cap, casually upended like a beggar's cap, is set at a slight distance from his feet. He wonders if the child is slow.

'We're not getting very far,' he says by and by. 'Where's your grandad? Where's Sam Trevis?'

At the mention of his name Trevis steps out onto the lawn from the nearby shed. 'Run along,' he says to the boy. 'Go on, go to the kitchen.'

The child wanders off with the same dreamy air: pearlescent, deathly, leaving his cap on the ground.

He picks up the cap and hands it to Trevis.

'I'm sorry, sir,' says Trevis, giving the fire a poke. 'My daughter's boy. He seems to dwell on a different star to the rest o' us. His mother's poorly wi' a swelling to her throat and I'm minding him today. I'll see to it that he don't get in your way.'

He inspects Trevis: his ruddy complexion and obliquely slanting cheekbones, his smiling eyes above a sad mouth. Trevis is tall and knotted, still young and firm-fleshed enough to be his own son. Yet he's a grandfather. 'How old is the lad?' he asks.

'He'll be seven come June.'

He feels it even now, the tack and drag of those last few clods of earth. He studies Trevis again. There's a delicacy, a sureness to him, in spite of his bulk. *A different star.* It's a good phrase.

'Can't your wife look after him?' he says.

'I'm a widower, sir.'

He hadn't the slightest idea. 'He's not in my way. I hope your girl gets her health back soon. Shall I ask Dr Gowring to call on her? There will be no expense in it for you.'

Though Trevis stands before him cap in hand, it's difficult to imagine anyone appearing less like the recipient of charity. 'Thank 'ee, sir,' he says. 'I'm heartily sorry 'bout Miss'ess Hardy.'

He flinches at the slicing impress of that gaze. Yes, Trevis is regarding him with keen interest. This man with the death's-head grandson and the ailing daughter. Trevis is looking at him as if he were simple, with pity, as well he might.

He casts around for something to praise in the heaps of dirt, the decayed greens. At the lip of the vegetable patch there's a sturdy, smooth-skinned rose, readying itself to put out its buttons come spring. 'That's a nice thing,' he says. 'Healthy.' Really, the rose is obscenely hale; it almost seems to tremble along its stalk. Then it comes to him. Onions and roses. *Down far in the earth, hidden its worth.* 'There's a bloody onion buried with it, isn't there?' he says.

''Tis a pretty country notion, sir,' says Trevis, 'and I've nothing agean it. Putting a bulb at the root strengthens the stock, and the rose gives vigour to the inon. See?' He crouches, plunges his thumbs into the mud, and reveals a bearded globe.

'Was this your idea?'

'No, sir. Miss'ess Hardy bade me plant it back-along.'

'I never knew.' How he hates it, suddenly, hates it with all his being, this country imprecision. This man must have a calendar somewhere, like every other modern man. Yet possibly he doesn't. He knows nothing about Trevis, either. 'When, exactly?' he asks.

'Let me see now. In September, maybe. We'd already had our first frost. It was poor weather for setting roses, but I was minded to humour her. She was that fixed upon't.'

His heart swerves from its beat. 'Well, perhaps there's some truth in the superstition. This bush doesn't appear to have done too badly.'

'Ay.' Trevis nods at him with grim good humour. 'And they do say that love can never endure where there's a garden without a rose growing.'

'Do they now?'

'Yes, sir. See, Miss'ess Hardy was right enough. The miss'ess always is.' His kindness and his pity are unmistakable. 'Leastways, that's the way it was with mine.'

A Visitor

HE KNOWS, WITHOUT BEING told, where he must go. Up
he climbs, up, all the way to the attic. He's been looking
in the wrong place. He isn't looking for forgiveness, but for love.
He sets his hand on the brass lock of Emma's bedroom and opens
the door.

She's there. She stoops to turn up the lamp, so that the shadow
of her head is thrown onto the ceiling and wall. The light shines
through the curls around her temples. He can see the pulse jumping
in her neck.

His breath snags, then rushes out, shocking him with its force. She
is as solid, as real, as she ever was in the early days of their married
life together. Time closes up before him like a fan. He seems to be
travelling very fast, over a great distance.

It's you, Em. Is it really you?

He's in Sturminster again, walking on the banks of the Stour.
He's crossed the river by the iron bridge and is coming up between
the trees. It's early evening, the moon just rising, but the posts and
walls and roads of the town still fling back their sense of the hot-
faced sun. He walks quickly, following the water. There is the dusky

house, standing apart. Black bats flit across the sky, whirring like the wheels of ancient clocks.

Em is waiting in the porch, wearing a white muslin dress with a tea rose pinned to the breast, her hair lit up by the blaze of the lantern. Through the open door he can hear the tinny playing of the musical box he bought her from a Rouen street seller while they were on their honeymoon.

Au clair de la lune,
Mon ami Pierrot,
Prête-moi ta plume,
Pour écrire un mot.

She's seen him. She's laughing. You're back, she calls. She bubbles and fizzes with delight. Oh, there you are.

Yes. He smiles. *I'm back. Here I am.*

In those years they lived at the edge of Sturminster Newton in the Blackmore Vale, twenty miles away, in a semi-detached house separated from the town by grass and grazing sheep. The Stour flowed past them at the bottom of a steep slope. The house was named, of course, Riverside Villa, and the name seemed not trite to him then, but romantic. There was a shared garden with a monkey-puzzle and a climbing rose; a pump that stuttered. The house faced west over the riverside path, the river at its foot and the water meadows beyond.

Every evening as he sat in his study he was electrified by the sunsets firing up the sky, like some vast foundry where new worlds were being cast. At dusk, after his work was done, he walked along the water. When he came home and looked up she was always there.

The hopefulness of that time! This kind of passionate hope is a property of youth. And yet he's heavy with guilt at having outlived it. *I'm fickle*, he thinks. But surely fickleness means getting weary of a thing while the thing remains the same.

Am I what you want, Emmie? This old man? If you want that other me, I'm afraid he's dead.

Oh, my love, she says. My own love. It doesn't matter. Come in.

She's here in white. Not pearl, or apricot, or plum. Not the colours of the after-sunset. She's here, as at the beginning of Creation. At the time they thought of that quickened period as nothing. They considered those days merely the prelude to better things to come – to their real life. They didn't realize that this was happiness.

Should I have stopped writing, Em? How would we have managed?

Don't mind that now, she says. Let's be comfortable.

I must fix that pump, he says. *I've been meaning to do it all week.*

Not tonight. Isn't this better? Sit down. You must be very tired.

He takes off one boot, then the other. He sits on the bed, heart racing. *Yes*, he says. *I'm rather tired.*

Tired of work.

Of work, yes.

But not too tired.

No, no.

He stretches out on the mattress. How flat this attic bed is, with its lacquered iron frame. It's a maid's bed, a girl's. Through the dormer window he can see the ghostly outline of the lingering daytime moon (or is it the evening moon at Sturminster?), the tops of the pines. The musical box is still playing its thin mechanic tune.

> *Ma chandelle est morte,*
> *Je n'ai plus de feu.*
> *Ouvre-moi ta porte,*
> *Pour l'amour de Dieu.*

Where are you, Em?
   I'm here with you, she says.

It happened long ago, but it isn't long ago. By the moon's sickly light it is still happening. In that other life Em lies on their bed beside him in the dusk. He faces her, blind with fear and longing, and puts out his hands. She's sheathed in her white dress. Its muslin panels are as weightless as air, parting at his touch like the wings of a scarab. They peel away until her body is bare. Her strong young shoulders are bare. Her stomach and thighs are bare and silvered. Her crackling hair is loose about his face. It's in his mouth. She's curled under him, or he is raised over her, trying to find her.

   'I love you, Tom,' she says. 'Do you love me?'

   'My Emmie,' he says. The moon has grown and looms at the window-square, only part of a moon, the curve sliced off its cheek by an adze. Emma's arms are around his waist. He meets the fierce kiss of her skin. His heart is too burdened, his body too wracked with effort, for speech. He feels as if every point of his flesh is being driven towards hers.

'Now,' she says, 'now. Please, now.'

Yes, now.

But his fervour fails. He's unable to close the angle between them. This was love: the woman waiting, the light on her hair. The pressure of her touch. But also this was love, the striving and failing.

As he hangs over her in agony, in a tangle of dread, something falls sheer, and crashes. They peer into the moonlit room. Everything is suddenly hard and bright. The new looking-glass that's been standing on the mantel, waiting for them to hang it up, has fallen to the floor. In a moment Em is out of bed, kneeling under the moon's sly ray, gathering the shards.

'Let it be, Emmie.'

'But a broken mirror is bad luck!'

'Nonsense. That's a silly old superstition. Come back to bed, my darling.' Though he speaks bravely he hears the fear sawing in his throat, the insane dry voice of terror. She's in the bed, crushed against him. Her limbs are cold. 'I'm sorry, Em,' he says.

'What is it? Is it me? Have I done something wrong?'

'No, of course not.'

He can feel her shivering all along his length. In a small voice she asks, 'Will we ever have children, Tom?'

'We will, I'm sure. In time. Please just give me time.' He tries to clasp her hand, but she pulls it away. 'You're more than I deserve,' he says.

'When you say that, I feel sad.'

'So do I. And I want to make you happy always — today and forever.'

Em rolls onto her back. 'Oh, Tom. You want so much.'

'I want very little. I feel as if I haven't enough staying power to hold my own in the world. He's looking at her face in profile: her set jaw and compressed lip with its upward thrust, the tilt of her forehead, half hidden by her hair. 'I'm afraid that you'll come to realize you've made a mistake in marrying me,' he says.

'That can never happen.' She turns and raises herself on her elbow. 'Never. I promise.'

'Don't promise, Emmie, or you may have reason to regret it.'

'Well, I do have a regret, already,' she says.

'What do you regret?'

'Only that our romance has come to an end.'

'All romances end at marriage, my love.'

She's as quiet as the moonlight on the boughs of the trees. She lowers her face and puts her mouth to his ear. 'I don't believe that, and nor do you. Tell me what you believe.'

'Oh, Emmie.'

'Go on. *Tell me*. "I believe."'

'All right.' He kisses her shoulder. 'I believe.'

'In my books.'

He kisses her collar bone. 'In my books.'

'In my gift.'

'This is ridiculous.'

'*Say* it.'

He kisses her chin. 'In my gift.'

'And in Emma, my wife.'

'And in you, Emmie.' He kisses her lips. 'You're the best gift of all.'

'I am. Now sleep.'

*

He folds her in his arms. He will hold her here forever. But she is already leaving. In her place is the darkness of her going, unconcerned and indifferent; the darkness which has already swallowed up his happiness, and is now digesting it listlessly, and is ready at any moment to swallow up the happiness of tens of millions of other people with as little disturbance. Everything will die. Everything will be forgotten. He can feel sorrow welling up in him, avid and obliterating.

Don't go, Emmie. As he clutches at her she twists in his hands. Her eyes are shiny with reproach. It's he, after all, not she, who is going, taken from her by something he can't control.

Weren't we happy back then, Em? he asks. *Weren't we?*

I was happy, she says.

Alone in his room that night he lights a candle and picks up his pen to finish his letter to Gosse. He follows the sounds of the house as it gets ready for sleep: the extinguishing of its lamps and pulling down of its blinds and the closing of its many doors, like the dismantling of an inconsequential stage set.

Hour by hour the world has been returning to him in its inescapable humdrum dimensions. He stares at his meagre limbs, his arms wrapped in their frayed shawl. It's still windy outside, though the moon has vanished.

When we walked together in the garden in September I couldn't see, my dear friend, that my time with Emma was limited. It has all run out. Love, youth. There was a finite amount of it and it's gone. I've used it up. What a bitter thing this is, that we can only learn the lessons we need to live our life by consuming its material.

In the past we've often talked about the craft of writing. Of course unlike you I'm no critic, and we haven't always agreed. You've always seemed to me admirably, even classically certain of the proper proportions of things, whereas I – well, let's just say that you've been the Roman to my – I'm not sure what. Something rougher, at any rate. Woad-covered savage, perhaps. Briton hacking at his stone. Hodge, with his mallet and chisel.

Writing a story generates so much waste. Even I, working with my crude tools, used to believe that what matters is getting rid of irrelevant details in order better to reveal some sort of essential shape. I was wrong, Edmund. The universe is chaotic. Time as we like to think of it does not exist. The interruption, the apparently extraneous event, is the significant one. That's where my attention should have been all along.

He raises his head, startled by a sudden blurt of wind in the darkness. It swells and subsides with a boom, like the note of a gigantic one-stringed harp.

I've never told you about a strange encounter I had twenty years ago. If I haven't done so before, it's because I didn't know, till now, what to make of it.

In those days I felt that a story must be curious enough to justify its telling; that none of us is warranted in stopping the hurrying public unless he has something more unusual to relate than the ordinary experience of every average man and woman. The whole secret of fiction, I thought, lies in distinguishing between the meaningful and the merely universal. The writer who understands exactly how exceptional or unexceptional his material is possesses the key to the art.

But I've come to see that there are moments in our existence which resist interpretation at the time. They look like digressions in the story we're constructing about our life. We only discover their importance much later. If we're very unlucky, too late.

It wasn't long after I'd published *Tess*. Emma resented that book. She resented me for writing it, for the fame it brought me. And I resented her – for standing in my way, for inserting herself into my dream, where she didn't belong.

One morning I was alone here at Max Gate. Em and I were in a sour humour with each other and she'd gone out straight after breakfast to pay a call. It was, I remember, an autumn day. The wind was up, just as it is tonight. I had the beginnings of a new novel in hand and again felt the impossibility, which always used to depress me while writing fiction, of getting anything resembling my original vision down on paper. I was sitting at my table with my shawl around my shoulders and the manuscript in front of me when our maid announced a visitor.

It's November, 1893. The wind is flailing the house corners, shaking the eaves and sending draughts scuttling over the threshold. There's a knock, followed by a creeping slice of light.

Molly appears in the crack of the door. She folds her arms, at once apologetic and obstinate. 'Sir,' she says, 'there's a person here to see you.'

'It isn't calling time,' he says. 'You know that.'

'Yes, sir. But there's a *person*.'

He senses a mystery. 'What sort of person?'

'I can't rightly say.'

'Well, is it a lady or a gentleman?'

'It's a man, sir. A man with hair black as – as boot polish.'

'As boot polish, eh? How is he dressed?'

'Very respectable, sir. A good suit. Also black.'

Respectable. He glances at his working corduroys. *Not like me, then*, he thinks. 'But?'

'But there's som'at about his . . . his countenance an' manner o' speaking, sir.'

'He's an American?'

'No, sir.'

Ah, he thrills. *A real foreigner.* 'Should I change, do you think, Molly?'

'You better had, sir.'

When he gets downstairs he realizes that he's still carrying his shawl. It's too late to go back up the stairs now.

He hangs the shawl over his arm and proceeds to the drawing room. It's oddly quiet, as if the wind has turned tail and run. As soon as he crosses the threshold he sees that he's in the presence of someone quite alien to him. His visitor is standing with his back to the grate, arms braced behind his buttocks. Though he's dressed from head to foot in western clothes of the deepest shade of mourning, it's apparent that he's not an Italian, a Frenchman, a Spaniard, nor even a Greek.

Removing his hat, the stranger bows. Molly was wrong. His hair isn't black, quite, but flecked at the crown with grey. 'Mr Thomas Hardy.' His voice is light and melodious. 'I am honoured to make your acquaintance. My name is Bān Qiáojí.'

'How d'you do.' He returns the bow with some clumsiness. 'I think, possibly, you aren't from Dorset?'

His visitor smiles. His smile is utterly devoid of irony. 'You are quite right. I have travelled all the way from my home in Shanghai to speak to you.'

'Your English is excellent.'

'Thank you. I've been a lover of English literature my whole life.'

Oh, God. *Literature.* 'Now, then – I haven't much time. Have you come for an autograph? If you'd be kind enough to pass me the book I'll write a message in it for you.'

'I have no book. I seek your advice on my story.'

'I don't give advice on other people's fiction, I'm afraid,' he says.

'Not fiction, Mr Thomas Hardy. A true story.'

'Are you some sort of journalist?'

The stranger gives him a look of frank horror. 'Oh, no. I am a murderer.'

'Good Lord.' He wonders whether he should ring, or run away. But curiosity gets the better of him. 'In that case,' he says, 'perhaps you should sit down. I can spare you a quarter of an hour.' He takes out his pocket watch and settles into his armchair. As an afterthought he wraps his shawl around him. 'I'm listening. Please start whenever you're ready.'

'This is most generous of you, sir,' says the stranger. He indicates the chair opposite. 'May I sit here?'

'Please do. I'm afraid I am unable to offer you any refreshment. I'm just an ordinary day-labourer, and these are my working hours.'

His guest smiles artlessly. 'I don't need refreshment. Your frank opinion is meat and drink to me.' He places his hat on a side table, tugs at the knees of his trousers, sits with the airy precision that characterizes all his actions.

In his pleasant voice he begins. 'My story is as follows. I am, as I have mentioned, a native of Shanghai. My family has lived in our old walled city for many generations. My father traded in cloth, like his father before him. Shortly after my thirtieth birthday he died, leaving me his business and his twenty boats. His last wish was that I should marry well. He had already chosen my bride. She was beautiful and belonged to a good family, far better connected than mine, which had fallen on hard times.'

'You are about to introduce a complication, I suspect.'

'You are a master story-teller, sir. My wife-to-be suffered from poor health.'

He fears he may have come across as abrupt and inhospitable – though if this man really is a murderer, that might be the least of his problems. 'I'm sorry to hear that,' he says.

'A childhood illness had left her with a weak heart. Still, she was the most elegant and ambitious woman I'd ever met. The match was advantageous to us both.'

'What was her name? In a story we must have names.'

'Xīnhán. In Chinese that means "bitterly disappointed".'

'Oh, dear.'

'Yes. After our marriage she came to live with me in my home on the Little East Gate. The house was built by my grandfather. It was enclosed by high walls and had a peaked tile roof and a courtyard, where we kept pigs and a chicken or two, leading onto a kitchen with a coal stove. The back was a patchwork of corridors and offices. My father was born there, lived there, and died there. I was born there, and had grown up there. Yet no sooner had I married than I must needs build a new one. My wife could not live in a merchant's house. She said that she couldn't stand the smell of the river.'

'You built her another, I expect.'

'I did, as far inland as I could manage, near the French concession. A square villa in the latest style, with a brick veranda and a garden planted with palms. Xīnhán named it Château Montigny. No sooner was the mortar dry than she set about cultivating our foreign neighbours. She had, she claimed, some French blood on her mother's side.'

'Most useful.'

'Oh, indeed. Our walls were covered with oils of spaniels and flying geese. At our parties we served oysters and Chablis instead of hairy crab and *huángjiǔ*. Within a few years she had made for me every connection I'd so far wanted and failed to make. We dined at the Hôtel des Colonies. We bought a brougham and attended performances of the Société Dramatique Française. We went to the racecourse with the British consul, whose French wasn't half as good as hers.'

'Too much circumstantial detail, Mr . . .'

'Mr Bān.'

'Less is more.'

Mr Bān blinks. 'Less detail, yes.' Giving the creases of his trouser legs a pinch, he continues. 'My profits had never been higher. But apart from an interest in making money, Xīnhán and I had nothing in common. We hated each other. We'd been married for over a decade, and we had no children. All attempts at reconciliation were hopeless.'

'That was a great pity.'

'It was intolerable. I began to spend as little time as possible at the house. Once my day's business was done, my steps often took me along the river to the harbour, where I would watch the lanterns being lit on the darkening wharf, and my own name occasionally greeted me from the walls of the warehouses.' A pause, not unhopeful. 'Will you allow me the lanterns?'

He bites his thumb, weighing things up. 'If I must.'

'While I stood there one evening,' his visitor says, 'I was surprised to see, coming towards me, a woman I'd known long ago, the daughter of the captain of one of my father's brigs. When I was a young man I'd admired her, but our marrying had been out of the question. I discovered that she now lived in a lane close to the Western Gate.

'I was embarrassed by this chance meeting but the girl, whose name was Lìxuě, seemed delighted to see me. She asked me to take tea with her for old times' sake, and her manners were so modest and simple that I felt it would be discourteous to refuse. Her apartment consisted of a single room with a canary roosting in a cage and a table where she painted flowers, by candlelight, on pieces of silk. Her father had died some years before, and this is how she kept herself.'

'I like the canary. Go on.'

'Following this encounter I often found myself turning into Hóng-zhuāng Nòng in the evenings to visit Lìxuě. As she sat over her painting and the bird fluttered against the bars of its cage we would talk of those we used to know in common. It was a relief to be myself again, and to remember days gone by in my father's house, and all our past dreams.

'Lìxuě didn't have two *wén* to her name, and no social standing to speak of, but it didn't matter. After I'd been calling on her in this way for three or four months, I realized that I was in love.'

He consults his watch. 'Six more minutes.'

'My story is nearly done,' says his guest. 'Shall I jump to the end?'

'Yes,' he says. 'Onwards. No further interruptions.'

'One day Xīnhán came home from the bathhouse where she spent her afternoons, and went straight to her bed. I saw that she was tired, but I was feeling angry and dissatisfied with our life together. That very evening Lìxuě had warned me, with tears in her eyes, that my visits had been remarked on by her landlady, and that, old friend or not, she thought it best I should stop calling on her.

'I followed my wife to the bedroom and stood there for some time staring at her motionless form. From the window I fancied I could see the lights of the wharf, and a ribbon of smoke rising from the lane where Lìxuě would, I knew, be lighting her fire to prepare her *cháhú* of tea. When Xīnhán began to complain that my hanging about the room kept her from resting, and to abuse me, as usual, for not thinking of her health, I told her that I wished she were dead. I said that I didn't care what happened to her as she was already nothing more than a corpse to me.

'We began to argue. It was the most vicious argument we'd ever had. My wife said that she'd known for a while that I consorted with the lowest kind of prostitutes and that so far she'd held her tongue only out of a sense of duty. She was going to return to her family at once, and I, son of pigs, could crawl back to the pigsty where I belonged.

'I said that she was a liar and that she was welcome to go. She said that she could prove it: she'd had me followed for several weeks, and knew where the *yāoèr* lived. She shrieked that she would expose my doings to all our foreign friends and that when I was revealed for the peasant I really was, no one in society would have me in their homes again.

'As she howled at me Xīnhán's distorted features turned red, and her brow appeared to burn beneath her lacquered hair. In the middle of this tirade she seized hold of her left breast, which swung loose, slack and veined, from the silk fold of her *zhōngyī*. She'd suffered bad turns before and I was immediately sorry I'd been the cause of this one.

'I told her to keep steady, and tried to put my arm around her, but she struck out in a frenzy. Then she fell back on the bed and lay there, gasping. Though her eyes were wide open she no longer seemed to see me. In the next moment her breath grew shallow and fitful, and rattled to a halt.

'I placed my hand on her chest. I thought that once in a while a faint movement disturbed its stillness – starting up for a few seconds and struggling to go on, then breaking down and stopping again. I knew that I should call the servants, raise the alarm, summon the doctor.

'I also knew that I could free myself of Xīnhán merely by doing nothing and letting nature take its course. So that is what I did – nothing. Perhaps five minutes later she let out a rumbling sigh, without closing her eyes. I sat by the bed for a long time, watching for any further signs of life, but none came. My wife was dead.'

His visitor inhales deeply. 'So you see, sir, I killed her. Or I let her die. There is no difference. And now, Mr Hardy, I need you to advise me.'

'I'm not sure I understand.'

'I used to believe myself a good man, but that's no longer possible. For the last two years I've been tormented with guilt and desire. I've mourned my late wife with every due observance, but I still think of Lìxuě. Needless to say, Xīnhán's threats were entirely empty ones. No one has ever discovered the true circumstances of her death. I haven't been punished in any way for my disgraceful failure, either as a husband or as a human being. I've continued to move in the highest circles, and my business has prospered.'

'What precisely is your question?'

'My question is: do I dare marry the woman I love, in spite of my crime, and enjoy whatever happiness might be left to me? Wouldn't that be an even worse offence?'

He shuts the case of his pocket watch. 'I can't answer it.'

'You can. Forgive me for contradicting you. You will please imagine my astonishment and relief when I came across your books, and saw that you had already written my story.'

'But I've never met you before.'

'That only proves that you have a knowledge of the workings of fate denied to other men.'

'I'm afraid I don't know what you're talking about.'

'I am referring to your story about Mr Barnet.'

'Did I write a story about someone called Barnet?'

'You did. You must remember. Mr Barnet, the flax merchant. First name, George.'

'George.'

'Mr George Barnet, yes, of Port-Bredy.'

He thrusts the watch back into his trouser pocket. 'Mr Bān, no such person as George Barnet has ever existed. Port-Bredy does not exist. If there are fleeting similarities between that foolish old tale of mine and your experience, then they are purely coincidental. I can't advise you.'

'But you, sir, know about life.'

'I really don't. I don't know the first thing about it.'

'That can't be. You have written many stories.'

'I know about stories, yes. But stories are not life.' His guest looks so defeated that he feels he must offer him something. 'The truth is that I've never been very good at life. Death left me in this world by accident.'

'It's my turn now to say that I don't understand.'

'When I was born I was blue all over. The doctor attending my mother pronounced me dead. I was tossed on a heap of rags in a corner of the room. But then the excellent woman who delivered me saw that I breathed, and wrapped me in my mother's shawl.' He fingers the wool around his shoulders. 'This one,' he says.

'May I touch it?'

'Well. Why not.' He steels himself not to shy away as his visitor extends a hand and lays it reverently on the shawl. 'I keep it with me to remind me that I'm as much alive as the next fellow,' he goes on. 'But frankly, I often feel I've never got the knack of living.'

'Still, Mr Hardy, you are here.'

'Yes. Here I am. I don't know if I have much more to say.' He's risen to his feet, and is on the point of ushering the interloper quietly to the door, when he changes his mind. 'Perhaps I do have something more to say, Mr Bān,' he concedes, overcome by a steep swell of weariness. 'I hate these visits, these intrusions into my day. Why do my readers think that they can interrupt my work on the smallest whim? Why do you all insist on treating my characters as if they were actual people? What could I conceivably have to tell you about murder, or love, or anything else? Everybody dies. I don't know any more about it than you do.

'Let me tell you what being a writer is like. It's like climbing a mountain. Every time you're nearly at the top, you lose your footing and fall to the bottom, and you have to begin again. You do your best. You climb and climb. And you always fail. At least, that's what I've found. I want just one thing: to be left alone to fail.' He's listed a little during this speech, like a skiff battling a wave. He feels spent. 'Do you truly believe that you killed your wife?'

'Yes.'

'Then I'm very sorry for you.'

Bān Qiáojí bows. 'And I am sorry for you, Mr Thomas Hardy. Everybody dies, but not everybody lives.'

He's been writing without stopping, and now he finishes his letter in a few swift paragraphs.

I'm ashamed, my dear Gosse, that I hadn't a single word of comfort to give that man, and that what he said meant nothing to me. Back then I thought of his story only as a story – a rather badly told story, the worst sort of over-embellished *literary* story, at that. It never occurred to me that just as my story was his, his might, in time, become mine.

We talk about marriage as a final state, safe harbour, in which we'll be protected from our darker urges. From doubt and suffering, and our own destructiveness. It's the natural, indeed the only ending our world writes for an honest love. Yet even honest men will, in extremity, deliberate indefensible actions. Not acting on temptation doesn't mean that we escape our longings. I'm not even a particularly good man. Who am I to judge?

I loved Emma when I married her. I know I did. And she loved me. We had such hope. But somewhere in our years together we became antagonists, sucking at the same dry soil, clawing over the same few inches of ground, until I felt that one of us had to fall if the other was to survive. Towards the end I believed that only her death would set me free.

It was an illusion, of course – the wild hope and the anger and the antagonism – all an illusion. If only I'd known earlier that these things had nothing to do with our actual selves! If only I'd taken a few days or months to notice Em as she really was, to allow myself to forgive her for falling short of my dream, to re-imagine her, I would have saved us both a great deal of sadness. Instead I turned away and behaved as if my real life lay elsewhere. And now I can't escape this knowledge: that at the very least love asks only that we don't avert our gaze, that we continue to *see*.

With Emma's dying it's as if an essential part of me has died too. I've written about suffering but suddenly I find that I don't understand it. It's terrible that pain can seem remote, even absurd, to all except the person feeling it. I've tried for so long to say that the world is like this, or like that, to insist on what I thought was worthwhile, and to ignore the rest. I thought that my work as a writer was the true story, and that everyone else's part in it, even Emma's, was a diversion. A distraction. I betrayed her in every possible way, Edmund, but most of all by behaving as if I, and what I'd set out to accomplish, were somehow separate from her. Unique.

How arrogant I was. If you look beneath the surface of any farce you see a tragedy. And if you blind yourself to the deeper facts of a tragedy you see a farce. Better not to attempt a distinction. Better to keep silent.

When I was younger I used to read the Greek and Latin poets. In their verses the dead stream to the shores of the Acheron like autumn leaves, like birds in flight. They are the shadows of themselves, mere ashes. These writers know what they are for. They must fan the embers of an old fire back to life. I can't do it any more. Words fail me. So much went unspoken between Emma and me. I want to get away from whatever words we used, and nearer to what we really meant.

Yours ever,

Thomas Hardy

As he lies in bed at midnight, half awake, the wind begins to rise up again, buffeting the windows. The panes quake. He drifts in the dark, listening to the crying trees. *Our life together wasn't a fiction, Em*, he thinks. *It was real, all of it. Every fanciful and unlikely thing. Our essences, our very selves, didn't change. You were real. I was real.*

In the same instant he feels the slightest touch on his palm. He won't look. He won't unvision what might be there. But his fingers close on something cold and frail, already turning to dust. He opens his eyes. A dry leaf from the old beech has blown into the room and settled itself on the sheet.

'Emmie,' he says, turning his face to the pillow, 'I thought it was you. I thought you'd come to tell me that at last you know.'

Mary

IN HIS DREAM THAT night he's standing beneath the ruin on the cliff. He lingers on the blowing sands and hears the shades on the distant bank, calling faintly. They are in plum, apricot, pearl, revolving like a crowd of dancers. He's distracted by their wan cries, by the warmth from the dying day, the touch of an arid wind on his cheek. Their skirts make a fitful phosphorescence at the edges of his vision. There's a figure advancing towards him, its contours vague; a field of blue reddened by a declining sun.

She's come. Her hair is gold, her skin is gold. She's of one piece with the air, its gold-blue undersurface. He goes to meet her, brimming high with joy. Only for a moment.

He's woken by a tapping on the pane of his room. Is it the rain? But it isn't raining now, and the wind has died down. *Emma.* He gets out of bed and stumbles to the window. All he sees is his own face hanging in the dark. Behind it a silvery shape bangs at the glass and is gone.

He clings to the sill, holding on with all his strength. He can't stand much more of this: his dead house, these dreams. Florence may think he's ill, but this isn't illness. It isn't anything.

'Mary,' he says aloud. 'Please help me.'

He will go to Bockhampton to see Mary. He'll go now. He pulls on his old corduroys and makes his way downstairs carrying his boots, still clogged with garden mud. On a peg beside the back door he finds a waterproof he doesn't recognize, and a wide-brimmed straw hat of the kind his father used to wear. They'll do. Once he's dressed he slips out through the side gate and hurries along the lane. Minutes later he's on the path leading to the railway bridge.

His footsteps send a cloud of moths swirling from the undergrowth into the air. He watches them as they rise into the thinning night, marvelling, briefly uplifted, as one might feel uplifted at witnessing a migration of souls. He has escaped. He's free.

Viewed from the bridge the modern town with its lit lamps appears smartly defined yet also undeniably trivial, its intersecting streets thrown like a net of fireflies across the dim outline of the past. Turning his back on Dorchester he starts to walk out past the mill, beneath the low barrows crowned with trees before and behind, crossing the crinkled waters of the Frome. In summer the current runs clear as the River of Life over pebbly shallows, rapid as the shadow of a cloud. In the pre-dawn, swollen by the recent rain, it's a lazy tick-ticking among the reeds and grasses of the water meadows where it dawdles towards the weir. After a few miles the rising road brings into view the darkness of the wood surrounding the hamlet of Higher Bockhampton. The tufted birches, the thick-boughed oaks, the creviced elms, together form a flat mass on the sky, in which the last stars flicker so wildly that their agitation is like the flutter of wings.

All around the wood lies the black heath, near relation of the night. In the breaking day the heath looks exactly as it has always looked: stony, pocked with furze. The sea changes, the fields change, rivers, villages and people change, but since prehistory this dimpled waste has never changed: swarthy and imperturbable, unmarked by pickaxe, plough or spade, it still seems to bear the first finger-touches of Creation.

At the very edge of the heath, at the end of a lane smothered in leaves that spill from the ditch on either side, is the little wicket opening onto the garden of the house where he was born. It's a low cottage with a pyramidal thatch broken up by dormer windows and a chimney standing in the very middle. Through the half-open shutters darts of fire- and candlelight reveal bushes of box thronging the walls, and the bare boughs of apple trees above. The creeper-covered doorway is as worn and rubbed by constant friction as a keyhole. He knocks his boots against the door-stone to shake off the mud and bits of leaf sticking to them, gives the door a push, and steps into the porch.

Henry is in the parlour, blending something in a kettle over the fire. It's rumoured in the village below that one of his eccentricities is to perform woman's work, even down to the baking of bread and cakes. He's never seen this till now, though he's long suspected that his brother, left to himself, has reverted to their mother's cottage ways.

'Hello,' he calls out. 'It's only me.'

Henry glances up from his cooking. 'Hello, Tom.' Thickset Hen. Reliable Hen. As ever, his brother betrays no particular emotion at seeing him. Henry is the one person he has never managed either to surprise or impress. 'You're just in time for breakfast. Will 'ee take this to our Mary?'

'What is it?'

'Mutton broth. I've chopped the onions very fine, the way she likes 'em.' Henry takes the kettle off the trivet and reaches for a bowl from the top shelf of the dresser. 'You look a right mommet,' he says, wagging his elbow to show that he should hang his hat and overcoat on the settle peg. 'I'm 'mazed Kate lets you go out like that.'

'She doesn't.'

'How is she? Mary's been asking for her.'

'Oh, you know. She's taken root at Max Gate. It might be difficult to dislodge her.'

Henry's face wrinkles in dismay. 'Try, then, Tom. Mary's pining. She's not eating.' He ladles out a bowlful of soup, wipes the lip with his apron. 'She's like a bloody caged bird. She misses her gaoler.'

'Do birds do that?'

'Oh yes,' says Hen softly, thrusting the bowl into his grasp. 'They do.'

Mary's room over the parlour is stuffy with smoke. An apple-wood fire with a stout branch at the centre belches its heat into the chimney in great puffs.

As children he and Mary used to climb the codlin trees in the orchard, scrambling up limb by limb. Mary's boots were always ahead of him, the striped apples clustered all about like eyes. He'd lose his footing, cry, *Mary!* Mary would turn and put out her hand.

The branch pops as it burns, darkened by soot, its growings all stagnated. Mary is dozing. Her rasping inhalations can be heard above the shattering wood.

'My Mary.' Setting the kettle broth down, he opens the window a crack.

Mary shifts in the bed. 'Tommy. You've come.' Her knuckles on the coverlet are a dreadful freckled blue. She gropes for his hand and tucks it under her chin. Hers is the only human touch he could ever endure. He can feel the wattle of her neck, her racing blood.

He cups his fingers around her face. 'Tell me if you get cold,' he says. 'I had to let in some air.'

'Oh, I'm all right.' She gives his palm a kiss. 'Don't look so sour. Hen's doing his best.'

'So I see. Has the doctor been lately?'

'He never seems to be anywhere else.'

'What's his opinion?'

'He says I've a congestion of the lungs. I might have told him that myself. I'm an old woman, it's the way of things.'

'You're not old.'

'I am, Tommy. You and me both.'

He stirs the broth, setting the transparent fragments of onion whirling like stars. 'I've brought you something to eat. Will you taste a little? I'll help you to sit up.'

'Just to please you, then.' Lifting her is trickier than he expects, because he's afraid of hurting her. Mary sucks the soup slowly through her gums. After a few mouthfuls she pushes the spoon aside and rests her head against the pillow. 'I've been uneasy about you,' she says. 'You've a bad habit of despairing.'

'I'm lost, Mary. I want to go back.'

'Back where?'

'To the past. I feel as if I've never seen things properly before. When I should have been paying attention I've looked away.'

'How do you reckon you're going to do that – go back?'

'By keeping perfectly still,' he says. 'By not moving.'

Mary smiles her mild smile. 'That's a good plan. Let me know if it works.'

He shakes his head. 'Ah, you're making fun of me. Mary, you've always told me the truth. Will you tell it to me now?'

Though her breath is laboured her eyes are bright. 'What is it, Tommy dear?'

'Did you all hate Emma?'

'I never hated her. She was a lovely thing when you first brought her to us. I thought she would bring you life.'

'Did I lack life?' But he knows. 'I did. Mary, I did.'

'She hadn't enough for 'ee, poor lass. She only had enough for herself, and you took that. She wasn't strong enough to stop you. You took it and made a shadow of her. Then it was harder to like her.'

'Oh, dear God.' He bows his head. He can feel the cold air of the December day on his neck. 'What shall I do?'

'You must learn to miss her, Tommy. That's what you must do.'

He holds tightly on to Mary's hand. He won't lift his head, he won't look up.

'I've the oddest notions sometimes, lying here,' says Mary. 'Today I've one of Father's tunes going round in my brain.' She hums a few bars.

'Why, yes. "The Seeds of Love".' He picks up the melody, his head still bowed, and they hum the first verse together. 'I used to dance to that in the middle of the parlour. Danced and danced.'

'But you cried while you danced. Do you remember? You were a funny boy.'

'I think I danced to hide my crying.' He raises his wet eyes to hers. 'You know me best,' he says. 'What's wrong with me? Why can't I be as other men are?'

She regards him soberly. 'There's nowt amiss with 'ee. You are the way you were made.'

'I'm afraid, Mary.'

'You can't be afraid. Not now.'

It comes to him that she means that he can't be afraid because she herself is afraid. Quietly, without troubling anyone else, in her usual way, Mary is preparing herself for death. He feels dizzy, as he does when approaching a piece of writing for the first time. It's the old panic at what he might have to uncover inside himself.

'Oh, Mary.' He grips her fingers. When he was six or seven, and outside with his father one winter's day, they came across a starving fieldfare. His father took up a stone and threw it at the bird. The fieldfare fell dead. He wouldn't let his father toss it on the midden but insisted on picking it up. He recalls its light bones, its fugitive warmth. 'Shall I sing to you for a bit?' he asks.

'You never sing any more.'

'Let me try.' His voice wavers, gathers strength.

> 'I sowed the seeds of love,
> I sowed them in the spring.
> In April, May and June likewise,
> When the small birds sweetly sing.'

Up and up his voice goes, striking a brightness from the dark of memory, rising beyond the little room, wire-taut.

> 'The violet I did not like
> Because it fades too soon,
> The lily and the pink I did rather overthink:
> I'd wait for a rose, come June.

> 'The gardener was standing by
> And told me to take great care,
> For in the middle of the red rose bush
> Grows a sharp thorn there.'

On he sings. He plucks at the rose until it has pierced him to the heart. The grass is trampled under his feet, rises up again. He thinks of the valley, shorn and stubbled, enduring the rains of winter; not yet thirsty for the rains of spring.

Mary's eyes have closed. He doesn't know if she's asleep or awake. 'Am I tiring you, my darling? Should I stop?'

Her breathing is slight but regular. Her fingers are still interlaced with his. He goes on holding her hand, stroking the small bones, as if his life depends on it.

He leaves Higher Bockhampton at noon, walking down across the water meadows into a quickening breeze. If Mary goes, there will be no trace of her. She'll have made no impression on the world. But the world will be lost. Mary, and Emma. Isn't it lost already?

I've been clever all my life, he thinks, *but cleverness isn't wisdom.* Fools are as happy as he's been. Happier, even.

At the bottom of the valley he stops in the leaze and squats against a stile with his back to the wind. He shuts his eyes and waits for his dread to subside. *I won't look away. I will remember.* But there are many recent things he doesn't want to see. That day, most of all: the day before Emma's death.

Why did we have to argue before you left me, Em? It was your last day alive, and I didn't know. I don't think you came to my room that afternoon to quarrel with me. I'll never find out now what you really meant to say. What you did say was worse than anything I could have imagined.

It's Tuesday, the 26th of November: not even a fortnight ago. He's in his study with his feet propped on the fender, eating his midday meal. It's a labouring man's meal. A slice, two slices, of bread and ham; a glass of well water. He's been at work all morning. He's glad to be able to down tools, to drink the water and sit, mind blank, in the warmth of the guttering coals.

No sooner has he finished his food than there's a jerk in the smoke of the fire, sending its rising skein bulging out into the room. It's been caused by the sudden opening of the study door. He glances up and sees Emma.

'I wonder if I might speak to you for a moment,' she says.

'I'm busy.'

Her gaze strays to his soiled plate, the crumbs of ham on his lip. 'You don't seem busy. You seem quite comfortable. I take it you've had a proper lunch.'

'I have, thank you.'

'Well. That's good.' She's clutching a paper scroll, which she touches to her breast. 'There's something I'd like to tell you,' she says.

He frowns. 'Of course.'

Em walks into the room and looks around unseeingly. She appears to be concentrating not on him, but on an inner event. 'I came to tell you that I've been—' Coming to a halt in the middle of the carpet, she puts a hand to the small of her back. 'That is, I've written – oh!'

'Are you all right?' he asks.

'A slight backache. Nothing out of the ordinary.'

'Perhaps you should rest. We can talk about whatever it is some other time.'

'I will not,' she says in a thick voice. 'We. Can. *Not*.'

'I'm working, Emma. I was going to make some corrections to a new poem. Would you care to hear it?' He finds the right page and gives her a propitiatory smile. 'I think you'd like it. It's about birds.'

To his amazement Emma flings up an arm, as if to ward him off. 'No, I *don't* want to hear it,' she says. 'Put it away! I don't want to hear *one word more from you*.' Her breath is coming in gasps. With her hand still pressed to her hip she shuffles over to lean against the mantel. The flameless embers paint the hearth with a red glow, staining her face and shoulders, throwing the charred triangle of her shape onto the wall. 'No more poetry, Tom. No more stories. I can't bear another minute of this . . . this *lie*.'

'What lie?'

'This marriage – this house – our life!' she pants.

He considers the changing lights in his water glass. 'I don't think you're quite well, my dear,' he says.

'I'm as well as I've always been. In fact at this moment I see things more clearly than I've ever seen them before.'

He gets up and reaches for the bell-pull. 'Let me ring for Dolly.'

'No. Don't you dare.' Her face is flushed. 'I'm going to speak, and you're going to hold your tongue and hear me out. Or I'll bring that inkwell down on your balding head, so help me God.'

Retreating to his chair, at bay, he shields his eyes with his fingers. 'Very well,' he says quietly. 'Speak. Maybe you can do it without having recourse to irrelevant insults.'

'That's right.' She expels an airless laugh. 'Rambling, vicious, mad old Emma! Poor, long-suffering Tom! How have you managed to stand being married to me these forty years, I wonder? The mad hag. The crazy shrew.'

'I've never thought of you in that way.'

'I should hope not. But you let other people think it and say it, and that's worse.'

He drops his hand and looks directly at her. 'I can't control what others think or say. I'm a public figure. This is a small town. When my wife forbids my own flesh and blood from setting foot in my house, there's going to be gossip.'

'Your sisters started it. Mary only cares for you, she's never given me so much as the time of day unless you happened to be standing there too. Mary, meek and mild! And Kate – Kate told me years ago that I'd failed you by not giving you a child.'

'You should have ignored her. Neither of us is to blame for that.'

'But I *do* blame you.' Emma's flush has darkened and spread over her neck. She's twisting her scroll this way and that. 'You're no proper husband. All those scandalous books. All that sex. What a joke! Outside your stories you've no life in you or feeling, Tom. You never had.'

'In my experience, people who think of themselves as full of life are usually brutal and careless,' he says.

'But to take so much care that you haven't managed it at all!' she flares out. 'You never meant to make me your real wife, did you? You've never loved me as I've loved you, never – never! In all the time I've known you, you've never truly given yourself to me. Even when you came to St Juliot – even then! – all your promises were empty.'

'I chose you above anyone else in the world, Em. I defied my family to marry you.'

'But why? *Why* did you choose me?'

'Because I loved you. You were the one person who believed in me and in what I might do.'

'Oh, exactly. You didn't choose *me*, Tom. You chose your writing. I know perfectly well why you married me. I was too young and too ignorant to see it at the time, but I do now!'

He's seized by a convulsion of pain. 'Em, don't.'

'You didn't want a wife, or a family of your own. You simply wanted a – a midwife to your books. Well, you've had your children. And I've had none.'

'Don't you remember those days, Emmie?' he says helplessly.

'I do remember. Why didn't you leave me there, where I belonged? Why did you uproot me and bring me to this loathsome place? It was all a lie. You've shut me away here and you've gone on writing while I've just had to put up with it all – your cold mother, your hateful sisters, this wretched gaol of a house!'

'I built this house for you, Emmie. Only out of love for you.'

'You built it for yourself,' she says. Her jaw is grinding. Still clutching her scroll, she lets go of the mantel and drags her skirts to the door. On the threshold she takes a long miserable breath. 'You can't love, Tom. You never could. You don't know the meaning of the word.'

It's not true that I couldn't love, Em. I loved, but I couldn't touch. I don't have that gift. I thought I could bring it all here in bringing you: the breeze, the sea, the shore – all your old sky and space. Our marriage wasn't a lie. It was never a lie. But I was always looking down. I was always writing. If I looked up, the fear was unendurable.

He's crouched against the stile with tears drenching his face, pummelled by the wind, when he realizes that he's not alone. A short way off he sees an ancient shepherd, leaning on a crook. The fellow has whiskers of the rare old mutton-chop pattern and is dressed from neck to knee in a drabbet smock. Jammed on his head he wears a straw hat identical to his own.

'Good day to 'ee,' says the shepherd. There are drifts of pillowy sheep in his wake, straying over the horizon like dirty clouds.

'Good day,' he replies, swallowing his tears.

''Tis a wild day. Blowy.'

He teeters to his feet. 'Yes. Very blowy.'

'Ye be lost, I reckon.'

'Not lost, no. I wouldn't say that.'

The shepherd tips his hat. 'Well then, good day, feller.'

'Wait a moment, if you will.' He wipes his cheeks and nose, glances up and down the grazing flock. 'You may be right. I'm looking for someone. Have you always lived hereabouts?'

'Ay, man and boy,' says the shepherd. 'I do mind so far back as to the time of Pa'son Moule at Fordington. My father used to supply en with lamb for's table.'

'Then perhaps you were familiar with the folk up Bockhampton way?'

'Well enough. Higher and Lower both.'

'There was a mason lived at the cottage on the heath. Hardy, his name was.'

'Hardy.' The shepherd scratches his chin. The whiskerless parts of him are covered in criss-cross lines like a map. 'I do mind en well. He was in a paltry way o' business. In those days he only had the one man working for en. But they were a kindly people. Once I and another lad did have to take some scrag end to en and the miss'ess did give we two slices of bread and butter and one with sugar on't. 'Twas a tasty bit. The old folk be'n't there now.'

'No, indeed. Tell me – do you know a Thomas Hardy here in the valley though?'

'Junior or senior?'

'Junior.'

The shepherd looks at him, looks away. He looks back at him again, and is evidently satisfied with his conjectures. With his stick he pokes savagely at a fat ewe which is encroaching on her neighbour's patch. Then he swivels his head from side to side and says decisively, ''E ain't got nowt to do with the she'p, as I do 'low.'

*

He walks on over the meadows, clinging to his hat, guided by the friendly line of the river. The wind is ripping across the skies, through the wide noonday. It's a speaking wind, nudging him along in noisy gusts.

Look up, breathes the wind. *Look up. Here is everything you've tried to say.* An oak sways above him, its limbs outstretched. Black rooks wheel overhead. *It doesn't need to be translated. You knew this once. How did you forget? How did you forget yourself?*

He finds that he's not crying now, but rather crying and coughing, or perhaps laughing: a long unloosened sound, as if he's shouting the wind's words. The world is all around him, and he's being blown into its embrace.

He lets go of the hat and opens his arms as it soars off.

What have I ever written about, Em? he laughs. *I thought I was writing about the world, but I was just writing words.*

A Promise

HE'S SHAMBLING BETWEEN laughter and tears as he walks up the drive of Max Gate. At the front door a tangle of cats nearly knocks him off his feet. He nudges them apart with the toe of his boot and only remembers after they've scattered that he's wearing the wrong coat and doesn't have his key. He tugs at the bell.

Kate opens the door. 'Well, I never,' she says. 'Look who's here. It's the native, returned. We were about to send out a search party.'

'I've been home. To the cottage, I mean. Katie, please don't scold me.' He feels untethered, as if he might float away. 'Mary wants you. You didn't tell me that she's so poorly.'

'You've had enough on your plate without being troubled with all that. I'm not going to scold you, foolish boy. Come in.' She shoots him a dubious glance before taking his waterproof. 'This isn't yours, is it?'

'It may be. I don't know. It could be the gardener's.'

Kate starts to shake out its creases distractedly. 'What colour were Mary's fingers, Tom?'

'They were blue. Bright blue.'

'Oh, Tom. Oh no. No.' She's folding the waterproof over and over. Once she's made a small wad of it she gives it another shake and begins again. 'I'd best be getting back,' she says.

'When?'

'If you know a thing's to be done there's no sense in delaying. I'll be off this afternoon. I've not much to pack.'

'Won't you stay a while longer?'

'What's the use?'

'What's the use of anything, Katie?' Her face drags downwards. He finds her hand in the folds of the coat.

'You're cold as ice,' she says.

'Ay, I'm bibbering. Leave that thing alone. D'you know what I'd like at tea-time? I'd like a proper fire, a cottage fire, made with wood. New wood, not coal. There's some in the lumber pile behind the kitchen.'

'I expect we can manage that. I'll ask Mrs Riggs to show Flor— to show Miss Dugdale where it is.'

'Not Mrs Riggs. Jane.'

'I can't be doing with this, Tommy,' says Kate. 'You may be many people but I'm only one.'

'Really? Just the one?'

'Let me go,' she says, herself again, wriggling out of his grasp. 'Two at most.'

He's upstairs in his dressing room, stripping off his muddy cords, when he hears Kate and Florence talking behind the locked door to Emma's room.

'I expect the niece will return,' says Florence, 'and that if she does, she will never leave. He is not the man to make her.'

'Much depends on you,' says Kate. 'What will you do next?'

'I'm not sure. I care for him, Kate. And I admire him more than any man alive. He is a very great writer.'

A small silence. 'Is he really? Everyone says so. Is it true?'

'Yes. People will still be talking about Thomas Hardy when you and I are dust.'

'Hmmph. He'll have to do his own dusting then.' Kate sighs loudly. 'Come on, Florence. There's no help for it. You'd better stay.'

'I'm never so happy as when I have someone to look after. But there's so much of Mrs Hardy here yet. I can't haunt another woman's house.'

'Oh yes you can, if there's no other way.'

'I wanted to be an author myself once. Well, at moments I still do. I have some money of my own. I've been considering getting a little London flat where I can write without interruption.'

'Ah, a woman with ambitions.' Kate gives her combative laugh.

'I'm foolish, aren't I? But if I'm to be reminded one more time that "dear Aunt" was a very great lady, and that I am quite a low sort of person, I will scream out loud. And he never says a word to stop it.'

'He's organized along different lines to the rest of us. I sometimes suspect that he doesn't see us as people. We're just paper figures, fitting into our allotted spaces like a jigsaw.'

'What does Mary think of it all?'

'Oh, Mary. Mary has always put up with him.'

There's a lull in the conversation. After a short while Florence says, 'I can't understand him. He was so lonely. And now he never seems to stop thinking about her. The paragon of wives. The late espoused saint, that shining example of humanitarianism. To cats, I suppose. He talks about "the girl who died twenty years ago".'

'Please don't go. You're doing him so much good.'

'Am I? I don't know what he expects from me. Living together like this has been out of the question for so long. But I'm beginning to doubt that he wants anything more than a companion and housekeeper.'

'Don't believe it. Didn't you hear him earlier? He quite has his youthful manner of speaking back.'

'There's his reputation to consider,' says Florence. 'You know what people are like in a small town like Dorchester, and how they talk.'

'That doesn't matter if it all comes right in the end. Be frank with me. Has Tom mentioned marriage yet? Have you reached an understanding? If you have, you can ignore the gossips.'

'He's done better than that – he's already married me in the grave. He showed me the corner of your family plot where I'm to lie.'

'The crazy old fool,' says Kate.

'I wonder if there isn't something in the air of Max Gate that makes us all slightly crazy.'

'So you *will* stay?'

'I don't know,' Florence says. 'I don't know! If I do I just hope I won't, for the rest of his life, have to sit and listen humbly to an account of *her* virtues and graces.'

Kate leaves that afternoon before tea. She's not wearing silk this time, but plain woollens.

'I'll ring up Tilley's for a car,' he says.

'Don't be daft. Shanks's pony is good enough for me.'

'Goodbye, then, Katie.'

'Goodbye, Tom. I hope I haven't tried to rule you too much.'

'You're like Caesar. You can't help it. I've liked having you here – I've more than liked it.' He swallows painfully. 'Your next battle is going to be the worst you've ever fought, old lady.'

'I know, Tommy.'

'Oh, Kate.' He's unable to stop himself. 'Mary,' he says. 'Mary – Mary.'

She takes hold of his wrist. 'My dearest boy, I know.'

'How can I help you? Please tell me.'

'Come and see us soon. Spend some time with her.'

'As often as she wants. Every week. Every day. Will you be back here?'

Kate looks suddenly stooped, braced like a furze bush in a blast. 'Oh, I expect so. Let's see how well you behave.' She rises up before he can object, seizes his shoulders and kisses him on the cheek. He can't recall when she last did this, or her ever having done it, for that matter. 'Get along now and have your tea,' she says. 'Don't keep that poor girl waiting.'

The first thing he notices on going to the drawing room is the fire-light. It's shining ferociously, juddering on the knobs and handles and lurking in zigzags on the delft tiles of the fire surround. The tea things are on the gate-leg table: cups and saucers and napkins and spoons and forks. There are slices of cake spread over the top two shelves of a three-tiered stand; filmy pieces of bread and butter clinging like pale yellow and brown postage stamps to the bottom. The teapot cover is open.

Florence looks up at him with a wobbly smile and puts aside the book she's been pretending to read. Her eyes have lost their rawness. There isn't a cat in sight.

'This is very pleasant,' he murmurs. 'An apple-wood fire.'

'Kate said you'd prefer it.'

'I do. Thank you.'

'Where are Beau-Beau and Comfy?' he asks. 'Where's Marky?'

'I've made a bed for them in the stable. Cats aren't really indoor animals, are they?' Florence pours his tea. It's Lapsang, perfectly brewed, not too dark and not too weak. 'I'm so glad you're feeling better,' she says. 'What will you have for supper tonight? I thought, as it's just the two of us, that we wouldn't dine, and that I'd let the girls off. There's cold rabbit, and there's an uncut ham.'

'Oh, rabbit. Ham. Whatever you decide.'

She hands him a napkin. 'Would you like some bread and butter?'

'Yes, please.' It's perfect too. So is the unpatterned cloth. 'Where did you find this tablecloth?' he says.

'In the kitchen press. Mrs Riggs says it's the right one. Isn't it?'

'Oh, yes.'

She takes a sip of tea before setting down her cup. 'What's the matter?'

'I'm sad, my dear. That's all.'

'Then we must discover a way of cheering you up. I'll read to you.' Florence opens her book.

'What's that?'

'*Great Expectations.*'

'Not today, thank you.'

'But you like Dickens.'

'I like him at the proper time. I don't want cheering right now.'

'What do you want, then?'

'I just want to eat my bread and butter.'

'Of course.' She rubs her finger along the margin of the page. 'I think, though, that you want something other than that. And that it has nothing to do with me.'

'I'm not sure I follow you.'

'Why am I here, Tom?'

'I asked you to come. Don't you remember?'

'I do. Do you?'

'Florence, please.'

'Here I am. But where are you? Where, really, *are* you? I'm ready to make you happy. But you won't *be* happy.'

'That's true. Right now I want to be sad.'

Florence claps the book shut. 'I've made up my mind. I'm going home tomorrow. We'll have rabbit tonight. And boiled potatoes. If you'll excuse me, I'll go upstairs now to pack.'

He should stop her, plead with her, perhaps, but he feels powerless to change anything or to alter what will happen in any way. He sits at the tea-table as if bewitched, staring into the fire while the green-grained sticks, sighing and muttering in the flames, cast their remorseless brilliance over the room.

In the firelight he sees his mother busy at her woolwork by the cottage hearth, the long coil of knitting rippling from her hands like an emanation of herself. *The fire's talking, Mother.* It's your own voice talking to you, Tommy, she says. His own hands are ordinary, smallish, curled-up hands, very much like hers once were.

Though he's dumb and hot with silence he can hear the fire spitting its judgement in a stream of words. *You weren't pure*, says the voice. *You weren't true. You didn't love. Love is patient and kind, love isn't provoked; endures all, suffers all. Love doesn't boast. Love never ends.*

He sits there until the sticks burn low and the fire has almost gone out. Around him is the stolid, empty house. He's never felt more insubstantial. Beyond the unlowered blind he can see the freedom he wanted vanishing like mist among the pines.

Florence has got the measure of him. *Yes*, comes the fire's ashen hiss, *but Emma had already got the measure of you long ago. You've no life in you, Tom Hardy. You never had. No life at all.*

It's getting dark by the time he climbs the stairs to his study. He gropes for his tinderbox, strikes a match and puts it to the lamp on his writing table. As the flame races up the chimney Emma's notebooks appear in a shudder of light. A week ago he couldn't face the sentence passed on him there. He'll accept it now. He already knows what it will be.

Taking up Emma's last diary with a dead hand, he opens it to the entry for the second of February, 1911.

He thinks he is someone. But I know that he is little, & commonplace. He is a common little man.

He is —

He moves his hand and reads:

He is impotent in body & soul.

'You're right, Em,' he says. 'You always were.'

He recognizes what this is. It's the beginning of the end of his life as a writer; the beginning of the end of his life. Nothing has lasted and nothing will last. There's no final meaning to be found in Thomas Hardy, in his stories or his poems; their strange geometries and excesses, their unstable fancies, their coincidences and contradictions – in any of these projections of his stunted self. He sees now what he must do. He's failed and he must learn to give it up: the house, his books. This body. Florence. All of it.

In his dressing room he puts on the trousers of his black suit, his braces; black socks, sock suspenders. Before he reaches for his shirt and jacket he adjusts the pier glass on the washstand. He rubs his grainy chin.

The beard of his youth and middle years has long gone. It never suited him: instead of making him look distinguished he simply looked like a man in hiding from the world. There's an inch or two of water left in the ewer and it takes him a minute to work up a lather from the dried-up cake of soap. He wields the razor with sure strokes, feeling the drag and scrape of the blade's edge through the foam, stretching the flesh of his neck with his fingers. Once he's cleared every fleck he splashes and pats his shorn skin, the wasting skin of a man who's had his three-score years and ten.

So, he thinks, *I'm only a writer, not a real person. But at least I'm clean-shaven. I'm dressed. On this final night, I can pass for myself.*

At half past seven he comes across an aproned Florence on her way to the dining room with a dish of potatoes. 'There was no need to change,' she says. 'We're just picnicking.'

'Still, I thought I would, since it's our first dinner alone together here at Max Gate. And our last, it seems.'

'Not dinner.' She's flustered. The steam from the potatoes has put a sheen on her nose. 'Supper.'

'I always dine. Let me help you with that.' He carries the potatoes to the table. There's a platter of blushing meat, already carved, in the centre. Florence has unearthed two silver candlesticks with new candles, and when he sees them he's glad that he's wearing his best clothes.

'How fine you look,' she says. 'If we're dining, then I'll get some elderberry cordial.'

'No quarrel has ever been repaired on elderberry cordial.'

'Did we quarrel?'

'I rather think we did.'

She nods seriously. 'Claret, then.'

'Stay put, my dear. I know where it's kept. I'll serve you.'

He returns with the wine and fills their glasses. They pick at the meat and potatoes in silence. 'Do you really mean to go back to Enfield tomorrow?' he asks at last.

'Yes.'

He tries to find a phrase that will convey both regret and the right degree of acceptance. 'It will be lonely without you,' he offers.

'You'll write,' she says.

'No, dear girl. Everything I've written is quite worthless. I've never managed to say what I wanted to say.'

'You *will* go on writing, Tom.'

'You can't know that.'

'I can. It's who you are.'

'I don't think so. I've been very bad at admitting to my own limitations. It's time for me to stop all that now. My life's work is finished.'

Florence says nothing. When the potatoes have gone thoroughly cold she fetches a tray from the pantry and begins to tidy away their plates and unemptied glasses. He helps her clear, thinking that almost anyone else – Kate, or even Henry – would have been able to handle this ending better.

'I'll carry that for you,' he says.

'I can manage.'

He follows her into the kitchen with a candle. Florence puts the tray down on the table and stares at it without speaking. It's dark, but she doesn't light the lamp. There's a truculence to her silence and immobility. He wonders if she's going to cry, and how he should respond if she does. Em never cried and he's unpractised at dealing with women's tears.

Florence doesn't cry. She appears, instead, to be fighting a war with herself. After some moments she turns to face him. 'I'm sorry,' she says. 'I am sorry for being so unkind to you today.'

'You have nothing to apologize for,' he says. 'I've been pre-occupied. I'm afraid I've neglected you all the time you've been here. You're a young woman still and there can't be much joy in caring for an old man like me. I don't blame you for leaving, Florence.'

She shakes her head. 'This is going to sound childish and vain. Please hear me out.' She joins her hands together, as if she's marshalling her strength. 'When I came here I was afraid, but I also had tremendous hope. I had a sense of what was due to me, you see.' A bleak smile. 'I thought you'd give me some definite sign that our future together was about to start. I expected you to make a fuss of me and to show me the sort of affection we've never been free to express openly. I really believed your need of me would take precedence over every other thing. When you didn't . . . well, when you didn't behave like a lover, I convinced myself that you didn't need me after all.'

'Florence, that's—'

She interrupts him with a grave look. 'Listening to you tonight, I realize that you're lost. Not to me, Tom. To yourself. I believe – no, I *know*, that I can help you. I think maybe I'm the only person in the world who can.'

She stops, and unclasps her hands. She isn't accusing him. There's no sign of her recent struggle in her eyes, just tenderness and youthful pride. He could still let her go. He could.

'Beautiful girl,' he says.

'I'm not beautiful. And I don't feel young. I felt young before, because I never knew what responsibility was. But I know now.' She's standing before him with her arms held out. 'Let me help you.'

A second chance at life. There's still time. He touches the tips of his fingers to hers. It feels as if he's being given a choice, but perhaps he isn't. Or perhaps the choice isn't his to make. 'Are you sure that this is what you want?' he says.

'Very sure.' She regards him levelly. 'But you must be sure too.'

'I've always been certain of your goodness,' he says, 'and of our sincere regard for each other.' He can't bring himself to utter the word *love*.

Florence lets out a small gasp of relief. 'So. That's settled, then.' Her eyes, enormous and glittering, are on his. She seems to expect a further gesture from him. He puts his thumb to the collar of her dress. The hollow of her neck is warm, its life beating rapidly. But as he leans forward to kiss her, she turns her lips away. 'Not yet,' she says. 'When I come back.'

'You'll be back? Do I have your promise?'

'Yes.'

'Oh, my dear. If I once get you here again, won't I clutch you tight.'

'Will you?' says Florence. She's at her most gallant. She's superb. 'I know you will. Goodnight, Tom.'

The Chosen

SATURDAY DAWNS CLEAR and bright over the crowns of the pines. The car arrives punctually after breakfast, lamps burnished, wings waxed to a high shine. He's pleased to see that the garage has sent the same chauffeur as before.

They drive to town at a ceremonial pace, on roads of brass left by the week's rain. At the station he leaves the boy to park near the siding while he queues for Florence's fare with the other weekend travellers. He buys the ticket for her, feeling its pliant newness under his fingers.

'I've given Flo and Jane their orders for the week,' says Florence. She's full of busy prattle. She's securing the clasps of her typewriter case but stops to tweak his collar. 'And a shopping list. You don't have to trouble yourself about all that. I'll come back on the Friday train, as soon as I've packed up my things.'

'I'll be here,' he says.

'Will you do something for me? Will you try to sit at your desk for half an hour every day? Just half an hour.' She brushes an imaginary speck of dust from his coat. 'Routine is important.'

He passes her the ticket, her bag, her gloves. He squeezes her hand shyly. 'Yes, my dear,' he says.

When they reach the barrier on the departure platform she puts her mouth up to his. Their lips meet. This is how the future will look: everything remade, reinvented.

He emerges from the station building to find the driver already standing by the car. 'Am I to take you home again, sir?' the boy asks, opening the door with a single swing of his arm.

'Not yet. I'd like to go to St Michael's in Stinsford first.' For a mile or two they crawl along crooked ways and past stone stiles. 'I believe I knew your grandfather,' he says. 'About twenty years ago. He drove a trap for hire. Was his name Debbyhouse?'

'Robert Debbyhouse, sir, same as my father.'

'Yes, that's right. He carried himself well, just like you. What is your Christian name?'

'I'm also Robert, sir.'

The Wolseley has come to a halt in the church close. 'There's something reassuring in that, at any rate,' he says, adding, 'No, please stay exactly where you are.' Leaning across the blazing leatherwork, he gives young Debbyhouse his fee. 'I'll let myself out. Don't wait, Robert De Bayeux. It's such a fine day, and I'm going to be mucky. I think I'll walk back.'

Beyond the churchyard hatch the family stones, only partly shielded by the branches of the yew, are darkened by streaks of rain. Next to them Emma's grave looks ugly and white. He gets down on his haunches and tries to rearrange the flowers at its head, removing a stray flint here and there from the chalky earth with his bare hands. He isn't able to do much. The grave is too fresh, too obviously an accretion of dirt.

He kneels before its exposed shape on the green, ashamed of the lilies and carnations in his wreath. They're the wrong flowers, not a lover's flowers. When summer comes, he must bring roses.

In the half-hour it takes him to walk home he begins to feel as if he exists neither in the past nor the present, but somewhere between these two illusions. Except for his own figure drifting through the meadow the valley is empty of any sentient thing, reflecting back sunlight hard as tin. He's enveloped by a vision in which he sees things not as they are, but as they will be – a future day just such as this, the dead month; the wet fields, the wind-warped upland thorn, and himself passing among them, invisible, without the disguise of flesh.

The vision won't leave him, even after he's crossed the threshold of Max Gate. The muggy little porch is as quiet as a crypt.

'Flo?' he calls out. 'Mrs Riggs?' There's no reply. Slipping off his shoes, he makes his way along the service corridor on damp feet. The kitchen is uninhabited. The range is dark, the curtains drawn. He glances around at the china on the dresser, the bewildering array of tools depending from the walls. On the centre of the table, under a net, he finds a plate of pork chops already stiffening in their own fat.

'Is anyone home?' he says.

He half expects to see Jane Riggs emerging from the pantry, but she doesn't come. Nobody comes. He's alone in the dumb, unresponsive house, absorbing a silence that has no edges. It seems to announce the end of all rational communication, all life.

He retraces his shining footprints to the hall. They're already shrinking, like prints on sand.

He stands and listens, as though he were still waiting for someone.

He studies the hat stand, the vacillating barometer, the armless cast of Venus. The more he stares, the less they seem to have to do with him. They're vanishing too. Where they used to be, there is the emptiness of the valley; that bare light, falling without interruption on the tight-lipped hills.

After a few moments he realizes, with a shock of relief, what the source of the silence is. The tall clock beneath the stairs has stopped. He opens the oak carcass and winds the spring till both weights are at the seat-board, consults his pocket watch and turns the minute hand to adjust the time. The lunar dial shows the right phase, a solemn new moon. He gives its face a rub with his sleeve and removes the key. The works of the clock start to stutter in his ear. Still trembling, he closes and latches the door.

A resolute *tick-tock-tick* pursues him as he climbs the stairs and continues down the passage to his study.

Here is the garden laid out in parcels of light and shade, the branches of the great beech spread against the December sky. Here is his shawl hanging from the back of his chair. On his table-top he sees his blotter, his ivory-handled pens in their tray, his inkwell. Opposite them is his calendar, still set to Monday the seventh of March, and beside that Emma's three black diaries and the exercise book containing her recollections, its edges faintly curled. Everything is in its usual place. Reflected in the central squares of the window he sees himself, his eyes beady and slightly glazed, nose large and twisted. He sees the coral stretch of the room, its paper layers hardening around him like the strata of some ancient rock. He's small and shrivelled up, moving over the rock with the quick jerking action of a bird – a robin or thrush.

He sits down. He pulls his shawl across his shoulders and reaches automatically for a fresh sheet of paper. At his elbow, where it should be, is the plaque he likes to stroke for comfort. *Write*, it says, *and with mine eyes I'll drink the words.* But he doesn't write.

How pointless and unimportant it all was: this house, the whole edifice, every brick and stone of it, the cloths and the clocks and the pots and pans and the flower beds, the tea services and silver spoons and curtains and pictures; each superfluous and unnecessary detail. Hasn't he only imagined living here? In spite of his plans and designs and refurbishments, he never gave his heart and soul to it. His real existence has always been elsewhere. And now that he's had to become the exhumer of his own life, forced to dig up its chattels and heaps of rubbish, he finds that they've disintegrated in his hands. Just fragments are left. None of it can tell him very much.

He has nothing to say.

His thoughts are interrupted by a tentative knocking at the door. Before he has a chance to compose himself it opens. Dolly stands in the doorway, dressed in a coat and outdoor boots and a surprising crimson scarf. 'I'm sorry to disturb your writing, sir,' she says.

'It's all right.' He points to the naked page. 'As you can see, I'm not writing. Where is everyone?'

'Cook is gone to market wi' Miss Griffin, sir.'

'What about lunch?'

'I'm to say it's in the kitchen.'

'Well, that's one puzzle solved. Why aren't you wearing your uniform?'

'It's my half-day, sir.'

'So. It seems we're both on holiday. You have your walking boots on, Dolly. Are you going out?'

'I'm going to Piddlehinton, sir, to visit my mother an' father an' the little 'uns.'

'Piddlehinton, yes.' He knows he's lost control of every aspect of this day, and possibly of the rest of his life. He resigns himself to surrendering to whatever comes next. 'I hope it's a good visit.'

'Thank 'ee, sir.' Dolly strokes her woollen calf with the top of her other foot, like a fly. 'I came to ask what I'm to say to 'em.'

'I expect you'll talk about the usual things. Perhaps not with the little ones, though that depends on their ages and degree of understanding of course.'

'No, sir. I meant, what I'm to say to Mother and Father about my place here, now that Miss'ess Hardy – now that . . .' She chews her lip. 'If I'm to be kept on, sir,' she gulps.

'Are there many of you at home?'

'Yes, sir. Too many, Father says. I'm third eldest.'

'Tell your father that you'll always have a place at Max Gate, unless you find one that suits you better.'

'Oh, sir.'

'Dolly, don't cry. Please don't cry, child. I can't bear it. I'd like to ask you something. Before you came to call me that Wednesday morning. Do you remember?'

Dolly swipes at her tears with her scarf. 'Yes, sir.'

'Did Mrs Hardy say anything?'

'Oh, yes, sir. I didn't want to leave her. I was all for ringing down to the kitchen, but the miss'ess wouldn't have it.'

'What exactly did she say?'

'She wanted you. She said it had to be you, sir.'

'Wouldn't it have been quicker to ring?'

'Maybe, sir. But she said it had to be you.'

It's almost midday. Dolly has gone. In his mind's eye he sees her crossing the river and climbing the sides of the valley into the north wind, red scarf flapping like a flag, till she rises out of sight. Everyone has vanished. He's left to himself in a silence, broken only by the ticking of the clock, which seems even more implacable than before. With every minute the world moves further away from his old life with Emma. Soon it will be gone forever. There will be new hours to fill, new meals to be eaten, new clothes to be worn. It will look like the same world, but it won't be the same.

Wind and rain, he thinks. *Sun and snow. March and December. Spring and summer and autumn and winter. Each year we take up our positions exactly where we've always stood. Has that kept me safe? Though I've resisted change, everything has changed.* He picks up Emma's last diary, turns it over in his hands. *Why did you come to my study that Tuesday, Em? You didn't set out to argue with me, I know. Look at this house, the shell of it. Look at me – I can't die twice. Whatever you say will be all right.*

He doesn't really hope for an answer when he opens it. He simply wants to hear Emma's voice one more time. He leafs through the pages at the back. There are scarcely any jottings for the present year. The final entry was written two days before she died.

25th November 1912

Yesterday was my birthday. I was too unwell to get up & hid away in my eyrie, listening to the birds hopping around me in the stripped trees. I feel every one of my seventy-two years. My back aches & my scalp itches & flakes almost past endurance. No one tells you that this is what old age will be like: the veins, the sleeplessness, the strange bulges arriving from nowhere, the humiliating nightly tussle with the chamber pot.

At breakfast time yesterday Dolly knocked at my bedroom door with Cook & Flo Griffin. Mrs Riggs had baked me an apple cake. I could only manage a bite, but when I took the morsel in my mouth a miracle happened. It was as if I was a child again, with Mother & Helen to make much of me.

Dear Dolly sits with me hour after hour & brushes my hair & pats my side with her cool hand, & this brings me some relief.

I don't see Tom these days. For my birthday he sent me up a signed photograph of himself. What to do with this paper husband? I've put him in a drawer.

Yet by another miracle we did meet this afternoon. I was lying on my bed at four o'clock when Dolly brought up a card. It was sleek & expensive & I guessed straight away that it was Rebekah Owen's. There was a message written across it, 'Will you not see *us*?' I asked Dolly to get out my good tea dress & not to fuss with stays but just to throw a few pins in my hair, & down I went.

It wasn't the idea of seeing Miss Owen that got me up, but the hope that Tom might appear.

For the next hour I talked with the Owens about stupid things. Houses. Tom's new play. Doctors, as if a doctor could have a cure for what ails me, which is the simple indignity of still being alive. Then, when I thought I would cry or faint, Tom himself arrived, all smiles – he was his old self, dapper in his tweeds. He didn't resemble a writer at all, but the dear husband I once knew. He greeted the Owens very amiably. All through tea though he would not look me in the eye. I disgust him now, with my thin hair & my loose sides & my pain. Or worse, he is merely indifferent to me.

How few my weapons are, not only against Miss Kitten & all Tom's hangers-on, but against his indifference.

Even so, I have lived in Dorset long enough to know a little about the old ways. When my pain first came on at the start of autumn I saw what I had to do. One morning I went to the gardener & said, 'Trevis, will you help me? We must plant a rose. Not a slip or a cutting but a young tree, we haven't much time. Can you get one?' He said that he could. 'Can you bring it to me by the day's end?' I asked. 'We must plant it tonight.'

As evening was drawing in he returned & said, 'I have your rose, miss'ess, & there's a rising moon to set her by.'

I remember standing in the garden as the hole was dug. Moonlight lay white as sand on the ground. By its shine each turn of the spade revealed hopeless terrified things, creeping & crawling over the earth. The shadow of a hunting owl flew whistling through the pines, followed by the shriek of a vole. It seemed to me that we are hardly better than they, poor earthbound creatures, with no language but a cry.

At last the pit was ready & Trevis lowered in the rose & spread her roots with a gentle conjuror's touch, fanning out the fibres in their proper directions for growth. He put most of these roots towards the south-west, for, he said, in the season to come, when the wind is blowing from that quarter, she would require the greatest holdfast on that side to stand against it & not fall.

'Here's an onion from the larder to plant by her root,' I said to him, '& here's something for your trouble.' But he smiled at me kindly & said, 'No, ma'am, I won't take payment for a charm like this, 'tis bad luck.'

'Then I hope you are repaid another way,' I said.

'Thank 'ee, ma'am,' he said, '& I hope that love finds you.'

Since then – silence. Nothing. Not a word from Tom.

What use is this kind of magic? It's nearly winter. A cold east wind is already stealing across the fields. I've waited too long for a sign from him. If I continue to depend on such worn-out tricks, I don't believe it will ever come.

This is my fault as much as his. I've waited for him in the wrong way, in anger & fear & despair, as you wait in a fortress for your enemy to surrender, not as you wait for a lover. As you wait at the top of a cliff, drawing your shreds & ribbons about you, while shadowy armies gather below.

Such a wintry sort of waiting. After forty years of marriage, what I think of my husband is probably no worse than whatever it is he thinks of me.

So. It's time to put old things in order. The enchanted country where we first loved each other is gone forever. We won't visit it again. There is no yesterday, there is only *now*. I must use my own wits, & try whatever ordinary human words can do to restore his sight.

I've glanced over the scrap I've written this last year & it's all I have. Yet it may be enough. However sharp my thorns, the truth is that they don't come up to my heart. Tomorrow I will find Tom & make him a present of my recollections, & then I will do what I should have done long before.

I will destroy these diaries.

He closes the notebook and gets up, though he has nowhere else to go. He sits down at his table again. It's too late to tell her that he's found the scroll which their foolish quarrel prevented her from putting into his hands.

It's all too late, Em.

What was real, in the end? What was true? Just this. The ticking of a clock, the ghost of a voice. The rest of his frantic, blindly labouring life has been built not on stone, but on sand. It's already disappearing, running through his fingers.

Look. A rose blooms in the darkness. Thin silks stir in the draught of the door. A bird sings in a cage. Stars flutter like wings. *Thou hast made my days as it were a span long: and mine age is even as nothing in respect of thee; and verily every man living is altogether vanity.* But if being alive were simply vanity, who would mind? It's much worse than vanity. It ends as it began, in silence. At its heart is the silence of eternity.

He stares at the sheet of paper on the blotter, its white indifferent face. Let the stone crack, the world erase itself. Let him sink back into clay, into fire, into the first wordless blank of Creation. He can't stomach his fate as it's been written. He's sick at the waste of it all.

But look, but only look —

As he gazes at the page the sharp sense of a lost day, some scene or vision now unaccountably removed, swims into view. He's at Sturminster, walking home through the water meads. It's midsummer. It's evening. He's been writing since early morning, and though he's taken this walk to clear his head he's numb with fatigue. His weariness is written in the arid wind that trails past him, in the skin of the stream, slackly stirred by its breath. He reaches the footbridge next to the pier, jammed with rotting lily leaves, where the current clucks into every hollow place.

There is the house, up high on the bank. He stops at his first glimpse of it. It's the same house, and not the same. It has the clarity of something recognized. The roof is crowded with swallows. They arrow off and drop among the willows at whose foot the river flows, rise again and fly in the curves of an eight above its gleam. A moorhen skims over the water, planing up shavings of crystal spray. He's distracted by the lingering heat of the afternoon, the touch of the wind on his cheek. The green meadow makes a fitful phosphorescence at the borders of his vision.

Look up. Look up now.

He looks up and sees her beyond the window, lamplight shining through her hair, like light through a brake. She has waited for him, after all. She's laughing, her rose-flush coming and going.

He walks on and she's everywhere, sometimes in front, sometimes behind, hovering a few feet from him, her contours vague, the all-embracing blue of her dress reddened by the declining sun. But he knows her, he's seen her. He goes to meet her, brimming high with joy.

She's beside him. Here she is: here.

There's only one question left to ask. It's the question that matters most in the world, and he's asking it over and over.

'You know I do,' Em says. 'You know I do.'

Downstairs in the hall the clock begins to strike the hour. The shifting of its gears is so loud that he seems to feel an answering vibration passing through his body. He counts the chimes one by one. There are twelve strokes, twelve blows. As the last note dies away, time opens before him with an eyelid's soundless blink.

Emma isn't out there. She's here, in him, as she has been all along.

It's not too late to say the things he should have said long ago. It can't be too late. *Can it, Emmie?*

He reaches for his pen. *I believe.* He opens his inkwell, dips the thirsty nib into the ink. *What do I believe in?* He puts his pen to the paper.

My darling Em,

It's been many years since I last wrote you a letter like this one, a love letter. I am very much to blame. I thought there was no sense in writing, but I was wrong. I know you'll forgive me because you understand what I am, how simple, how unseeing. I was trying to put together a picture that was always right in front of my eyes.

I love you, Emmie. I've loved you from the day we first met: that never-to-be-forgotten day. (Never again, I promise.)

When I was young and hopeless you called me to life. And

now that I'm old and hopeless, even though your going felt like my own death, I find that my heart still beats. It says *Emma*. Calling and calling: *Emma, Emma, Emma*, until I'm not sure if it's the sound of my heart, or you summoning me, as you summoned me once before – to speak.

My own love, do you remember the paths around Beeny? How we sat on the cliff where the grasses grew tall, and chattered? You were dressed in brown, or in blue. I wore a white hat, I think. Your cheeks were peony pink. No, rose pink. Your hair was bronze, or copper, or gold, the liveliest of metals. Such soft womanish hair, curling about your face. You were breeze-blown, and we didn't know how many hours had passed. It began to rain.

We became a story, which I thought had ended. But here I am, still telling it.

It's difficult for me to grasp what it means to love you after you are dead, and what I can possibly put into words that you'd want to hear. I'm afraid of annoying you with my clamour, the foolish clamour of the living. But if you'll let me, I would like to begin.

Ever your most loving husband,

Tom

It's twelve o'clock on a Saturday afternoon. He turns the sheet of paper over so that it's new again. He confronts its sheer face.

Here is his hand, poised above that hostile surface, ready to start the climb. Here, beyond the glass, are the black lines of the beech veining the December sky. In the space between its branches, like the infinitely repeating lattice of a crystal, he sees the shape of the words he doesn't yet have. He believes – he can't help but believe – in their persistence, in the power of his words to give him safe shelter.

The winter breeze is stirring towards him across the wet mead. He lowers his eyes as he drives his pen forwards, welcoming the effortful friction of the steel on the page. *You alone exist. You alone are real.* His heart beats fast. He writes:

How you call to me, call to me.

It's a calling, or a calling forth, that won't ever stop, now that it's started. The voice is speaking, in transparent syllables that assure him that the life he is going on with is not just made of scraps, that it still advances, that it is part of something larger and more substantial than himself.

Saying that now –

Oh, what is it saying? That past and present, absence or presence, are one and the same. That he will only know reality when it has ceased to exist. That the world lives on. That nothing will be lost.

The radiance on the water, the shadowless spring fields, and Emma – here they are, asking for his love and his clear-sightedness if they are to shine.

The words come to him quickly.

Saying that now you are not as you were
When you had changed from the one who was all to me,
But as at first, when our day was fair.

Who can say what remains, when everything that was is taken away? *I still live, I breathe. Dearest Emmie, isn't this moment enough?*

Yes it is. Why, it is.

Now, he thinks. *Yes, now.*

He will go on writing to her. He will write today and tomorrow, and the day after that. If he has to, he'll fill a book with his cries.

ACKNOWLEDGEMENTS

*T*HE CHOSEN IS A fictional, but I hope essentially true, impression of the days immediately following the death of Thomas Hardy's first wife Emma in November 1912, and of Hardy's writing of *Tess of the d'Urbervilles* some twenty years earlier, in 1890. It is also the story of how some of the greatest love poems written in English, the 'Poems of 1912–13', came to exist.

Though *The Chosen* is based on the known facts of Hardy's life, I have taken the occasional chronological liberty. Edmund Gosse visited Max Gate in September 1890, rather than in March. Hardy later gave a guarded and slightly misleading account of *Tess*'s bumpy journey to publication; what is certain is that by 25 November 1889 the manuscript, representing about half the story, had been rejected by three magazines. He appears to have settled down to complete it in the late summer of 1890, submitting the revised first half to *The Graphic* by 8 October and the rest by the end of that month. But he must have done some writing in the meanwhile to wrap things up so quickly, and this is what I imagine him doing – with Gosse to kick-start him, and with Emma's help. John Tudor Laird's *The Shaping of 'Tess of the d'Urbervilles'* (1975) was an invaluable guide to the evolution of Hardy's most famous novel.

While Hardy's negotiations with Macmillan for an *édition de luxe* of his work – eventually to become the 'definitive' Wessex Edition of 1912–13 – began in late 1910, the title of that edition was only decided on at the beginning of 1912. I've condensed by a good year a much longer process that also involved his ongoing revision of the proofs.

The incident of Hardy's Chinese visitor (who made a confession similar to the one in my story) happened towards the end of Hardy's life, rather than in the autumn of 1893 as he was beginning *Jude the Obscure*. It's noted by his former doctor, Frederic Bazley Fisher, in an appendix to Cecilia Marjorie Fisher's monograph *Life in Thomas Hardy's Dorchester, 1888–1908*, published by James Stevens Cox (1965).

The 'black' diaries which Emma Hardy kept from around 1890, chronicling her dissatisfaction with her marriage, were burned by Hardy not long after he discovered them. We know of their existence because Florence Dugdale (who would shortly become his second wife) mentions the find in two letters she wrote to Edward Clodd in 1913. The diary entries in *The Chosen* are therefore entirely fictional, though I've drawn on Emma's surviving letters in *The Collected Letters of Emma and Florence Hardy*, edited by Michael Millgate (1996), for their tone, and sometimes for their content.

Emma also left behind a manuscript memoir that recalled her youth, and how she first met Hardy, which is now part of the Thomas Hardy Memorial Collection in the Dorset County Museum, Dorchester. She had finished this record of happier times by 1911, but I have imagined her still writing it in 1912. Hardy included an excerpt from her description of their meeting in the biography he prepared in secret for publication after his death. The full text of Emma's memoir was edited by Evelyn Hardy and Robert Gittings in 1979, as *Some Recollections*, the title she herself gave it.

Many of Hardy's own words appear in *The Chosen*. I've quarried his fiction, poetry, verse dramas, personal notebooks, interviews, letters, manuscripts, and his self-authored biography, published posthumously, under Florence Hardy's name, in two volumes (1928–1930). Hardy's carefully constructed version of his life is collated as a useful single text, with Florence's revisions, by Michael Millgate in *The Life and Work of Thomas Hardy* (1984). I am grateful to the librarians of the Bodleian Library, Oxford, for so helpfully providing me with scans of Simon Gatrell's *'Tess of the d'Urbervilles': A Facsimile of the Manuscript, with Related Materials* (1986), and to the Harry Ransom Center at the University of Texas at Austin, for a beautifully clear digital version of Hardy's manuscript of 'The Bird-Catcher's Boy' in the Thomas Hardy Collection. The cornerstone of *The Chosen*, though, are the 'Poems of 1912–13' themselves, which Hardy began to compose very soon after Emma died, and brought out in his 1914 collection, *Satires of Circumstance*.

I owe a profound debt to Thomas and Emma Hardy's biographers, especially Robert Gittings, Denys Kay-Robinson, Michael Millgate, Ralph Pite and Claire Tomalin. If anything in *The Chosen* feels authentic, it probably originated with them. Emma's aperçu about marriage to a man of genius being both a privilege and a misfortune is Millgate's, in *Thomas Hardy: A Biography Revisited* (2004). Her rather tart conclusion as to the 'very grave fallacy that novelists understand the personal application of their own novels' is taken from John Fowles's essay 'Hardy and the Hag', in *Thomas Hardy After Fifty Years*, edited by Lance St. John Butler (1977). Hardy's reflections on the classical writers in the chapter called 'A Visitor', and on authorship in the chapter called 'The Voice', were inspired by Will Eaves's brilliant essay '*The Odyssey*', in his *Broken Consort* (2020).

I am further grateful to Martin Stephen at the National Trust for supplying me with the complete Historic Buildings Survey of Max Gate, and to the volunteers at the house for putting up with my daily summer visits till closing time. The late Faysal Mikdadi, Academic Director of the Thomas Hardy Society and an ever-welcoming presence at Max Gate, often shared thoughts about Hardy and Emma, and kindly sent me a copy of Emma's story *The Maid on the Shore* (The Thomas Hardy Society, 2018).

Writing a book is a labour of love. Warmest thanks go to my editors at riverrun, Jon Riley and Jasmine Palmer, best of readers, to my endlessly encouraging agent, Bill Hamilton, and to Nick de Somogyi, my incomparable copy-editor, for their support at every stage.

Some rec[...]

I think possibly som[...]
what my early life wa[...]
account of my family, [...]
when I was young, h[...]
met my husband. I c[...]
when I was three years [...]
way into the country [...]
are taken to see the se[...]
were very great when [...]
them I can never for[...]